A Master Plan of my Love Life

By Anne Beatson

 FriesenPress

One Printers Way
Altona, MB R0G 0B0
Canada

www.friesenpress.com

ISBN
978-1-03-913980-0 (Hardcover)
978-1-03-913979-4 (Paperback)
978-1-03-913981-7 (eBook)

1. FICTION, LGBTQ+, GAY

Distributed to the trade by The Ingram Book Company

For my precious nieces: Kaitlen,
who encouraged me to write this unique story,
and Sagan, who typed lots of notes that I wrote on my travels.

Table of Contents

1 1
2 15
3 23
4 39
5 54
6 65
7 78
8 83
9 100
10 115
11 131
12 145
13 159
14 170
15 183
16 193
17 213
18 216
19 224

1

"Don't even think about it." Anthony's words were a warning, "I can't take this anymore; you need to stop organizing my life and stop meddling with my love life."

Imelda moved towards the kitchen, shrugged her shoulders while correcting him, "You don't have a love life. How long has it been since you brought a girlfriend home?" His mother continued, "I can't trust you to find your perfect match, and I want grandchildren."

Anthony's expression was of disbelief, "I'm twenty-six years old, a fact that you continue to ignore." He couldn't be more frustrated; this battle with his mom was becoming a chore. "Believe me, Mom, you can't make any choices for me in the love department, and you definitely don't know the sort of person I need. When I do find my irresistible life partner, you will be the first person I'll tell." He was constantly warning her to stop her matchmaking and meddling.

"I only want to see you settled." This was Imelda's half-hearted attempt to apologize to her son.

In his calmest reserve, Anthony warned her again as he walked out the door, "You've started this vendetta, and you're leaving me with two choices: to stay or to leave. If my work schedule was less busy, I would be packed and gone by now. I'm warning you,

Mom, if this silliness continues, I will move somewhere far away from you."

Anthony settled in his Jeep, and as he was backing out of the driveway, he felt he had shed a layer of skin. Apart from his mom's sad attempt at matchmaking, his life was good, and, for the most part, he didn't mind sharing his time with her. Things became unbearable when he came home from work to find strange women—whom he had never met—who were invited to dinner by Imelda. On one occasion, he was really embarrassed when his mom couldn't remember the woman's name. It was the last straw, and his diligence to her prying was necessary; he did everything he could to stay away from home.

The scenario was ridiculous, as Anthony discovered Imelda was inviting women she had met on the street for dates with her single son. She believed she should conduct interviews of potential wives as they would be living in her house.

One young lady who was invited to dinner was asked, "I hope you want children, my dear. Anthony is looking for a girlfriend who wants to start a family soon." Anthony glared at Imelda. The astonishment was unbearable.

He was so uncomfortable that he had to say something before the charade continued, "Let me introduce myself; I am Anthony. What's your name?"

"Janice Young."

"Well, Janice Young, my mother is suffering from idiocy. I assure you that I am not looking for a wife, but I am going to spend the evening with some friends. Have fun, you two, and enjoy your meal." Anthony couldn't wait to leave.

Torn between anger and confusion, Imelda adamantly yelled out, "I want grandchildren!" She sounded like a broken record, and Anthony wasn't staying around to argue.

Poor Janice was truly embarrassed and stood to leave. She thanked Imelda for her invite and immediately grabbed her coat and purse, and walked out the door.

What was my mother thinking? Anthony wondered as he drove away. She knows nothing about these women, and the sad thing was that she knows even less about me! Anthony's single life was copacetic until her ridiculous arguments started to grate on his nerves, and he hated her singular approach to obtain grandchildren.

Anthony's career, however, was a different story. He had been fast-tracked to his present position as regional sales manager for Quick & Easy Foods Inc., a unique food distribution outlet that sold meal ideas using fresh produce and offered varying suggestions to change the epicurean experience.

He had worked for Quick & Easy Foods since Grade Eleven, when he was hired as an entry-level clerk who stocked the shelves and cleaned the store. He worked hard and demonstrated that he was capable of so much more, which was evident in the creative and innovative ways he marketed the products. With his friendly attitude, sense of humour, and excellent customer service, he assumed more responsibility. He proved dependable, and willingly helped his associates, for which he was promptly promoted to assistant manager. He achieved this success by the time he was eighteen. As soon as he got his degree, the company promoted him to store manager. At twenty-four, he was a district manager in Vancouver, a position he held for less than a year. As the company was growing so quickly, he was offered his present promotion as regional sales manager based in Victoria, Vancouver Island.

Anthony was pleased with his progression through the ranks, as well as his increased earnings. He continued to work very hard, but he hadn't forgotten the overwhelming difficulties and challenges that new recruits faced. He arrived at the new Nanaimo store, and, with his usual flourish and his entrance premeditated, he proceeded to gather the staff for a meeting.

"Good morning, peeps. Welcome to the new store! We are all ready to start work, I hope?" Anthony was aware that two of the store's cashiers were missing. Sophie Cardinal, the store manager, had taken the calls from the absent staff. Initially, she was worried they would need a lot of time off, but they assured her they would be healthy enough for duty in a couple of days.

"Mr. Lynwood." Sophie waited until she had his attention, "Markus and Janine were in a fender bender last night and ended up in Emergency, so they won't be able to attend the meeting today."

"Thanks Sophie, do you have any news on how they're doing? They're not badly injured, I hope?" Anthony was concerned that this new store might get busy very quickly, so he decided to stay overnight.

"No, sir, they assured me they'll be back at work in a couple of days. Markus hurt his arm and shoulder, and Janine shot forward and bruised her chest." Sophie assured him that they would cope for a couple of days.

"Sophie, please copy your notes and pass them on." His concern for their well-being was real. "And keep me informed of their progress."

"Yes, sir, I will."

Sophie and James had spent the previous two days training the staff, filling shelves, and becoming familiar with the till. Anthony walked around the aisles to make sure they displayed the products as per the plan-o-gram that best indicates the placement of retail products on shelves, in order to maximize the sales. This also unifies the right quantities, and that everything was perfectly presented and ready for day one in the new store.

"Grab a coffee or water, everyone, and we will start the meeting shortly." Anthony looked around the room and assessed that the questions about the absent pair would better be discussed over a ten-minute coffee break.

Anthony was considered an excellent organizer, and he spent a few minutes showing Sophie how he would merchandise a particular end-cap. "If you discover a better way of stacking the product, please feel free to do it your way. I need to stress that when new products come in, they must be on display as quickly as possible." In his relaxed way, he shared his talents and enthusiasm.

"James seems to have a knack of displaying the merchandise for maximum effect; he insists we don't put a super-large item next to a tiny item, or stack product too high." Sophie got Anthony's attention. "He's also very helpful when any of the clerks ask questions, and he doesn't hesitate to respond quickly with a job well done attitude."

"I'm glad you found such a diligent worker here! Keep me informed on his progress. In the meantime, how is everything in general?" Sophie gave him the thumbs up. "Did your delivery correspond to your order? Were there any problems?" Sophie shook her head. "I don't like surprises," he said, "so if there are any immediate problems, please tell me as soon as you come across a discrepancy."

Anthony saw the time and announced, "It's time, everyone. Let's get down to business." He suggested that everyone rejoin the meeting.

"Yes, sir." Sophie smiled as she went to the only vacant seat, which was next to Anthony.

"My name is Anthony Lynwood, and we are here today to have a meet and greet session, so I'm here to share my expectations with you, and you can share yours with me." He looked at the expressions on their faces: some looked quite nervous, so he continued. "We all need to work together, as a team, so don't be afraid of sharing your ideas or asking any questions."

James Prescott asked, "How do we best explain what this store is all about?"

"The meal concept is simple. We aim to reduce the prep-time for our meals, keeping costs affordable. The customer buys all the dried fixings, chooses a sauce base, and finally adds a protein to create well-balanced meals that suits their families' tastes. The mix and match concept is endless." Anthony had everyone's attention.

"Imagine a fresh hamburger with fried onions and barbeque sauce. Now, replace the sauce with a Cajun, a Thai with sweet peppers, or a hot Korean sauce. Another popular suggestion is lasagne noodles or cannelloni pasta shells, or crispy yellow peppers that can be filled with a combination of taco-seasoned chicken and vegetables, served with melted cheese on top. Or, fill them with ground chicken and Jamaican curry with sour cream, garlic, and chives."

"Encourage the customer to try the assorted batter mixes to create individual flavours by adding fresh fish, bananas, or, even a hamburger. To assist the customers and reduce the prep time, we can pre-bag products in small amounts." Anthony was on a roll, "Our batter is sugar-free, and that means diabetics and special diets can also enjoy it. One of my favourites is fresh asparagus drizzled with chocolate and sprinkled with sea salt."

"I hope this helps, James." Anthony then explained that the hot spices were batched together, as were the mild spices. "To help the customer calculate the approximate quantity needed, read the labels on the products, become familiar with what goes with what. The smallest estimate is for two people. It takes a little practice, but I'm confident all of you will get the hang of it."

James added, "Another great selling point is that dried produce takes up very little space in a pantry and has a super long shelf life."

The meeting was off to a good start. With the presentation of seasonal products, everyone was able to join in with ideas on merchandising, and clerks who were new to this business accepted that Head Office might override some of their suggestions. For the most part, all employees felt competent to voice their opinions.

"It's almost time to open, sir." Sophie wanted the staff to be ready.

"Sophie, first of all, my name is Anthony." He whispered. "If I can't take your call, then send a text without delay." Anthony was looking at her to make sure she understood. "Secondly, and I must reiterate, if anything happens in this store, please contact me immediately."

She was certainly aware of Anthony; he was bordering on dreamy with his classic good looks, golden-brown hair, and tailored suit. His six-foot-three frame was always perfectly groomed, and his friendly smile put everyone at ease.

"There's a new cell phone on your desk, Sophie, do feel free to use it for personal calls too. We only pick up the tab for Canadian calls, no U.S. calls, I'm afraid, unless you have a long-distance app. This laptop must be dedicated for company use only—for security reasons—and you'll get regular electronic updates that are sent directly to your system. If you do use it for personal storage, be aware that the updates from head office may overwrite or destroy any information it does not recognize. For convenience, we all use our cell phones to store personal information instead of our laptops."

"Look through your laptop and check it out. When you go into the programs, you should find it easy, but take the time to read the online manual. If you have any questions or experience unexpected glitches, let me know. I would also appreciate your feedback regarding the software, so give me your opinions, if you can." His information session was detailed. "If you recommend any changes by way of improvements, I will contact you directly so that we can discuss it. Again, keep me informed, please."

Walking around the store, he noticed how clean everything was; he saw how the shelves were stacked and he was happy with the displays.

Sophie knew her stuff, and her confidence assured Anthony that the future held promise, and she was ready to be the store manager. "I will make sure to run everything past you. I'll do as you ask." She replied, "How do we forecast sales items?"

"Just follow the instructions on the laptop. When you access the sales section, choose the forecast option." Anthony assured her it was easy. "Check it out; it's user-friendly. We've tried to answer your questions in it, and it's one more way of sharing ideas. As you run low on product, enter the items immediately and have your order ready bi-weekly. Again, if you need anything, Sophie, call me."

As he got to the door to leave, he waved his goodbyes to the staff and told Sophie he was staying in Nanaimo in case she needed any help. He had no doubt—in fact, he was certain—that Sophie and James would increase sales and eventually take this store to the next level. Anthony knew he had chosen wisely when he matched these two together.

"Was that my phone ringing?" Sophie had just remembered her new cell phone and rushed to her desk. Unpacking the phone took a couple of minutes, and she checked the call list and saw Anthony's name.

"Hi, Anthony, you called?"

"I forgot to mention to your staff that we have a pecking order. All problems that occur in the store should be handled by you, the store manager." He waited a few seconds, "I want you to call me if there are any problems you may need help with. I know sometimes staff situations can get out of hand, and I will get involved when necessary; just let me know if there is a situation, good or bad.

"One last thing, if you do come across a predicament with staff that needs to be addressed, I want an email detailing the problem, what action you applied, and what the outcome entailed. I won't broach the problem with your staff. We, that's just you and I, will discuss the problem and come to an amicable resolution, at which time you will address the issue, in confidence, with your clerk. I would only get involved if there was no clear means forward."

Sophie agreed. "I'll address this at my next staff meeting. Was there anything else?" He could hear the excitement in her voice.

"I wanted to mention my first impressions of the staff we employed. They are a mixed bunch, but they're all willing to pull together, and that is a big plus. Let me know who you choose to promote to assistant manager."

"I will. Thanks, Anthony." Sophie stared at her phone. Her boss's boss was very nice and kind, and, she could not get over how attractive he is in person. Up close, she noticed his eyes were grey in the middle with a thin black line around his iris. She was perched at her desk in her tiny office, daydreaming about him, and hoping her new district manager would be just as easy to get along with—Anthony had forgotten to mention who he had hired for that position.

Sophie walked around the front of the store as James was stacking products and filling spaces. The store was busy but steady. She couldn't help but notice that he was an artistically creative merchandiser, who could produce something great out of almost nothing. His current presentation was geared towards kids, as he pointed out to Sophie that he has three younger siblings, two sisters and a brother.

Sophie watched him, and her first instinct was to join in and help James make the model. She was impressed with his ideas. What a great selling feature, she thought, to utilize and promote the products. She noticed that James had his artistic hat on, "Very creative, James," then she asked, "Do you need some help?"

"No, I'm almost finished; what do you think?" James stood back. His smile was evident as he was proud of the end result. With candy boxes, he had fashioned a car and train masterpiece.

"I love it." She was impressed. "I'd like to know how this kind of presentation will work for us, so keep an eye open for the kids' reactions."

It didn't take long. One of the kids was throwing a tantrum—he wanted to take the whole display home, and James walked over to find out who was causing the commotion.

He bent down on one knee. "Well, young man, I made this train." James explained, "I'm so sorry, but these boxes of candy belong to the store." The little boy looked so sad, as James continued to explain, "I can only make one train, and it must be kept on display here, in this store, for all the kids to see."

The little boy stopped pushing his mom and stood quietly, waiting for James to tell him more. "What you can do is be a good boy, be nice to your mom, and ask her if you can collect the packets when you shop here."

The little boy wiped his tears away and looked up at James, asking, "If I can save the candy boxes, will you help me make that train, like that one there?" He was persuasive, and James couldn't hide his smile.

"First of all, I think you need to ask your mom if she will help you buy the packets each time you come into the store."

"Mommy, can we save candy boxes?" James waited a few seconds as he watched the boy and his mother, who said she would love to help him collect the boxes. They were both happy with James' solution. As they moved to the checkout till, James continued to talk to the young boy to help him stay calm.

"Maybe, young man, you can do some chores to help your mom, and she might buy an extra box sometimes." James suggested, and then asked, "So, what's your name?"

The little guy looked at James with a wide grin and said, "Adam."

"How old are you, Adam?"

"I will be five in a few weeks." The little boy was chatty, "I'm going to have a birthday party. Do you want to come?"

"I'm too old to come to your birthday party," James told the little guy.

"My mommy will be there, and she's old too," he pleaded.

"Well, Adam, we are looking forward to seeing you again." James looked at his mom, and she beamed as he helped the clerk bag her purchases.

"Thank you, James, your magic works! And my name is Karen," Adam's mom replied. When she got to the store's entrance, she called, "We'll see you soon. Thanks again, James!"

Adam was still waving at James from across the car park.

Sophie walked over to James, "I'm more than impressed; your customer service was above and beyond." Sophie asked, "Have you worked in sales or merchandising before?"

"This is my first full-time job; although, I have worked part-time since I left high school," James explained that he wasn't work shy and that he had been slowly trying to do some UVic courses in biology, but found learning at home difficult with his sisters and brother always close-by. He explained that he wanted a career in medicine—to work in the paediatrics field—but funds were a huge problem which he had no way of overcoming. "If possible, I'll work full-time, and hopefully, I'll have enough money to pay for tuition at UVic next year. Until then, I'll concentrate on getting my own place." Then, as an afterthought, he told Sophie he intends to apply for grants and bursaries from local foundations. Sophie was hung on his every word.

She didn't know how quite yet, but she intended to help James get into university. Maybe, she thought, he could get first dibs at any potential overtime.

"By the way, Sophie, I got the idea for this display from the pirate's treasure chest poster over there," he pointed to a nearby wall. "See the car and a train sticking out of the top?" He was pleased that Sophie had noticed his creation, and he put the 'icing on the cake' when he commented, "That lady will be back to get candies for her son; it was an easy way of up-selling."

Sophie took a photo of James with her new phone and explained, "We'll keep a record of your ideas. Let's use this format for merchandising seasonal products." Sophie made a note of the interaction between James and the customers. "Anthony will be back here next week, and I can't wait to show him what you've done." She also asked James to record anything they could discuss in their monthly meeting.

"James, we need your expertise to organize the storeroom." Sophie mentioned while she still had his attention. "We need to know exactly when our next order will arrive and where we can put the stuff."

The office was very pokey, and there wasn't enough room to swing a yoyo. It didn't help that all the empty cardboard boxes were stacked at the back door. As they walked, Sophie began taking mental notes of the adjustments they would have to make in the upcoming week. Her thoughts were disrupted, however, when she heard a huff and sigh coming from one of the cashiers.

"James, can you please help Joey? He looks flustered, and I think he's having a problem with his till?" Sophie noticed Joey was shaking his head as James walked over to the till.

"Okay, Joey." James said, "The POS is working fine. If you can, try to remind all customers that we have tap, then your job will be much easier." James was very helpful by talking calmly to Joey and going through the steps with him.

"What's a POS?" Joey asked while getting frustrated.

James moved Joey away from his station and explained, "A POS is short for 'point of sale' and remember, Joey, you must give every customer a receipt to close their transaction." James then helped Joey with a few customers until he felt that he had got the hang of it. Joey was grateful that James took the time to show him how everything worked. James had figured out the problem as he went on to explain further.

Sophie again praised James for his easy manner and his ability to handle problems. She couldn't help but notice that he had a genuine rapport with the other clerks. He was a super nice guy.

"What do you need, Kelly?" James asked when he noticed her tensing up. "Let me help; we've been so busy all day, and I think we're all a little tired. Let's do this cash-out together." They recounted Kelly's cash but her problem wasn't with the cash; it was with the till.

"This crazy thing isn't working, and all I need is my end-of-day totals, and I can't remember how to do it." She was frustrated, and James suggested she take a few deep breaths. She had mastered the sales input in the till, and her customer service was excellent. She used every opportunity to promote the impulse sales items she chose, and kept her area organized.

"The easiest way to remember this procedure is to write down the sequence of keys you need for the totals." James wrote it down and told her to put it into her cash box.

"Thank you, James, that was painless, I wished I'd thought of that." They laughed at the simple solution. Kelly was aware of his good looks, easy charm, and captivating smile—she thought he was every girl's dream.

Sophie made sure everything was closed correctly for day one, and all the staff were cashed out and signed out. She told James it was time to close the store, and they did a sweep to make sure everything was in place and cleaned and that everything was locked away.

"Hi, Anthony, I wanted you to know that the day went better than expected. I'm going to assign duties and prepare for tomorrow. It will run like clockwork when the cashiers get familiar with the set-up."

"Glad to hear it, Sophie. Is there anything I can help you with?" Sophie's news of the first day was music to his ears.

"Where will the new product be stored? My office is too small." Sophie wondered aloud; she didn't want to burden him.

"At the back of the cooler, there are lots of boxes that need to be flattened, and some need to be put away or stacked in the storage room. When you flatten the boxes, you will see the door to the storage room." Anthony explained. "The lighter boxes go on the top shelves, and the heavier product goes on the bottom shelves. I left sticky notes to help you all organize. The boxes that you flatten should be returned to the delivery van for recycling."

"I thought that door was the back exit." Sophie didn't think there would be a storeroom entrance.

"You're right, Sophie. All deliveries come to the rear exit, which reminds me, when a delivery truck arrives, you need to be there." Anthony then explained, in detail, the importance of rotating products and the tracking sheets that must be altered accordingly. If there were any discrepancies or anomalies, both the manager and the driver need to initial the changes.

"Thank you so much, Anthony. I appreciate all of your help."

"It's my job. Have yourself a relaxing evening. Good night, Sophie."

In his hotel room, Anthony was working on a new store location. The consensus at head office for the store's location was between Comox and Campbell River. He needed to spend some time becoming familiar with the demographics of these areas, so he decided to head north sometime soon to start planning the next outlet.

2

As Anthony turned into the driveway, his shoulders were tense. He was anxious, and his gut was full of dread as he slowly approached the front door. Imelda was sitting at the kitchen table nursing a box of tissues. She was crying again. It was obvious to Anthony that she was suffering from depression or anxiety; why else would she continually cry? He never knew what to expect when he arrived home, but this tearful scenario was becoming the norm.

Three years earlier, Anthony's whole life changed when his mom was diagnosed with thyroid cancer. When he found out the severity of her disease, he drove from Vancouver, where he had been working for a few months as a district manager. Luckily, he got the news several weeks ago, that he was relocating to the Island, where he had already found an apartment within walking distance to the ocean. He was excited and wanted to share his news with his mom, but when he arrived at his family home, he found his mom lying on the couch, in tears. His father was nowhere to be found.

"Where's Dad?"

"He's gone. He left me. Oh, Anthony, I'm so scared." She was sobbing her heart out, incoherent, and it was difficult to understand what she was saying. "I need him now more than ever." Imelda cried out angrily, "How could he be so cruel?"

"Did Dad say where he was going?" Anthony was bewildered, "What did he say when you told him you had cancer?"

"He told me that he has met someone who doesn't laze around all day wallowing in self-pity, the way I do." Imelda wiped away her tears. "He also pointed out that I have no energy or inclination to do anything with my boring life." Her sobbing continued, "I told him that I was diagnosed with thyroid cancer, and he told me he didn't believe me." Imelda was in a terrible state, "He was horribly bad-tempered, and that was the way he told me: he was leaving, and he never wanted to see me again."

"What did he expect of you?" Anthony was confused, especially after finding out that his dad was living with another woman. "How long has he been seeing this woman?" Imelda shrugged her shoulders, shook her head, and continued sobbing. Anthony was furious, "Do you know her?" Imelda shook her head again.

"No, I don't know her; today was the first I've heard of her existence. He came home early from work, went directly to our room, packed all of his belongings, and he told me to sell the rest. He said he was trying to get out of here before I got home."

"Where is he now?" Anthony was ready to battle with his errant father.

Imelda shrugged her shoulders, "I don't know where he's gone, and I don't know who his girlfriend is; I didn't suspect him of having an affair." Imelda was in a terrible state of anxiety, "What did I do wrong?"

"I'll speak to Dad. In fact, I'll call him now." Imelda told him there was no need.

"Let's get one thing straight, Mom. His behaviour was out of your control, and he's the only person accountable for his actions." He hated seeing his mom like this, "I am going to call Dad, get him to explain . . . This is so unlike him. We need to know the real reasons why he's abandoned you." Anthony was in a quandary; he always believed his dad was a one-woman man.

"I already tried to contact him. His cell phone was left on the kitchen counter."

"I will call him at work." Imelda had already tried that, only to discover that George had taken early retirement.

Anthony held her lovingly, "Mom, we'll survive this together." With no hesitation of his sincerity, he told her his solution, "I'm going to move back home, so I can help you. If the treatments are hard on you, I'll lend a hand when I can."

Anthony knew the promotion to Victoria was imminent, so he asked Alexis if he could move immediately to be with his mom. Alexis, his boss, did what was necessary to make his transition to the Island as painless as possible.

After her surgery, Imelda went for radioactive iodine treatments and chemo, which caused her to lose some of her hair. She had a hard time reconciling her situation. She was having long bouts of depression and self-esteem issues, which was way more than Anthony bargained for. She felt desperate and scared, but she tried to hide it from her son.

She was, however, proud of the man he had become, and for his sake, she was trying to hold her world together. She didn't want to be a burden, but she also didn't want a psychologist's help to make her feel better. She was irrational.

During her recovery, when Anthony came home from work, Imelda usually cooked a meal and they would spend their evenings together. They would put on some cheerful music and play cards, chess, or even Monopoly. They both played to win and the cheerful bantering that went on during the games was quite loud at times.

Three years after her surgery, Anthony was still living with his mom—not where he imagined himself living after university.

Imelda's physical health was improving; she was getting stronger now that her treatments had finished. He was ready to find his own place again, but Imelda had become clingy, she was lacking self confidence. He didn't know how to rectify this problem; and if he dared mention a psychologist, she stormed out of the room.

One day, out of the blue, an envelope arrived in the mail with Anthony's name on it. He opened it to find a letter from a lawyer, which contained a surprise document. His father had legally handed over his half of their property to Anthony. Prior to their separation, Imelda and George had made a Will, stating their only child, Anthony, would inherit their property. George wanted Anthony to inherit his half of the family home as part of his parents' separation settlement.

Anthony was sad and disappointed that his dad was avoiding him, and he was unable to thank him for the generous gift. It was obvious that George deliberately left his phone at Imelda's house to sever all ties with his family. Father and son were always so close, which confused Anthony when his dad left without saying a word. He found George's behaviour puzzling and out of character.

George was undeniably aware of how difficult his ex-wife had been with his refusal to hand the house over to her, but it was a huge relief to Imelda when he finally agreed to give his half of the property to Anthony.

Imelda wanted to ensure that her husband could not surrender any of their joint property to his new family, so George transferred the title deed to his son before he remarried. If anything were to happen in the future, Imelda wouldn't have to handle any liens on the property. She was content with this new agreement. She needn't sell the house to pay off his new wife, who Imelda was determined, wasn't entitled to anything. Unfortunately, she now believed she had complete control of the entire house.

George had no intention of returning to Imelda. When he decided to leave his half of their property to Anthony, he hoped some day to reunite with his son, but so far his letters went unanswered.

However, Anthony was frustrated as he believed his father had never once tried to contact him, and the lawyer who sent the letter refused to discuss his client. Anthony wished his dad would have just called him, or at the very least, texted him to let him know he was okay.

The property was so huge that Anthony thought of dividing their home into two independent suites. The entrance was impressive and furnished with a six-foot oval walnut table with a vase of roses in the centre. To the left of the hall, the kitchen was modern with banks of drawers instead of cupboards. Every appliance was installed, and they even had a wine cooler fitted into an alcove. The open plan dining area furniture consisted of a long wooden table with eight old-fashioned upholstered chairs. The room was light, as two sets of patio doors lead into a sunroom that boasted a television, record player, and desk with a laptop and mouse. The formal reception room was to the right of the hall, where an opulent marble fireplace surrounded a wood-burning stove. An elaborate crystal chandelier was the focal point in this room, where three plush sofas were spaced in a u-shape around ornate glass coffee tables. The real wood furnishings were large but not opulent, and the drapes had wooden pelmets. Shelves consisted of assorted books with jackets that gave colour contrasts to the off-white décor. The stairs were wide and had a landing that joined four oversized bedrooms, each with walk-in closets and en-suites. The whole house reminded Anthony of his dad.

Imelda kept her home spotless; all the walls were white, but the decor was starting to look drab. It was not as welcoming as it used to be, but she was determined not to renovate or decorate to brighten the place up. It was easy to see that pictures had been removed from the walls. It needed a coat of paint.

Anthony craved privacy, and the longer he stayed in this house, the more desperate he became. He looked around his old bedroom, its powder blue walls lined with shelves of comic books and littered with kid comic book posters. He still had his childhood Superman comforter, which was not exactly a suitable choice for a young man. In three years, nothing had changed; the whole house looked like it was trapped in a time capsule.

When he offered a sensible solution regarding dividing the house, Imelda blocked him at every turn, refusing to take any of Anthony's suggestions seriously. She wanted him to stay, but her lack of consideration or cooperation had caused a huge rift between them. He had tried so many ways to make her understand his predicament.

"Imagine, Mom, me bringing home a partner and admitting that I live with my mom. It's hard to believe that any partner would welcome such a great offer." He added sarcastically, "I truly believe we could amicably divide this property."

"I don't understand. Are you ashamed of me?" Imelda was defensive. "Who cares if you bring your girlfriend home, and your mom lives here?"

"I do." He was abrupt and thoroughly aggravated.

The first thing that came to his mind was *The Big Bang Theory*. Howard lives with his mom, and his life is hell; it was a relief to all the viewers when she passed.

"For goodness sake, Mom, please try to understand? I want my own life! I don't want to bring a date home and have you asking embarrassing questions. We need a solution, and we need it quickly."

She didn't care what he needed, "I'm telling you again, it isn't going to happen."

"You've become very self-centred in your old age. You don't need a four-bedroom house with four bathrooms, and you don't need to be tied to mowing the lawns. This house needs a family; it's far too big for one person, so another option would be to sell the house, and you move into an apartment." He waited for her reaction, but there wasn't one. "I can get a townhouse close by. What do you think?"

Imelda dug in her heels as she refused to think about any of Anthony's ideas.

"I don't want to tell my future spouse that we have to live with my mom. I can't think of how I would explain that we cannot make love as my mom is in the next bedroom. 'Always wear your pyjamas in case my mom is wandering around the house.'"

"You are over thinking these issues." This was Imelda's favourite comeback.

"When I arrive home at the end of a busy day, I'll want to have intimate moments with my spouse." Anthony warned her, "The way things are right now, make this idea impossible. It's absolutely unacceptable, so our circumstances will change, sooner than later, I promise you."

"I would never interfere!" Imelda said calmly.

Anthony angrily replied, "That's a lie. I don't believe you—you're the world's worst busy body." Imelda glared at him. She was fuming as he told her, "You are self-centred and manipulating, and for me to regain my sanity, I must move away from here. I want my independence, and some day in the near future, I will have it."

He believed the solutions he offered were sensible, and he had no problem living next door to his mom. He wanted her to realize it was time to make changes to her life, allowing herself to move on instead of living in limbo. After her split with George, she lost all her friends and she locked herself away in the house, which was unhealthy.

"It's late, and I have a long day tomorrow. Please think about downsizing. Good night, Mom." He went to his room.

Thinking back to his early years, he had a hard time remembering his happy childhood. He recalled that he had fantastic grandparents, and Imelda always insisted the whole family get together at Christmas. He recalled getting lots of presents and his grandpa Evan Lynwood made a big fuss over him.

But when Imelda's brother died in an accident at work, she cut ties with her parents. Not long after that, she cut ties with George's parents too. There were no photos or mementos of any of Anthony's relatives, which was strange, but he couldn't remember what actually happened to his grandparents. He did, however, remember that they died. That's what his mom had told him, so it was pointless to try and contact anyone to help him take care of Imelda.

The one thing he knew for certain was, his mom's demeanour was not improving—not only was she crying more often, but she directed her growing frustrations at Anthony. She became irate and would scream her displeasure when he talked about moving out. He considered hiring a companion for her, but if he couldn't put up with her antics, how would a stranger cope?

Every day, his mom's temperament was getting worse. Anthony wished he had stayed in his own apartment; he certainly regretted surrendering his lease. Without Imelda's permission, there was no one and nowhere to turn to for help or advice.

3

Driving around Vancouver Island in the springtime was insanely beautiful. Wildflowers of perky pinks to yellow daffodils and baby bluebells crowded the parks and ditches, all intent on finding the sun.

After completing his degree at the University of Alberta, Anthony worked for a few months in the Edmonton store, and then he moved to downtown Vancouver, where he would occasionally meet his buddies in Gastown for a pub crawl. He didn't crave a social life of bar-hopping, and he couldn't believe his luck when he was offered his present position on Vancouver Island, as he looked forward to moving closer to his parents. On the outskirts of Victoria, he had found a two-bed apartment overlooking the ocean. He would never have tired of the view. With the beach on his doorstep and the smell of the ocean, it was all soothing to his senses, making it a difficult decision when he finally surrendered his lease to move into his parent's house, in downtown Victoria, to care for his mom.

Anthony loved all aspects of his job, especially the perks of sightseeing, as his travels took him to some of the most picturesque sites imaginable. The coastal road to Sidney had amazing ocean vistas, with fishing boats, ships, ferryboats, and, occasionally, pods of orcas and humpback whales that could be seen during the summer months.

His job often took him further north to Nanaimo, where the highway cuts through small seaside towns and villages. The busy ferry terminal successfully caters to tourists, where restaurants with sea views were most popular, but the sights off the beaten track were also stunning. Coombs, with its Old Country Market, sells large varieties of home-grown produce, and brags several goats living on the roof of the market, making it a comical sight. Heading south, Ladysmith brags a uniquely layered campsite to afford all the sites with a sea-view, and its swimming pool was a natural rock formation.

The main street in Parksville had small shops and greenhouses full of perfect blooms, where the smell of lavender was often associated with the array of wildflowers.

Parksville Park avidly catered to young kids, with its mega activities—like mini golf—and picnic areas that included a beautiful beach and ice cream parlours. The town also hosts a special four-day sand sculpting competition, a must see for all visitors.

Anthony's initial trip to their newest acquisition, the Victoria store, was planned with emphasis on building a motivational foundation. He was also working to create an innovative and original merchandising itinerary; that was individual, eye-catching, and hopefully will encouraged friendly competition between the stores. The store manager, Stuart McIvor, was waiting for Anthony to arrive.

Sitting in the car park, Anthony quickly read all of his notes as he had not visited this store since it opened two weeks earlier. When he approached the door, he could see the staff actively preparing to start their day. They had all the components ready to open the store, and with less than twenty minutes to opening time, Anthony walked up to the checkout area.

"Good morning, everyone!"

Anthony's friendly greeting got the attention he needed as they all gathered around. "I asked you all to have your questions and suggestions ready." His request held a challenge, "Who wants to go first?"

Stuart started, "How can we create awareness for this store? We notice lots of people walk by, but we're not busy. We need something eye-catching, maybe?"

"What are your best-selling products?" Anthony asked. He had a few ideas, but he wanted the staff to put their thinking caps on.

"I think kids' candy is a popular item." Stuart looked around at the other staff, hoping for a suggestion or two. "We sell a lot of curry-based items, and the recipes are great—in fact, it's the best curry I've ever made." Stuart had tried several different recipes and was zoning in on Mexican tacos. "The next best seller is Mexican-Mix; it's a medium-tasting recipe that appeals to the teenagers, and now the younger kids are asking for it. The shrimp tacos are the front-runner because they taste so good, they are perfect, and even for younger kids, they're full of flavour without being spicy hot."

Anthony smiled and just had to ask, "Are you saying that our recipes give you an inclination to cook more meals?"

"It's so simple and with far less additives than frozen meals." He continued, "I have some recipes that I would like to submit for consideration, and this may help sales if we can offer a new recipe every month."

"Submit your ideas to me, email me all the components and directions; I think you may have hit on a new trend. Great idea, Stuart! I think that will work."

"Hayden, what do you think?" Anthony could see he wanted to put his suggestion forward. As soon as Hayden started to share his ideas, he got everyone's attention.

"Depending on what's happening locally, our seasonal sales should reflect the event. For example, when the rodeo comes to town, we should promote beef jerky. I know this because I worked on the rodeo circuit for three years. We need the jerky close to the till as an impulse item, and we can nudge the customer by reminding them that we're selling jerky."

"Okay, Hayden, give us some more suggestions." Anthony liked the way this guy thought.

"We can ask kids to draw or colour something seasonal. It'll be Easter in a few weeks, and for the most creative, artistic efforts, the kids can win prizes. We can feature their pictures on that spare piece of wall with no shelves."

Hayden was sketching his ideas on a piece of paper, "The kids can paint or colour this." He held up the sheet with a rainbow outline on it. "A candy, chocolate, or chips packet can be coloured at the end of the rainbow." He showed everyone what he meant to achieve.

"I'm willing to print off the pictures and deliver them to the elementary schools, with printed instructions and that they are to be dropped off at our store. This will give parents an opportunity to visit us, and when the kids bring in a picture, we can give them a balloon with our logo."

Anthony was impressed, "Stuart, what do you think?"

Stuart's reply was swift and supportive, "Hayden, that's a brilliant idea! You're in charge of organizing this competition." Hayden grinned and informed everyone he had lots more ideas. Stuart realized he had a star employee. "I'd like to see some of your other suggestions."

Stuart asked Anthony how to order balloons. "Leave it with me. I'll order for all the stores, and I'll deliver them on my next visit."

Anthony checked the time, "We need to open in a couple of minutes. I'm looking forward to hearing more great ideas. I intend to be here for the whole morning, come and share your thoughts, okay, team?"

"Stuart, put on your thinking cap and try to work on some merchandising techniques." Anthony shared Sophie's and James' ideas.

The store opened, and while Anthony was walking around, checking products, Stuart tagged along. "Anthony, I think I have a good idea."

"Okay, Stuart, let's have it."

"I was thinking about impulse sales. When the customer has done shopping, and is at the till, we need to utilize this counter space better—display some tempting goodie bags that we can make up, which aren't on our shelves. It's a good way of up-selling. What do you think?"

Anthony encouraged him, "Show me how you would do this."

"First of all, look at the amount of counter space we can use to create our display." Stuart grabbed some candy sticks. "If we put three boxes of these candy sticks side by side, it should be enough." Stuart suggested the candy sticks alone didn't work, but they should sell if they could be added to some chocolates and nuts to make all the grab bags different.

"We have a huge assortment of Easter eggs." Anthony went to the storeroom and picked what he considered to be best sellers. He created a simple display, but incorporated a huge assortment of chocolate.

Hayden came along with an array of tea and tisane packets. "Place these behind the candy. What do you think?" He asked while organizing the merchandise. "For St. George's Day, we can make a catchy display of English cookies and candies. For St. Patrick's Day, we can use all green products. For Canada Day, we can have local Indigenous artists in the store, displaying their wares, which we can sell to holidaymakers throughout the summer and possibly Christmas."

"Hayden, look at the assorted rock candies. You can display them like this," Anthony used a couple of empty water glasses to place the candies in, "Or you can sort out individual candies in separate containers. It's your call."

"Hayden, I think you have great ideas! Looks good! Make a new impulse rack every week and record the sales. Don't forget to record sales of the product for the week before and the week after." Anthony was pleased with the ideas the staff had suggested. "Take photos and send me copies that include the increase in sales per product."

When it was almost time to leave the store, Anthony called Hayden to have a quick chat. They walked outside the store. "Hayden, I want you to share your ideas with me, and only me. You're so creative that's why I would like to work with you on how we can make things happen." Anthony was blown away with his suggestion of inviting Indigenous local artists to the store.

"Please don't discuss this initiative with anyone. If I can get the backing we need, I will make sure you get the credit for your ideas." Anthony also reminded Hayden to think of prizes for his Easter contest. "Get some help to make up grab bags with assorted Easter and regular candy."

"Hayden, please remind the staff to greet all customers as they come into the store. People prefer to shop where the staff is friendly."

Walking around the store, looking for discrepancies in the merchandise, Anthony couldn't find any concerns, "I'm taking off now, Stuart, but before I leave, can I have a word in private?"

The two men walked out of the front door, and Anthony shared his idea, "I have a suggestion, and I hope you agree with my decision to promote Hayden to assistant manager. He's knowledgeable, creative, and the kind of guy you know you can rely on. What do you think?"

"I agree with you; he deserves it." Stuart seemed happy, "Can I tell him?"

"Yes, but I would like you to teach him most of the manager duties, starting today. That way, when you need a day off, your store will be in good hands," Anthony said, "and if you have any problems, call me."

He walked to his Jeep and drove to the harbour where he parked his vehicle. The sun was shining, and there was a mild breeze; he wanted to stay outdoors, so he found a bench where he could eat his lunch in peace. He saw the harbour taxi leave. It crossed his mind that he would have preferred fish and chips, but it was too late, he missed the boat.

His phone rang, and it was Sophie. "Hi, Anthony speaking, how can I help you?"

"It's Sophie. In ten days, I have to attend my aunt's funeral. She had been ill for a very long time, and when I was a kid, she took care of me after school when my mom worked. Will it be okay for me to attend?"

"Yes, of course, Sophie. You must go, and you have my condolences." He wanted her to know the policy for close family members who passed away. "This company prides itself on family unity, so the same applies to all members of your staff."

When Anthony asked her if she had chosen an assistant manager, Sophie didn't hesitate, "I do have one candidate in mind."

"Who is the lucky recipient?" Anthony already knew who he would pick, but who would she choose?

"It's James. He helps staff and customers without being asked, he uses his own initiative, and he is reliable. The products are always stored in date order, and he does a block and face as he walks around the store. Most importantly, all the customers love him; he's nice and polite." Sophie continued to sing his praises, "And we are all happy working with him; he's a very special young man."

"I'm so happy, Sophie. I agree with your decision. We're on the same page, and guess what? I have his nametag ready. I was blown away when you told me how he handled Adam's hissy fit."

"How are Janine and Markus doing? Have they come back to working full-time yet?" Anthony asked. Sophie confirmed that Markus was working full-time, and Janine was still on limited duties. "You can always ask Janine if she wants more hours; she can sit and prepare assorted candy bags for two three-hour shifts. If that proves to be difficult, keep your eyes and ears open, and see if anyone would fit in with your staff. Don't forget seniors or students for part-time hours.

They talked about Anthony's next visit to the store. "I'm impressed you noticed all the positives in James." He was relieved, as he really liked James, "Good choice, Sophie!" It was also his intention to promote him to store manager when the new stores are ready to open.

Anthony got back to his office, then he remembered something, and he caught Sophie before she left the store. "Sophie, before you take off, I need you to teach James how to complete an end-of-day memo tomorrow. Let me know how he does."

It crossed Sophie's mind that James was being trained for store manager, but she would do as Anthony asked, it may help pay for his university courses.

"If James has a problem, ask him to call me at home." He said goodbye to Sophie, assuring her that James would get his promotion.

Everything was going so well at his work, but the problems with his mom were escalating. She was being unreasonable because she was afraid of being alone, but if she didn't want to be alone, they could be next-door neighbours. He didn't understand why he couldn't get through to her. He sat for a few minutes in the car park near the gas station when his phone rang. He could see it was Imelda calling him, again.

"Okay, Mom. Mom, you must stop crying; I can't understand what you're saying." He waited a few seconds.

"It's your dad. Oh, Anthony, he was in an accident and was rushed to the hospital. He called me and asked me to go and see him."

"Mom, you can't go to see him. What about his wife? How did you find out about his accident?" Imelda continued to cry. "Mom, I'm on my way home now. Wait for me, please, Mom. Don't do anything until I get there."

He drove home quickly, and as he reached the driveway, his mind whirled, wondering what he should do. His dad had severed all ties to his son, and Anthony decided not to visit his dad in hospital. He saw his mom's pain, but he was unable to understand her acceptance of all the nasty things this man had done to her. From the day George walked out on his sick wife, Anthony never wanted any interaction with his selfish ass of a father.

"He needs me." Imelda tried to convince Anthony as soon as he entered the room.

"You're out of your mind, Mom. You need to pull yourself together, think about the consequences. What you intend to do is unthinkable; he was lying to you and cheating on you. He was so busy with his new woman that he never once considered your feelings." Anthony tried so hard to get through to his mom's sense of what was right.

"The most reprehensible, unforgivable thing he did was to abandon you when he found out you had cancer and upcoming surgery. Where was he when you were having surgery for thyroid cancer?" Anthony was exasperated, his tone a little higher, "I can tell you where he wasn't!"

"George called me. He asked me to go and see him in the hospital." Imelda began to argue, "He wants me to go to him."

Anthony was frustrated and decided to be blunt. "When you were in the hospital fighting cancer, he was in another woman's bed." Anthony told her again to think about what she was saying.

When he entered the kitchen, he apologized. "I'm sorry, Mom, but I am so frustrated because you won't listen to sense." Anthony poured a drop of brandy, and he offered it to his mom. He hoped it would calm her down, but she simply turned away, refusing to look at him.

"I know how you feel about him," her tone was loud and intimidating, but she needed her son to understand. "And just so you know . . ." she yelled even louder, "I have never stopped loving him."

"He didn't care if you lived or died." Anthony didn't want to continue arguing with his mom and opted to go for a shower. He said he wouldn't be long and that while he was in the shower, she should think about her situation. Imelda looked dreadful with her puffy eyes and her hair dishevelled, but he needed her to be sensible. "I must be frank . . . he cheated on you for a couple of years and married the woman, and you'll take him back?" Anthony waited to see if she was listening, "He'll probably do it again. Mom, you need to muster up some dignity."

She needed to realize the consequences of accepting him back. After all the heartache he caused, how could she trust him? Anthony knew she was lonely, but reconciliation with her ex was too much to think about.

When he got out of the shower, he dressed and headed down the stairs to continue the debate. He called her, and he got a horrid sinking feeling when she didn't reply. It dawned on him just how determined she was to see George. She must have gone to the hospital.

Anthony wanted to walk out the door, now more than ever. He wanted to leave his mom and get as far away as possible from all of her drama. Her purse and phone were gone, and she was gone. She had convinced herself that she still loved him. He couldn't imagine who would have called her to tell her that her ex-husband was in the hospital.

He thought, "What kind of situation are you getting into, Mom? I don't know what to do now." Saying it out loud didn't help at all. He grabbed his phone and called the hospital.

"Someone called my mom from the hospital to let her know my father was admitted earlier today." Anthony waited until the nurse answered.

"I'm sorry, sir, who do you wish to speak to?" the nurse asked.

"I need to know if you admitted a patient by the name of George Lynwood."

The nurse asked, "Is Mr. Lynwood a relation of yours?"

"He's my father; I'm Anthony Lynwood."

"Are you coming to the hospital to see your father?" she asked.

"Is he seriously ill? Why was he admitted?" Anthony was told that his father was in the ICU and that he was being monitored.

"He has been heavily medicated and sedated, and regarding his condition, the doctor is the only person who can answer your questions. I'm sorry, sir."

He told the nurse that he would get there as soon as possible.

The drive to the hospital was easy as there was a lull in traffic at that time of day. He asked himself what he was doing. He truly wanted to support his mom, but this situation was completely out of hand.

When he arrived at the hospital, he followed the signs to the ICU units.

He found a nurse. "I'm looking for my father, George Lynwood. He was admitted today."

"He's in Room 15. Turn left." The nurse pointed to the sign.

"Thank you."

Anthony walked into the room. It was a little bigger than a cubicle, but he could see his dad from the doorway. He was on his back, motionless, with tubes taped to his mouth and chest. Several machines were monitoring him.

A lady asked, "Can I help you?"

"I don't know. Who are you, and why are you here with my dad?"

"I'm Mrs. Delia Lynwood," she volunteered.

He hesitated to walk a little closer to the bed. "I'm Anthony Lynwood."

Awkward didn't describe the atmosphere.

"My mother got a phone call to let her know he was in ICU." Anthony took a very deep breath, "She assured me the call was from him. Obviously, it was not." He looked at his father, with all the life support machines active around his bed. "I am sorry to have disturbed you." He turned to leave.

"Just a moment, Anthony, are you not going to ask how he's doing?"

To Delia's surprise, Anthony answered scathingly, "I don't care."

"But he's your father. His prognosis is not very good." Delia shared.

"The day he walked out on my mom was the day she found out that she had cancer." Anthony looked at the floor and continued talking in a quiet monotone. "She had surgery and several che-motherapies after that." He looked at Delia, "Dad accused Mom of telling lies about her cancer and that he didn't have any feelings for her. That she was lazy and useless. He tried to destroy her. Oh, and he also told her that he had a new woman in his life. I assume that's you?"

"Oh, I'm sorry, Anthony. I didn't know about your mother having cancer." Delia looked sincere.

"No matter, I came here looking for my mom." Anthony headed for the door, "He walked out of my life, too. I had no way of contacting him; the least he could have done was to send me a text." He continued to stare at his dad. "I never want to set eyes on him again!"

"But he's your dad, and he's in an induced coma. He has a pulmonary embolism—a blood clot to his lung—they don't have much hope for his recovery." Delia thought she should stress how ill he was.

"He was my dad, but he gave up that right when he chose you over me. It's been three years since he left, and he chose to ignore me, he could have phoned or texted. I didn't know if he was dead or alive."

"He's a good man, and he had his reasons for leaving your mom. Please, give him a chance to explain." Delia tried to help him understand.

"No, it's too late for that. I honestly don't care if he makes it or not. Please, don't contact me or my mother."

By the time he walked to the car, his head was aching. Where was his mom? Her behaviour was unpredictable, to say the least. He tried calling her again, but she didn't pick up.

With no knowledge of any places his mom knew, Anthony didn't know where to start looking for her, so he drove straight home. He opened the front door; with no need for a key. "I went looking for you," he called out, "I thought you had gone to see Dad."

"I changed my mind. I went for a walk instead." Imelda didn't say where she went, and Anthony was suffering from a lack of curiosity.

He was, however, hopping mad at her deception. "Yet again, you lied to me. Mom, you have become a stranger to the truth. When Dad arrived at the hospital, he had suffered a heart attack and a blood clot. He was not in an accident; he was unconscious, so he didn't call you, and he didn't ask you to visit him." She sat looking at the floor. "Every time you open your mouth, I hear lies,

lies, and more lies. What are you hiding? Why lie? Tell me why he left you!" She began to cry.

Anthony didn't wait for a response, "I met his new wife, and I left instructions for the hospital staff not to call this number if anything happens to him."

"What was his wife like?" Imelda asked hesitatingly.

"She was worried about him. She was sitting at his bedside and waiting for some better news." He wanted to blast his mom for her duplicity, having him believe that she had gone to the hospital.

It was difficult, but he kept his tone respectful, "I found myself in an uncomfortable situation, and I had no intention of introducing myself to his wife." He threw his jacket on a nearby chair, "How could you?" his voice was quiet but angry, "I asked you to wait for me so we could talk it over." He grabbed a water bottle from the fridge, "Instead, you just took off!" Imelda didn't say a word.

"Her name is Delia," Anthony said. Imelda glared at him. "I suggest you stay away from her. If I find you locating his wife, I will leave here without a forwarding address." His eyes didn't leave her face, "Is that clear, Mom?" She didn't answer him. "Is that clear?"

"Why would you think I would try to get in touch with her? I assure you; I have no intention." She stood up, and on her way upstairs, she told him, "I have no intention of contacting your father, either."

"I wish I could believe you, but you admitted that you want him back, that you still love him." He got to the bottom step of the stairs and turned to face her, "For your own sanity, forget about him." She looked up at him like a petulant child, "If he comes here, Mom, I will leave. That's a promise, not an idle threat."

"I don't want to talk about him anymore. I'm sick to death of your accusations, and I don't want to argue with you, so I'm off to bed." Imelda replied with teary eyes.

His gut told him not to trust her. He wanted her to move on, make new friends or find a new beau and start living again. With her cancer in remission, there were copious numbers of support groups who wanted to help her, but Anthony hadn't realized, until now, how stubborn she was. Imelda had convinced herself that George had called her, but that was impossible. It was another lie.

Anthony's decision to move back home was the worst decision he had ever made. It was futile arguing with Imelda as she was deaf to all suggestions regarding their situation. It's unbelievable how she lacked self-respect, which was especially apparent when she decided to invite women to have dinner with her son.

With his head hung down, Anthony admitted that his home life was crappy and getting worse by the minute, but he had a burst of imagination, silly thoughts invading his mind. "Next time—if there was going to be a next time that Imelda invited him to dine with a potential spouse; he should wear a full cowboy outfit with a Stetson hat." It would be hilarious. Imelda would not be able to handle it; she would go nuts when he demanded she pass him the spittoon. This crazy thought tickled his funny bone!

He headed to his room to work on some sales projections, but he was so exhausted, he face-planted on the keyboard.

At four a.m., Anthony was pacing the floor, and thinking aloud, "I need to get away. She has manipulated me for the last time. After meeting Delia, he refused to accept reconciliation between his parents." He looked up, "Lord, help me. What can I do, where do I go from here?"

Absolutely nothing had changed. Every suggestion he made that would allow him some independence was thwarted, and Imelda kept crossing that dividing line. She needed to have control, which was evident, as she wanted to choose the woman who would provide her with grandchildren. She wasn't making sense, but then it crossed his mind: what if his dad had seen this side of her? Maybe he felt trapped in some way.

Anthony was convinced she had gone batty! She thought he could be forced to have grandchildren yet he may not be able to sire a child. What stupid nonsense would her back-up plan consist of then?

Anthony was convinced his mom was living in La, la, land. He knew he had to go to work, but that was the easy bit; he loved his job. The alternative was to stay home, and every time he thought about his mother's confession, he was convinced his father would be there when he got home from work.

After his shower, he left early for work. It was a long drive up to the northern shores of the Island to Port Hardy to visit an established store. He filled up with gas, grabbed a breakfast sandwich and a coffee, and turned the radio up. He was heading north, on a five-hour drive, to visit Jade

Anthony had very few friends, so he mostly kept to himself, but after the recent dealings with his mom, and all of her problems, it proved that he didn't have the knowledge or experience to deal with her issues. He was certain she needed to see a doctor. It was typical melancholy, and crying had become the norm, but when he suggested she needed help, she adamantly refused. His perception of their problems was simple, he needed to move out, but that was easier said than done. She needed help, and he didn't know where to turn or how she would cope if he abandoned her now.

4

He left home earlier this morning, while his mom was in bed, without telling her what his schedule was like. She started phoning him when she got out of bed and she called him often, throughout the day.

He finally grabbed his phone and reduced the volume. He booked into the Richmond Hotel and decided to give himself some space, hoping to come up with a solution, his primary objective was to take a break from the endless confrontations with his mom.

Recently, his dad had been in his thoughts; it was so out of character for George to dump all of his responsibilities. Being away at university, Anthony was unaware that things had gone sour between his parents. George always had the patience to play a game of chess, go swimming, and challenge Anthony to race across the pool. During his teen years, they often got on their bikes and headed off for an ice cream fix. Why would he walk away from his son?

Another pastime they shared was woodwork, and George's favourite was building birdhouses, and Anthony loved to paint them. Several neglected hand-painted plant pots, in an array of sizes, littered the patio deck. They were the focal point of the yard.

George was a proud father who was caring and loving, and this was how Anthony remembered him. It was so hard for him to believe that these two people were his parents. He didn't recognize either of them.

Anthony just wanted to ask his dad why he left home without any warning and why he never contacted him to tell him why he walked out.

Anthony had made it painfully clear to Imelda that he can't and won't live under the same roof as his dad. He was persistently reeling from the shock of his mom's admission that she still loved her ex-husband.

When Anthony finally called home, his mom answered, "I have so much work to do here, and the drive was too long, so I'll see how it goes and I'll probably be home by next Friday."

That was not what Imelda wanted to hear. "Anthony, I need you home. I cannot stay in this house alone. I'm scared."

"Don't be ridiculous. I have no intentions of babysitting you; I have to work for a living." He believed he had no option but to be firm with her. "This can be a trial period, Mom. Remember, you can choose one of the following options: you can sell our house and move into an apartment, go live in a senior's complex, or split our house into two halves, and I will be your neighbour." Anthony added for good measure, "You are spoiled for choice, but you have to decide soon. If you refuse, I may sell my half of the house to a stranger." To Imelda, it was an idle threat.

"I've got to go now, Mom. I'll call you in a couple of days." Anthony didn't wait for her answer; he ended the call, and blocked her number. His phone was always on when he was working, and Imelda tried to contact him several times. Later that evening he texted her to let her know he had decided to stay away for the long weekend.

Imelda called every hour. She was determined that Anthony must come home; she needed to know what he was doing all the time. Thanks to her interference, he was living in a ridiculous environment that resembled a sideshow at a rodeo. He decided to stay away from her until he could figure a way round their problems. He kept his phone on after he blocked her number on his cell phone. He must accept calls from his staff, and handle calls that were work-related. Each time he checked his voicemail, the messages were all from his mom.

It was no use. He couldn't think of one good reason for calling her. So, he didn't.

Jade Cardinal, the store manager, was cleaning the cooler. The second Anthony walked into the store his brain went into work mode. "Good morning, Alice." He addressed the young clerk as he walked through the office door before asking how things were going. "I'm here to see Jade. Do I spy a new face on board?"

"I'm sorry, mister, but you aren't allowed in there. It's a staff-only room." The new guy, Brett, addressed him again. "Please, mister, I need you to leave this part of the store . . . now!"

"What's your name, young man?" Anthony asked while smiling, "I'm Anthony Lynwood, and I'm here to see Jade."

He didn't see her in the store, and he was sure she was working today. Anthony asked, "Where is she hiding?"

"She's cleaning the cooler because several cartons of milk were not sealed properly. So, she went to clean the cooler. You can't go in there." Brett was serious.

Anthony turned to leave the office. He called Jade's name, "Tame your new bodyguard." Anthony laughed, "He just ordered me out of the store."

Jade was watching, and as he walked around to the front door, she stepped out of the cooler and welcomed him, "Well, hello stranger! Let me introduce you to Brett."

"Brett, come and meet Anthony; he's my boss from our head office." Jade saw them shake hands and clarified, "Brett is here as a trainee janitor." Anthony looked at her in amazement.

Jade asked Brett for his help. "Please, check that the floor is clean and finish wiping the shelves in the cooler. Oh, Brett, polish the glass doors, inside and out. We need them super clean and shiny so we can put new cartons back on the shelf."

"You know how difficult it is to get staff around here?" Jade complained to Anthony, "I asked personnel if I could hire a bright young man with more abilities than disabilities." Although Brett had a form of dyslexia, Jade announced that he could function quite well by memorizing colours and performing repetitive tasks.

"He has a developmental disorder, which can cause a learning complexity in one or more areas of reading, writing, and numeracy.

"It's Brett's first week here, and so far, he has kept his head down. He's a quick learner, and he's always asking questions. Unfortunately, he's only allowed to work part-time, as he has a personal aide who sees to all his needs.

"He's learning the products, and he's doing a great job keeping the shelves stocked. He remembers to ask for help to complete the necessary steps." Jade continued, "All the clerks look out for him. We're pleased to have him on board." Jade was happy with her protégé, "He makes up all the bags, weighs them very carefully, and attaches the special colour-coded recipes and shopping list for fresh meat and vegetables."

"He can do all those duties and be a bodyguard to the boss. I'm impressed." Anthony grinned.

"He loves the company here. He's a sociable character and working here is a major contrast to his lonely life; and his personality fits right in with us. They walked around the store talking about the new items on back-order due to the supplier's limitations.

"Jade, I'm taking a couple of days to do your store assessment. I know, I'm a few days early, but I was in the vicinity."

Jade had an excellent rapport with Anthony, but she couldn't let that one go. "You were in this vicinity?" Jade challenged him,

"You're telling me you came on the off-chance?" She burst out laughing. "Other than me, who else do you know that lives this far north?"

"I have booked into the hotel here in town." His smile didn't reach his eyes.

'Do your worst!" She teased him, "I wondered why you hadn't returned my calls. I assumed you must be doing your rounds."

"Can I borrow your desk?" Anthony was always polite, "The two new stores that have just opened came up with a list of ideas on up-selling: counter displays, impulse items, competitions, and seasonal displays." He powered up his laptop, "Let me show you what I've gathered."

They covered most sales tactics. "It's almost time to close," Anthony replied and had decided to invite Jade to supper at his hotel. He thoroughly enjoyed her company, more than any other woman he knew.

Seated at a table, they ordered a pot of green tea. "I've been giving lots of thought about local Indigenous artists. It's important to make sure it's authentic, and this could be a great way to connect emerging artists with vacationers looking for original artwork."

"Indigenous artists should have the power to reshape their own urban spaces," Jade was educating Anthony, "They reflect their contemporary and traditional values, stories, experiences, and ideas, in this lasting and tangible way."

Though Anthony had the basic idea, he needed help with the concepts that Jade was trying to verify, "The artists in all store districts will be able to create and promote their own ideas. I believe that would work. What do you suggest?"

He was mulling over the fact that vacationers wanted original artwork, and what a bonus to see how these items were fashioned. "I'm suggesting we invite artists to sell carvings, cards, jewellery, clothes, and other items that are solely resourced from our First Nations artists and crafters."

Jade was amazed, "Do you mean only one local artist per store?"

"We have limited space, and one artist per store would work for starters. And remember, we can't take up store space, we can only use the excess space we find."

Jade needed clarification, "Are you suggesting we open a gallery type section, where they can create their art and sell it in the store?"

"Maybe, we can also consider seasonal end-caps, especially if the store is smaller and space is at a premium." He then stated, "Possibly three months in the summer and one month before Christmas."

"That would be great," she agreed. "During the summer months, say, from April to September, that's when the Island has lots of tourists. We can offer a tiny bit of the store where artists can create their art." Jade was always looking for a way to promote her cultural arts and crafts.

"It can also benefit the artist when the rains start. Their artwork can stay dry," she pointed out. "It's a great idea! What do you think about the overall concept?"

Anthony was also thinking of other options, particularly if the artist didn't want to spend time in the store, pre-packaged containers, and price tags might work.

"Tourists want original artwork," Anthony said, "it's a winner; ever since this idea was first mentioned I've been gathering ideas and making Alexis aware of what we hope to achieve. When we get back to the store, we can figure something out." He ran Hayden's ideas by her. "Hayden suggested that we rotate the different artists and crafters to get more people involved.

"I have also asked Hayden not to discuss this idea with anyone. I will introduce you two later. He's a smart kid with buckets full of ideas."

"He sounds great. But first, Anthony Lynwood, you come here with a face like a wet weekend. You're not your usual boisterous self. And you asked me to dinner? Are you feeling okay?"

"My mom's being a pain and my dad's in a coma. I'm feeling stressed, but that's because I'm still living with my mom, even though her cancer is in remission. Oh, Jade, I hate going to that house. I'm craving my independence again."

He gave a forced laugh, "It's a nightmare living with her, especially when she keeps inviting strange women to our home to meet me. Women she doesn't even know show up for dinner because she wants to choose her daughter-in-law so she can have grandkids."

"Oh, what can I say about that?" Jade burst out laughing. She would have offered to help him, but she had no clue how to handle his problem. "You moved in with your mom to help her through her cancer recoup." She watched his expressions, "and you're still there three years later?" He looked at her very seriously. "You need to leave, Anthony. You're doing neither you nor your mom a favour by staying."

He nodded his head. "Yep, I'm bursting to leave. I keep trying to escape, but she blocks me." Jade laughed out loud. "Honestly, she's so confrontational! She's either yelling or crying for attention, and she'll do anything to get her own way."

"You used the word escape. Does she lock you in your room or shackle you to a wall? And you said she blocks you? Anthony, she's half your size!" Jade told him she had a vision of Steve McQueen on a motor bike at the end of the movie *The Great Escape* being chased by his mom. "All joking aside, you need to talk to her. She sounds like she isn't coping with her lifestyle. Maybe she should apply for a job as a correction officer?"

"Jade, you are not funny!" But they both giggled.

Anthony continued with his tale of woe. He told her how his dad abandoned his family. "It was so out of character for him

45

to walk away, and at that time, I was working in Vancouver, so I didn't notice if he confronted Mom. Well, I wasn't aware if he did—he never said a word to me."

He told Jade about his dad's new family and how he met George's new wife at the hospital. He told her the story about his dad lying in ICU with a lousy prognosis.

Anthony went on to explain why his dad used the house as part of his parent's divorce settlement. George refused to hand the house over to Imelda, and Imelda eventually agreed that Anthony was to be given the deeds to half of the house. "So, I own half a house, but my mom won't hear of moving on or starting anew. She opposes all of my ideas when it comes to altering the footprint of the house. She's so stubborn and so difficult that she has finally driven me away. I walked out."

"It's time for me to go." Jade checked her watch. "I'm working in the morning." They both started laughing.

"Thanks, Jade. I needed a friend, a good listener who doesn't judge." Anthony was holding her jacket. She was hoping for a kiss or a hug. She wasn't disappointed when he hugged her and wished her pleasant dreams, as he was her best friend who was always there when she needed him. Jade felt they shared a good rapport, and she hoped she could always be there for him, especially now, when he needed it the most.

The northern shores of Vancouver Island are rugged. The untamed craggy shoreline has a jagged beauty that is complemented by the way the ocean frames the shoreline. Visitors who care to linger can enjoy the solitude of the vast untouched forests in the several campsites within the secluded beaches, giving everyone the opportunity to experience paradise. They get the chance to see the plentiful and varied species of wildlife that can compete with any travel magazine.

As Anthony walked along the sandy shore, enjoying the peace and quiet, he made plans for some small changes Jade requested. Although the gulls were noisy and the wind was blustery, Anthony didn't want to leave this idyllic spot. Most locals boast a simple life amid this stunningly beautiful terrain. Wherever you turn, you have oceanic vistas perfect for spotting whales, and the noisy gulls hovering overhead waiting for the fish to appear. The majestic and most revered of all birds was the magnificent bald eagle soaring across the sky, looking for prey. Standing by the water's edge, Anthony could see the reflection of the early morning sun shimmering off the water.

Two local fishermen came close to shore in a small motorboat and cast their lines, sitting back to wait for a bite. The locals are known for their ability to catch fish; it's an element of the survival skills that were passed down from their ancestors.

Anthony had a flashback as he remembered his dad taking him fishing for his tenth birthday. They went to the pier in Sidney, and George had stocked up the cooler with snacks. He swore Anthony to secrecy because the candy and pop were not Mom-approved. Neither of them was successful fishermen; Anthony couldn't remember ever catching a fish, but they enjoyed being there together, sitting on the pier, watching the sea otters play.

The wind was blustering again. He walked a little further down the sandy beach and came across a boy and a girl with kites; he could hear their mom calling them for breakfast and warning them that they were going to be late for school.

A huge rock on the shoreline was calling him to take a few minutes and watch the ocean. He sat comfortably on his jacket. The sea had a fascination for him like no other, and he decided that he would like to live in a place like this, close to the shore. Waves were constantly hitting the rugged rocks, and the gushing sound was mesmerizing, enhancing his senses and increasing his awareness of the smell of saltwater, enticing him to go swimming. It was too cold this time of year, so he hadn't considered packing swimwear, but he wished he had. His favourite pastime was snorkelling, especially around these rugged northern shores. He would recommend swimming in the ocean to anyone, but this far north, they'd have to invest in a wet suit as the water was bitterly cold.

The thought of moving to a seaside location, with its endless views, may entice Imelda to move. This was another excellent alternative, an idea that hopefully, she may consider, and at this juncture, anything was worth a try.

He contemplated how to broach this solution; he was no expert, and he's too soft by far when handling her. Considering that his sanity depended on her cooperation, he felt he should try to make a deal with her. He could find a house or an apartment, on the ocean, to show her the possibilities. His problems begin when Imelda became teary-eyed. He immediately gave in to her wishes, hoping she'd eventually compromise and move from their present house. This could be his ticket to independence and possibly give him a chance to have a relationship.

His mom was clinging to a love that had disappeared, dissipated, and had gone sour, gone forever. The house belonged to the past too. He was ensnared when his mom refused rent or a payment of any kind. Anthony had always been an avid saver but never stingy. He was very generous, especially for a good cause. It was good to be rent-free, which made his present financial situation very good.

His phone began to ring, bringing him back to the present. "Hi, Jade." Something happened that she didn't want to explain in great detail, over the phone. "Yes, I'm about twenty minutes north. I'm on my way."

"Thank heavens you're still here." Jade quickly related the story of an accident. "One of our senior customers was in the car park loading his groceries into his car. A truck, pulling into park, backed into him. The truck driver insists it was an accident. I called the cops and an ambulance, and when they arrived, they took the hurt customer to the hospital. Oh, Anthony, I hope he's okay."

Jade was able to get Brett in for a couple of hours to help out while she dealt with the car accident.

"First thing, I'll call the hospital to see if we can help in any way." Anthony was already dialling the number. The hospital refused to comment on the man's condition, but they assured Anthony that the man was being attended to in the Emergency room.

"Yes! Anthony, that's his car." Jade pointed, "It didn't suffer any damage at all. He was bent over to load his groceries in the trunk when it happened. I hope the man is okay."

Anthony opened the car door, but Jade stated that the police had already gone through the vehicle. He opened the glove box and grabbed the customer's identification. As the store was incredibly busy, Anthony decided to step in to lend a hand while he considered his next step.

They spent their time filling and refilling products, checking the expiry dates, and moving all the soon-to-be outdated products off the shelves. They cleared out the storage room and separated the high and low volume sales, and the products that were seasonal were packed or put on sale. They stored any re-useable, nonedible products in boxes.

Brett came into the store and asked for his list of duties for the day. His list was colour-coded, but when he found the product, he asked for confirmation that he had the correct list. His extra help made everyone's job easier, and they finished all the chores by closing time.

Now the store was closed Anthony had decided to drive to the hospital with hopes of finding the customer, even though he had no way of recognizing him. When he entered the hospital, the duty nurse informed him that usually only family and friends were allowed to visit, but she would talk to the patient to see if he was accepting visitors, by pure luck, he welcomed the stranger.

Anthony was led to Mr. Keel's room. "He's a tough old gent, and he's doing fine. His legs were extremely bruised as the truck driver hit him with his bumper," the nurse stated, "but there's good news . . . no broken bones! He was very fortunate."

Anthony introduced himself, and asked if he could help in any way, and that's when the nurse asked if Anthony was taking Mr. Keel home.

Anthony brought his Jeep to the Emergency entrance to pick up Mr. Keel. The older gentleman was very gracious, "I can't thank you enough, young man!" he stated as Anthony lifted him into the Jeep. Sheepishly, Mr. Keel asked if his car was still in the parking lot.

"Your car is right where you left it."

"Can I get it tonight?" Mr. Keel was on a strong drug, and driving was out of the question. "Please," he was pleading.

"No, the nurse said you're on medication and not able to drive." Then Anthony had a thought, "But, I'll call Jade and ask her if she can bring your car while we make a welcome cup of tea. How is that for a deal?"

"Thank you," Mr. Keel said, "I live on my own, so it would be hard to get a ride to my car."

Driving a little way along Ocean Drive, they came upon a tiny bungalow perched on a craggy mound. It had the most beautiful view of the ocean, and the beach was his front lawn. "Well, sir, you couldn't have chosen a nicer spot for your house." It was perfect. The men made their way into Mr. Keel's home, where Anthony put the kettle on and brewed the tea.

"The Missus passed away twenty-two years ago. This little piece of heaven was our dream; it's so peaceful here. Many times, we'd sit together on the cobbles, watching the waves. Even now, after all these years, I sit in that same spot and I think about her. I've never had a notion to sell it; I feel close to her here. We were in love: young, happy, and content until she went to see the doctor and was told she was expecting a baby. We were the happiest folks alive. Then the saddest thing happened later that same day, she also received the results of some earlier tests, and they found she had leukemia. Annie and baby were both put to rest three months later."

Anthony stayed for quite a while, listening to his stories.

"It was interesting how little some things have changed over the years. I'm in my fifties and so set in my ways. Every day is the same as the day before."

After a while, Anthony assured Mr. Keel that his car would be delivered the next morning, first thing. He asked Mr. Keel if he was retired or if he still worked.

"I was an accountant in my younger days, and now I work part-time. I dabble a little, submitting tax returns to Revenue Canada, and generally helping folks out here with their personal taxes."

"It's great to be able to help your neighbours like that! But, it is time for me to go.

"It was so nice to meet you Mr. Keel." Anthony genuinely enjoyed his company.

"Now that we're friends, you can call me Sammy."

"Okay, Sammy. I'll see you tomorrow," Anthony confirmed before leaving Sammy's home and driving away.

When Anthony arrived back at his hotel, he called Jade, and they arranged to drive Sammy's car back to him. "Oh, Anthony, I have his spare set of keys, the police have his keys and some documents which I will pick up for him."

"I've known that man for several years, and this is the first time I've known his name!" She described him as quiet, passive, and pleasant. Anthony thought of him as interesting, caring, and very friendly.

"I'll drive to his house in the morning, and you can pick up his keys from the police station and bring his car. Then I'll drive you back to the store." Jade had no problem with that arrangement.

"Get some sleep, mister," Jade advised. "And I'll see you tomorrow."

While Jade was driving Sammy's car, her foremost thoughts—as they had been these past couple of days—were with Anthony. She thought of how he must free himself of his battle-axe of a mom, he's a grown man who needs his own space. She had never met his mom, but she sounded like a master manipulator.

"Come on in, lass. I have your hubby here waiting for you. We're having a cup of tea." He poured an extra cup and handed it to her.

"Mr. Keel, how are you feeling today?" Jade asked, wanting to help him. "I was worried about you, especially after seeing the accident yesterday."

"I don't want any fuss. I felt sorry for that young feller; I was sorting out my trunk and I was bent over and he wouldn't have seen me through hi rear view mirror."

"You're getting around pretty good, I see. I was worried that the accident badly damaged your legs, but you're walking around just fine. No broken bones, eh! You are a lucky man!" Jade thanked him for her tea and sat down at the kitchen table.

"No broken bones," he smiled, agreeing with Jade. "That young man in the truck was driving slowly, so I don't think it was intentional." Shaking his head, "It was an accident. I must thank you for calling an ambulance to get me to the hospital and for bringing my car to me." He added, "Call me Sammy. I would like that."

"Well, Sammy, I'm Jade. I'm the store manager, and Anthony isn't my hubby; he's my boss."

"Thank you both for all of your help." They continued their friendly conversation until their tea was done.

Sammy followed them to the door. "I'll be coming to your store again soon. I hope to see you both again."

As Jade and Anthony drove back to the store, they discussed Sammy's accident. Then the discussion turned to Sammy's home and its location. "I want a house like his on the beach, and I'll get one sooner or later. That's the good news. The bad news is . . . how do I get rid of my mom?" They both laughed heartily and had a fit of the giggles all the way back to town.

"She's my mom, and I wanted her to be part of my life—but she has to stop matchmaking! She has no idea what I'm looking for in a partner."

5

He took a deep breath and said, "I'm gay. I have zero interest in women, romantically, that is."

"That must be awkward for you," Jade commiserated.

"She doesn't realize what she's missing. Her life stopped when Dad left. She needs a new start and a damn big push to help her restart it. She needs something to get up for in the morning and someone special in her life. She actually stays in the house most of the time, with occasional trips to the grocery store. She never goes to dress shops or buys new shoes, and very rarely she goes to the hairdresser and even the dentist."

"Does she know about you being gay?" Jade threw caution to the wind as she already knew the answer.

"You had to ask, didn't you?" Anthony laughed. "You figured me out, but you still had to ask." She didn't answer but waited for his reply. "She doesn't have a clue."

"When were you going to tell her?" Jade loved this man so much, but now she knew he wasn't romantically interested in her at all.

He couldn't pretend to guess his mom's reaction; she was unpredictable. He confessed he had no clue on how to approach his mom.

"Are you planning to stay here this weekend?" Jade asked, slightly changing the topic. "I'm thinking of going snorkelling, and you're welcome to come along." Though she knew nothing romantic would happen between them, she loved his friendship even more and wanted him to stay for as long as possible. She was wondering how she could keep him around longer.

"I didn't bring my gear." Then he explained, "I went walking to the point, earlier, and smelling the salty air, swimming crossed my mind, but it's too cold for me." He told her that he had no plans to go swimming without his wet suit, but he wanted to go beach-combing and just hang around the beach for a couple of days.

"I'll take that. It'll be great fun spending time together." Jade laid down the law. "Rule #1: no business. Rule #2: no fishing." Jade knew he'd ignore Rule #2, but would eat, sleep, and drink Rule #1.

"Jade, you're beginning to sound like my Mom!" They both laughed.

"What about Rule #3? No discussing my problems. I am actually working on a master plan of my love life, and I honestly don't need anyone's help."

"Did I hear you correctly? You are concocting a master plan of your love life?" Jade laughed, "You are crazy, eh?"

Anthony remembered when James was interviewed for his job, how he admired his good looks, his dark brown hair, and eyes, not to mention his smile. In fact, James bordered on perfection.

"It's probably too soon to ask who the lucky man is." Jade was reticent. Anthony was a reserved person who would not be comfortable telling her about his dreams.

Although Anthony usually shares his feelings with Jade, he wasn't ready yet. He had met someone he believed was "the one," but he needed to get to know him better. Anthony became lost in his thoughts, instantly thinking of James who must have some inkling how he feels. Sometime soon, Anthony intends to spend time with James, he needs to know if they are feeling the same chemistry; but right now he was on tenterhooks, curious to find out if James feels the same. He'll soon know when he plucks up the courage to ask him out on a date.

"If he'll have me, I'll be a very happy man." He told Jade.

They spent the whole weekend together. Jade invited Anthony to a barbeque at her apartment; she wanted to show off her newly renovated kitchen and her new deck. She bragged about having air-conditioning and Anthony was impressed. As it was Sunday evening, and she had to work the next day, they agreed it was time to call it a night.

"This weather makes me sleepy," Anthony said. He got up and grabbed his jacket. "See you tomorrow, I'll call in to say goodbye before I head back to Victoria."

The next day, Anthony had reluctantly decided to check-in with his mom since it had been quite some time since they spoke. After leaving Jade's store, and before he hit the road, he checked his phone and Imelda had called him. He returned her call, "Hi, Mom!" When Imelda didn't answer him immediately, he asked, "Are you okay, Mom?" He didn't particularly want to discuss his sexuality with his mom on the phone. He had decided to take Jade's advice. It was time to speak to her in person regarding his being gay, just in case she reacted badly. Her hesitation to answer his call was soon solved.

"I just wanted to make sure you were okay, and I also wanted to know when you are coming home." Imelda then mentioned that she had planned another dinner, as she had met a very nice girl.

"Stop right there. I'm not coming home." This time he gave it to her full bore, "I don't want to come home, ever! I'm not eating dinner with a stranger, so I'll drop in for more clothes if and when I am in the area."

She started to argue about how lonely her life was without him.

"Make friends, join a bowling team, take up golf; you owe it to yourself to get a life." Anthony's suggestions were ignored, as usual.

"You need to get some professional help, and until you do, I have no intentions of living there with you. That house reminds me of Dad. What we need, Mother, is a fresh start. When I get back to Victoria, I'll start looking at the property listings; we both need a new home and certainly not together."

Imelda abruptly ended the call. Anthony was annoyed as he began driving south—his mother was making him crazy. He wanted to be anywhere except where she was.

After stopping for gas, Anthony called her again, "Please, listen to me, Mom. I don't want to quarrel, so don't ignore my calls, or we will not be able to talk amicably, which means there will be no solution to our predicament. I need my own place." Anthony immediately realized she had hung up on him again.

He was almost at Nanaimo when he decided to call on Sophie. He needed to find things at the store that needed attention something to distract him. Above all, he was hoping to see James. He had a good reason to stay overnight, and he chose to get a hotel room.

It was mid-afternoon, and the store was bustling with shoppers and their kids. Anthony realized they had the Easter colouring competition well in hand.

As he walked through the door, he was greeted by James, "Wow, we didn't expect a store visit so soon."

"I was actually driving past Nanaimo on my way home from Port Hardy. I was working there for a few days, and then I took the weekend off to be a beach-bum." Anthony elaborated, telling James about the sandy beaches, the old fishermen, the houses on the beach where Sammy lives, and Jade and her bodyguard, Brett.

"I can see you've been getting busy," Anthony mentioned as he looked around the store. "Do you need a hand with anything?" Anthony took his jacket off. "We have dedicated tills, and I don't want to do a cash-out/cash-in, so find me a different job."

"Kelly needs help," James replied. "She was filling the chips—we got a new merchandise plan-o-gram—and because of the customer volume today, we have all been struggling. She was also helping us on the floor, showing customers some of our best sellers. She's mega fun to work with, and she's good at her job." James was insisting the staff be recognized, particularly when they do tasks without being asked, and show their innovative and creative skills, especially when the store was so busy. "Kelly is quite a gem!"

"Thanks, James. I'll go find her. Is Marcus here today?"

"He worked six days straight." James was not overly fond of Marcus. "Did Sophie know you were coming?" Anthony shook his head.

"I wanted to ask if we could find a nice restaurant tonight and have a chat," Anthony suggested trying not to show how nervous he was. Then as an after-thought he asked, "That's if you can spare the time?" Anthony had obviously surprised James.

"I've no plans for tonight. There's the Fish Palace; it has good food and its close by."

"That sounds perfect. Thanks, James. Now, put me to work!"

Anthony didn't care if his job was five pay scales above the clerks; if he could make things run smoother, then he'd roll up his sleeves and get on with the job at hand. He found it easier to show the junior staff that he knew what he was doing, by occasionally taking off his 'boss' hat. They could watch and learn how to handle the difficult customers, and witness excellent customer service. They would learn what's expected of all staff. It was a big incentive to the staff, when they saw how well Anthony could handle things. If you have the smarts, and if you are eager to work, a promotion was an achievable goal.

Kelly was grateful for Anthony's help. The containers she was stacking were too heavy for her small frame. "Kelly, wait, let me show you an easier way." He showed her how to split the cartons and move smaller amounts. "Now that was easy, eh?" Kelly was smiling. "When you split a box of any product, remember to write the total of the remaining packets on each box, as well as the date and your initials. It makes for an easy audit. When you take product out of the box, change the number accordingly."

"Anthony, come meet my friend!" James urged him to meet the little tyke, Adam. He introduced Karen first, and then Adam, who held his hand out for a handshake. He was so cute that Anthony wanted to pick him up for a hug.

"James has been so good to us since we moved to this area. It's not easy making new friends, and he lives close by, so we see him often." Karen knew what James was like, "Adam hero-worships James, who takes him to play in the park when he has a day off. You would think a handsome young man like James would have better things to do, but he is patient and kind to my son; he's a very special person. Although, there are times when I feel guilty dragging him away from his studies."

"It was a pleasure to meet you, Karen, and you too, Adam." Anthony was so impressed with James' work.

Adam, though, had the last word! "I've been collecting boxes so I can make a car for my room. James will show me how to build it, and I want it to be like that one." He pointed to the car on the shelf.

Anthony passed Karen a ten-dollar bill. "Add this to his collection, please. He deserves a treat for being so grown up and wanting a handshake." Anthony excused himself from Karen and Adam to continue helping in the store.

As they checked the back doors and security alarm, Anthony commented, "You have everyone eating out of your hands! You're doing a great job, man!"

"It's time to relax, though," James said, "we've had a very busy day. You make all the jobs look easy, and I'm glad you came here today." James and Anthony had decided to head directly to the restaurant after work. He was singing Anthony's praises as they made their way to the Jeep.

"I've worked for this company since high school," Anthony informed him, "I've had lots of practice, in fact, my old boss used to send me to pacify any irate customers. I got all the grumpy ones, but I didn't mind. I can take a lot of agro before I lose my cool."

They arrived at the Fish Palace, where they served chicken as an alternative, although chicken wasn't on the menu. They were shown to a booth and given menus. "Would you like to order a drink while you browse the menu?" the waiter asked.

Anthony told the waiter that this was his first visit. The waiter helpfully recommended a glass of Stella Artois. "How often do you see Adam? And the reason I am asking is . . . he's a real character. I don't know many little kids, but Adam is one of a kind. I'll never forget his handshake. He looked me in the eye, smiled, and greeted me properly."

"I've only known Karen for a few months since I got this job. We live close by, and sometimes I take Adam to play in the park to give Karen a break. She shared her story with me of how she tragically lost her husband—who was in a nasty car accident on his way to the hospital to greet baby Adam." James could see that Anthony was interested, and he continued, "She found it difficult to walk into an empty house, with her new baby in her arms, when her whole world had collapsed. She's had a hard time, but she's bringing Adam up to be a great guy."

"How tragic, poor Karen and poor Adam, he never knew his dad. Does she have family in this area?"

"No. She was an orphan, and no one adopted her." James looked sad as he explained, "Karen met her husband when they were both in foster care as teens. Her husband was left at a fire station when he was born, and he had no records of his family either. It's a very sad story. He was her life. She's a very smart lady and I enjoy spending time with her and Adam."

The food arrived. "Oh my, this is a feast! Where do I begin?" Anthony's appetite was affected by James' story.

"I should take a doggie bag home. My mom isn't the best cook."

James looked at Anthony, unbelieving, so he had to ask, "Do you live with your mom?"

"I left home when I went to university. When I got my degree the company put me on a fast track, where I worked in Edmonton for a few months as store manager. They quickly transferred me to Vancouver, as the company was expanding rapidly. I was there for a few months training to be a regional manager. Eventually they needed to relocate me to Victoria.

"I was already moving to Victoria, when my mom got cancer, and my dad walked out on her the day she was given the prognosis. He found a new partner. Can you imagine? When she arrived back from her doctor's appointment, my dad had all his stuff packed and was on his way out the door. Dad accused her of telling lies about the cancer and being useless and lazy." Anthony went on to tell him that he moved back in with his mom to help her recover. "Now I'm desperate to move out because she's driving me crackers!"

James was hanging onto his every word. He listened as Anthony described how his mom was obsessed with finding him a wife. "My mom insists she wants grandchildren at all costs." Anthony explained, "It's hard to believe I was introduced to so many prospective brides, who I've only met once."

"I can't imagine! We're in the twenty-first century, why have you waited so long to tell her that you're gay?" James shook his head. "Sorry, I'm being presumptuous, but I'm surprised, I just assumed . . . how come she hasn't figured this out for herself?"

"Don't be sorry—you're correct! I am wary as my mother and I are not on the same planet or in the same universe. How can I produce grandkids unless I adopt some?"

James asked outright, "Would you be willing to adopt?"

"I would love that, if I have the right partner." Anthony would love a family. "Putting up with my mom's crappy behaviour for the last two years, I don't feel like I have any options. I can't have a relationship the way things are. When my parents split, I should have moved closer to her, instead, I got my old room back. My dad surrendered his half of the house to me during their divorce to ensure I got half of the title. It was hard trying to understand why he never contacted me." Anthony couldn't resist, "I just want to be rid of the house and my mom. I know it sounds harsh, but if you knew her, you would run a mile."

"What about you? Is your life perfect?" Anthony waited for James to speak. "If you say yes, I will cry."

"My life is far from perfect. I have two sisters and a brother. My dad's from Seattle, and my mom's from Brazil." James told Anthony about his dad having an alcohol problem, "It's been going on for years; I don't know why my mom puts up with him. When I was ready to head off to university, I found out that my dad had drunk away all of my savings. I came home another day, and he had sold my laptop." James had every right to be disappointed with his dad.

James admitted, "Believe it or not, I'm a huge fan of *World of Warcraft*, but all my toons were gone. It was my escape-to when I was feeling down; I found it was easy talking to the other players because you don't know them, and they don't know you."

"You, too, eh? It was my favourite game to play; I just needed to make more time." Anthony was very quiet after that, as he waited for James to continue.

"I lost the whole game, and because I couldn't afford another computer, I had to say goodbye to my hobby. Apart from the first couple of games, which were on DVD, the rest were downloads. That trouncing was excessive and would cost far too much money to recreate." James refused another beer when Anthony offered, but he asked the waiter for a coffee. "I couldn't afford another computer; I was so mad at my dad."

"You've had it tough too," Anthony commiserated.

"I have to drive back to Victoria tonight," Anthony said as he smiled at James. "Put me out of my misery. Are you in a relationship?"

"No." James grinned.

"Well, I'd love to spend more time getting to know you, if you'd like? I've enjoyed this time together, thank you." Anthony didn't want to leave this handsome man.

"Do you have a set schedule? Or do you go where and when you are needed?" James asked.

"I usually try to book as many store visits as I think are right for the company, but I can change my plans if necessary. Alexis, my boss, has always been very accommodating."

"So I may see you more often?" James asked with a grin.

"I'd like that." They stood outside the restaurant after Anthony paid the bill, and slowly made their way to the Jeep. On the drive back, they chatted for a while. Anthony couldn't believe how easy it was to relax with James; how this evening was so much more exciting than he had originally thought.

"Anthony, what do you think of taking me up north with you the next time you go? I have some time banked already. You made the beach sound wonderful, and, by the way, I love swimming and snorkelling. It would be great fun," James was asking for a date. They exchanged numbers. Anthony walked away on cloud nine! He hadn't met anyone interesting since he moved into his mom's house.

"See you soon, James, but as it's not company policy, we are just good friends."

"That's okay by me." They shared a tight hug. "Good night, Anthony, and thanks for supper."

Over the next few days they found out that they enjoyed the same movies, and had fun watching the latest James Bond. Anthony had spent the last few nights at a hotel in Nanaimo, and while James was working, Anthony was driving to Campbell River one day and Comox the next day, to survey the areas for the next two stores. When James finished his shift they had supper, and took long walks getting to know each other. They discussed their dreams of owning a boat, and living by the ocean. Anthony's master plan was on the first step to fruition; he had found James.

"How come this is your first full-time job?" James was a go-getter not a slacker.

"I've been taking courses at UVic on a pay-as-you-go system, but it was difficult working full time and doing school work in the evening. So I need more money to eventually pay for the courses, and I'm being optimistic saving for full time university. It's my passion to become a doctor, preferably one who works with kids."

Anthony assessed James goals and decided he will try to help. Maybe Quick & Easy will offer a bursary; he will talk to Alexis.

The rest of Anthony's trip back to Victoria was filled with ideas of how to talk to his mom. She would never accept that he was gay, but that never bothered him when he was living far away from home. His thoughts went back to James and their amazing evenings. He must convince his mom to sell the house or consider the other options he offered. He felt trapped. He will be twenty-seven next month, but with James around, he'll get so much more out of life than he was getting now.

He pulled into the driveway. It was very late, and the house was in complete darkness. He walked in quietly, leaving his case and laptop on the counter so that his mom would know he was home.

Once inside the house, he was having second thoughts; he should have opted for a motel. His next step was to lease an apartment, but he needed to talk it over with James. They can look together.

He went to bed excited and restless, remembering to put the alarm on.

6

"I'm up! I'm just getting dressed. I have a very busy day today and I can't be late." Anthony had promised himself that he would tell his mother this week. No more secrets. As far as his mom goes, he was a practicing procrastinator, and he was very good at it. If this problem was work-related, he would have handled it immediately.

"You were very late coming home last night, I waited up until eleven. Where were you?" Anthony didn't want to answer, his whole body cringed. He didn't have a clue how to deal with this woman.

"If you must know, I went on a date last night." Anthony's smile was genuine.

What he definitely needed was some intimate, one-on-one time with James. He was a perfect mix: his fabulous sense of humour, his love of family, his amazing personality, and his eye-catching good looks; and his ambition to become a medical doctor. Anthony liked him a great deal, and he was looking forward to their next date, Sunday was their day off.

"Okay, Mom, how's this for a scenario? If I met someone and got married, what will you do?" She didn't answer, so Anthony continued, "I certainly don't want you sitting there when I get in from work. Married people need intimacy and privacy, not a nosey relation hovering around them. You'll need to stay in your room and stay out of my business."

"How stupid; I own half this house." She was, yet again, in a mood for a fight.

"I hate the thoughts of you waiting up for me, Mom; there's absolutely no need. But what I hate most of all is when you delve into my private life."

He was putting his laptop on the counter and saw a pile of mail addressed to him that his mom had opened.

"This happens again and again, you opened my mail! You're an interfering busybody. I refuse to discuss my work or my private life with you, and from now on, my mail will be forwarded to a mailbox."

He wasn't getting through to her, so he explained that they got along much better when he was at university. "Have you thought any more about selling this house?"

"Don't sound so melodramatic. What a ridiculous idea. Why would I do that?" Imelda sounded patronizing.

"Have it your way. You've made this situation as painful as possible. You refuse to believe how much I hate living here with you." He ran upstairs and gathered his clothes, shoes, and toiletries, which he packed into a suitcase, before placing his suitcase into his Jeep. He came back into the house, collected his laptop, phone, and wallet.

"I'm gone. Don't try to contact me. I will block your calls. We have nothing more to discuss unless you are willing to sell this house."

"You took off for a few days away. Wherever you went for your little break was irrelevant; we are back to normal. We'll be fine, you'll see." Imelda was impossible, like a petulant child. "I don't want to sell the house. You can't make me. Why should I?"

"You are not normal! You're selfish and inconsiderate, and your life choices are ridiculous and childish! You obviously choose to live in this house alone. This house is clearly more important to you than me."

"You'll be back because you have nowhere else to go," Imelda spouted in confidence.

"I assure you that I won't come back here. I want a home of my own." Anthony was seething. "A home without you and all your ridiculous notions!"

As he got into his car, she yelled out to him, "Where are you working today? Or are you going on another secret trip?" He pretended that he didn't hear her. He started the engine and backed out of the driveway.

The drive to his office was twenty minutes. He picked up a large coffee on the way.

"Dad, you were brave enough to leave. I may have misjudged you. I'm too soft with her, and she's become more selfish and argumentative. I want my life back."

Anthony's priority was to find himself an apartment; this was the second step in his master plan. He knew that he would never move back in with his mom. He had finally met someone who he believed would make him happy, but he needed to be in his own place. Anthony smiled as he remembered telling Jade about his master plan and how it was coming along. He was free of his mom, at last, and it felt amazingly good.

Because he had spent the whole evening with James, he didn't complete Sophie's store evaluation, so he called in his office, where he settled in a cubicle, with his laptop open he quickly completed all the criteria. Sophie was in his radar for district manager.

While in the office, he went over the projections for the new Port Alberni store. He would contact Bruce Chow, the new manager, to arrange a meeting so they can go through the store inspection together.

Anthony got up to leave, and he almost jumped out of his skin when he heard, "Hi, handsome! Wow, you're honouring us with a visit?" Alexis crossed the room like she meant business.

"How far did you get with the plans for Port Alberni?" she asked.

"I just finished browsing over the projections. It's in a great location, and I'm going there today. I'll stay until I have it all organized. It will possibly take the whole day, and then I'll send you my usual report." Anthony liked his boss. She was always pleasant and considerate and very business-minded. When Anthony introduced her to business acquaintances, she insisted he called her his colleague. She never ever liked to be called boss.

"Thanks. I'm looking forward to it," she replied. "Who did you hire for Nanaimo? I plan to go there next week."

"I hired Sophie Cardinal. I've been keeping a close eye on her; she's so good with the staff, has excellent management skills, and I look forward to promoting her. At the same time we hired a young guy, James, he has great potential. He has shown his capacity to manage the store, and I will promote them both."

"I'll let you know what day I intend to go to Nanaimo, and now I'm looking forward to meeting them. Will you please come with me? Please, Anthony?" Alexis usually had fun when she spent time with him, but his workload was hectic. "Please?"

"Okay, I will fit you into my busy schedule . . . if I must!" his pouty expressions and condescending tones were comical to her.

"You must! I will call you." She walked away, laughing.

On the way to Port Alberni, Anthony was thinking how lucky he was, and James was the reason.

When Anthony arrived at the Port Alberni store, he was surprised that Bruce wasn't there to greet him. Their meeting wasn't until later in the day, so Anthony decided to get on with the task at hand and help unload the stock. By the time this was complete, it was close to meeting time, and yet, Bruce had still not shown up and had not called. "Not a good start," Anthony said aloud.

As Anthony fumed, his phone began to vibrate—it was Alexis. "Anthony, I have Mr. Bruce Chow here; your manager arrived about fifteen minutes ago. He had a problem with his car. He went to look for a new car, but he didn't manage to find one he liked. His old car died on him. He said he had been trying to contact you, but your phone went directly to voicemail."

"Oh, and my mistake, he isn't moving to Port Alberni until next weekend," Alexis laughed at her own mistake. "He seems like a genuine sort of guy. He's apologized so many times. Shall I keep him here?"

"Alexis, ask him if we can meet tomorrow at the office at nine o'clock." Anthony realized he had forgotten to turn his phone on again.

"Hi, James it's me. Can you talk?"

"Yes," James wanted to call Anthony last night, but he chickened out. He didn't want to come over as pushy or needy, but he desperately needed someone to talk to—he had urgent problems that he knew he must discuss with Anthony.

"I wanted to let you know that I ended up having an awful row with my mother. She won't consider selling the house or dividing it into two separate apartments." Anthony continued with his tale of misery, "I drove out to Port Alberni first thing this morning as I had arranged to meet Bruce, the new manager, only to find out he was sitting in my office in Victoria waiting for me. Now I have to meet him in the morning."

"I hope your day goes better than mine," the silence became a sure-fired give-away.

"Are you there, James? Talk to me." Anthony's gut was churning.

"I'm here. Oh, Anthony, something happened to Karen in the middle of the night. She phoned me and asked if I could pick up

Adam from the hospital. When I arrived there she was sedated, with a bevy of doctors around her, trying to figure out why she collapsed."

James reminded Anthony, "Today, Sophie went to her aunt's funeral, so I had no choice; I had to bring Adam to work with me." James wanted to cry, "I don't know what to do, as I can't get any information from the hospital; they're doing a barrage of tests. I'm so sorry, Anthony."

"First of all, James, I'm on my way. I will be with you as soon as I can get there." Then Anthony had a thought, "Ask one of the junior staff to take care of Adam and stay with him at all times, as we are not insured for unattended children. Call me back ASAP."

James sent a text to Anthony saying that Kelly had offered to help. He was grateful to Kelly, but the hospital would still not discuss Karen's condition over the phone.

By the time Anthony set off, the highways were pretty busy. After a few minutes, James called to confirm the situation, "Kelly is taking care of Adam. They're sitting in the office with colouring pencils and wads of paper."

"Perfect. Now you need to keep all the customers happy. Do your best, James, and tell Adam I'm coming to pick both of you up, so that all three of us can go see Karen."

"You are a wonderful man, Anthony Lynwood."

Anthony was driving to the speed limit. All his concentration, though, was on Adam. Anthony told his car to call the Nanaimo store phone number.

James answered. "Oh! James, I forgot," Anthony said, "if anyone comes to pick up Adam before I get there, don't let him go with anyone unless they have court documents. On second thoughts, don't let anyone take him."

"I won't. Thanks again, Anthony."

The store was ready to close as Anthony drove up to the front door.

"Where is the little man?" He followed James to the office and called, "I have a treat for any kids who want a kid's meal with a toy."

An excited Adam yelled, "Do you mean me-e-e?"

"I sure do, little man." Then he told James that they were going to the hospital, and, hopefully, they would get some answers as to what happened to Karen.

"James, did you know Karen was ill?"

James shook his head, "She told me she was tired all the time. I didn't think to push her. Sometimes, she would call me and invite me over for supper. She looked like she had the weight of the world on her shoulders. I would just play with Adam until bedtime and leave so she could get some rest."

"Let's eat first before we find out what happened to your mommy," Anthony said as they approached a fast-food restaurant. Adam was excited to go through the drive-thru. The three of them ate in the Jeep on the way to the hospital. When they arrived, they parked the Jeep, and Adam clung onto James for dear life.

They approached the front desk, "Hi, my name is Prescott. Last night, my friend Karen Greene was admitted. Can you throw some light on the situation?" The clerk asked him to spell her last name. "It's Greene with an e."

"The doctor needs to talk to you, Mr. Prescott. Please take a seat. She'll be here momentarily."

"We've done a stream of tests but are not getting answers quickly enough," The doctor explained that Karen was not responding. "I can only give you information when I receive it, and right now, we're waiting on her blood work. It won't be long. Her MRI results aren't here yet, but Dr. Lightfoot is the specialist in charge."

"Can we go in to see Karen? Adam, her little boy, needs to see her, and so do I." James gave a sense of urgency.

"For the child's sake, you can take him to see his mommy. If, however, he becomes too upset that she won't wake up, you'll need to take him away. She's in an induced coma, and we're doing everything possible to bring the swelling down in her brain, but we need her test results."

"Mr. Prescott, I'm Dr. Lightfoot, the neurosurgeon," the specialist explained by giving them a list of things that may have caused it, but until they received the MRI results, they were at an impasse. "We knew Karen had a small tumour that we were tracking; however, the test results have revealed that it has grown very rapidly and has become very aggressive. We are doing everything we can to bring down the swelling."

They thanked the specialist, but before Dr. Lightfoot left, she suggested they take Adam home to bed.

"When I brought Karen in last night, I didn't notice if she had her purse with her," James explained to Anthony and that they needed a door key to get Adam's clothes. Doctor Lightfoot told him to ask the nurse, as she left Karen's bedside.

"Hi," James approached the nursing station, "Could you please help me find Karen Greene's purse? I need her house keys to get Adam some clean clothes."

"Just a moment, young man; we need to verify who you are and how you're related to Karen. Is this young man your nephew?"

James filled in all the information that he could. "I'm Adam's emergency caregiver. Ask Adam who I am, please."

The nurse turned to Adam. "What's your name, young man?"

"Adam Leon Greene," he said the words slowly. She then asked him lots of questions until she was satisfied. "My daddy was also Adam Leon Greene, isn't that right, James?"

"Yes, you look a lot like your daddy," James said smilingly.

"I'm going to let you take her keys, but, just so you know, it's not hospital policy for me to hand over Karen's purse. For Adam's sake, I will give you her keys and will hold the rest of the contents in Security."

Then she looked at Adam. "Will you be a good boy for James? And maybe he can bring you back tomorrow to see your mommy?" Adam's distress was obvious. Her heart was peeling inside of her chest. As there was nothing she could say to make things better, she changed the subject. "Do you go to school, Adam?"

"No, my mommy teaches me at home. She would be too lonely without me." Adam thought about school, "When I go to Grade 1, my mommy says I can go and play with the other kids. She wants to go to work then."

Adam was a great kid, and all he wanted was his mommy to wake up. "Can you wake my mommy up now, please? I want to tell her about the car I made with James."

It was getting late, "It's past your bedtime, young man," the nurse said."

James began deferring Adam's questions. "We are going to take you home now, Adam." He swung the little man upon his shoulders. "Say good night to the nurse," James assured Adam that they would be back to see his mommy the next day.

When they arrived at the car, Adam settled into the back seat. "James, I don't know much about kids, but he needs a child's car seat. The stores are still open; let's get one. Can you sit with him for now?" Anthony was committed to helping James in any way he could.

The three arrived at Canadian Tire, where they found a booster seat. At the same time, they grabbed some snacks and juice. They had finished their errands in no time and were standing in front of Karen and Adam's apartment door.

"Here's the key; I hope it's the right one," James pushed the apartment door open. Anthony walked in with Adam sleeping in his arms, and he quickly went to find his bedroom. It was a tiny room, and the first thing Anthony noticed was a car made of candy boxes. They immediately tucked him into bed and left a night light on before quietly leaving the room.

"I got hold of Sophie, and she assures me she can handle the store tomorrow. I have no idea what I'm going to do," James felt Anthony's arm around his shoulders.

"We will figure it out together. You need some sleep after being at the hospital all night, and I will sleep on the sofa." Anthony was hoping to find some documents to help locate family members or friends. "Get some sleep now; you look wiped. Tomorrow, we'll sort ourselves out," Anthony had an awful gut feeling that when Karen woke up, she would think he was snooping into her personal belongings.

The men woke early; Adam had slept for a full nine hours and joined Anthony on the sofa.

"Hey, buddy, what would you like for breakfast?" Adam gave Anthony a wide grin, which told Anthony that he really liked breakfast. "Do you like cereal?" Adam shook his head. "Do you like eggs?" Adam shook his head. "Okay, I give up. What do you like?"

"Beef ravioli with cheese sprinkles on it?" Adam was testing Anthony, who soon caught on.

"I can only make pancakes," Adam admitted he loved pancakes. James, who had gotten up just after Anthony, was busy in the kitchen making coffee.

"James, where's Karen's phone? It wasn't in her bag, and neither was her wallet."

"Let's spend some time searching, although Karen told me she met Adam's dad in a teen orphanage. She said she never knew her parents and was brought up in a foster home until she was ten. She was taken back to the orphanage for unknown reasons, where she met Adam's dad. There were just the two of them, and he looked out for her; he was very protective of her. I think she's a wonderful lady."

"Did my mommy get some orange juice?" Adam told James it was his favourite.

"I'll make pancakes, and you call the hospital, James. Let's see how she's doing today. If she's awake, she'll be able to tell us who to call." Trying to get organized in a tiny, strange kitchen was difficult for Anthony, especially since he was a large guy. "Let's get breakfast over with, so we can head off to the hospital and hopefully, we'll find her phone before then."

James sat at the table. "I should try to call her missing phone first," he dialled Karen's number, and her phone started ringing. "Anthony, we found her phone," he said. They searched the sofa and found the phone under some cushions.

"It needs a password."

"You can try 'Adam.'" It seemed like an obvious choice.

Anthony's next suggestion was Greene, but neither unlocked the phone. "Adam, does your mommy have another name?"

"I call her mommy," Adam was trying to help, and both men wore huge smiles.

The pancakes were done, and Adam found the syrup. Anthony found Adam a juice box and sat beside him with his coffee.

"Do you have another name?" Anthony asked.

"My name is Adam Leon Greene. It's just the same as my dad's name."

James was holding the phone. "I hope we don't get locked out. Here goes," he keyed in Leon, and it worked. While James searched her phone, Anthony wanted to start his search.

"Okay, James, I'm going to have a look around." Anthony carefully began opening drawers, trying not to disturb the contents. "James! I've found a letter; it's addressed to you." Anthony handed it to him.

James was hesitant to open the letter. "Do you think she knew how ill she was? Why else would she write to me?"

James,

I received the results of my brain scan, and there was a tumour. I was going to tell you, but I was hoping for a miracle, and now I may have waited too long. The doctor advised me to have it removed several weeks ago, but he thought it was too late even then. I had no-one to take care of Adam, so I couldn't go in for surgery. Please, help my little orphan. He will be put into a care facility, so if it's possible, please visit him sometimes and keep an eye on him if you can. I am handing over his welfare and care to you. If there are any problems, please take your concerns to the Child Welfare people. I know this was a lot to ask of you, and I will understand if you cannot help. He adores you, James.

I have left some papers, my bank information with total access, and a list of Adam's favourite foods. Again, I know this was a lot to ask, but you are so caring, and most importantly, I trust you. I know you are too young to be bogged down with this responsibility, and I would have loved it if you were older and settled. I would have imposed on you to welcome Adam to your family. My lawyer, Eric Gould of Graham & Gould, knows my situation, and he'll help you with whatever you need.

When, or if, you visit Adam, remind him of me and how much I love him.

Love, Karen Greene, (Mommy)

Anthony also read the letter. They stood with tears in their eyes, which they had to wipe away when Adam put his empty plate on the counter.

James gave Karen's phone to Anthony as he composed himself. While Anthony scrolled through her phone, he only found one personal number—James' number—other than the doctor's office there's a few other community and business numbers.

"I need to call my office," he dialled the number. "Hi, Alexis, I need an enormous favour. I can't make it into the office today, and the new store manager Bruce Chow needs to be taken to Port Alberni to inspect the store. Can you help me? Please, Alexis? A friend of mine was rushed into the hospital last night, and I don't know if she's going to make it."

Alexis had no problems doing as Anthony had asked, and she offered to help in any way he needed. He said he'd call her when he got to the hospital, as the test results should be in by then. He didn't tell her who was sick, and she didn't ask.

7

Anthony, freed up from his busy schedule, stayed at James' side, to help him through this tough time. He wanted to take some of the responsibility, as he was explaining to James, "First things first, we go to the hospital and see if we can talk to Karen. Between the two of us, we'll be able to take care of Adam until she comes home."

Deep down, they both knew that Karen was dying. Why else would she have asked James for help? Her letter said it all. They both hoped that Karen, under the care of Dr. Lightfoot, would be able to have her tumour surgically removed.

James looked up to Anthony with tears streaming down his face. He smiled and said, "Thank you so much, Anthony. I don't know how I could get through this without you."

"My heart goes out to you, James. I'm here for you, and I'm willing to take half the responsibility for Adam, and help in any way I can."

When they arrived at the hospital car park, Anthony grabbed Adam and perched him on his shoulders as he called out, "Are you okay, little man?"

"I want to see my mommy," he was excited to be back. As they made their way to Karen's floor, Adam said, "I want the nurse to wake my mommy."

A nurse heard what he said, "Your mommy needs you to be a good kid. She needs to sleep, and I have given her some medicine for her headache." She looked at the men, "We need to talk, so I'll get a nurse to stay with Adam."

"Doctor Lightfoot is on her way, she'll explain the details, but I'm afraid Karen's condition has not improved. Her tumour is growing so quickly that it's believed surgery was no longer an option. But again, Dr. Lightfoot will be able to explain this in greater detail."

The nurse paused for a few moments so they could absorb the information, and she asked them to wait for the specialist.

Dr. Lightfoot explained there was little hope that Karen would regain consciousness, and she warned them that it was just a matter of time before she passed. The neurosurgeon asked if Karen had a directive, and the nurse said there was one in her purse, and her signature matched her driver's license.

James told the nurse, "I need to call her lawyer to see if he has any information as to what we should do." She saw the way Adam was looking at James, and she almost cried, "Karen told me that Adam's father died when Adam was born, the same day, as a matter of fact."

"Go and see her; she looks peaceful. Adam will have a hard time as he can't wake her, so please be tolerant with him," she kindly smiled as she waved to Adam.

James looked like a little lost boy. "Anthony, will you call the lawyer? If Karen is going to be ill for a long time, I'll take care of Adam. I'll hire a caregiver who will see to his needs. I must meet with her lawyer, and Anthony, please, will you come with me? I know it's asking a lot, but I need you."

"Of course, I'll stay with you. I'm going nowhere, and I can be here as long as you need me." Anthony was sincere. After seeing Karen, he realized she was gravely ill, and he was expecting the worst. No matter the outcome, he would stay with James.

James thanked him again, as two large arms gave him a hug.

The three of them were sitting at Karen's bedside, waiting for the doctor.

"James, can I have a quiet word with just the two of you?" Doctor Lightfoot signalled for the men to follow her to the doorway. "Karen was awake for a little while this morning, but her pain was extreme. We had to give her opiates to make her comfortable."

"How long will she be in the hospital?" James' naive question caught Dr. Lightfoot off-guard.

"You are going to have to brace yourself, for Adam's sake. Karen is not expected to survive. Her tumour is causing multiple organs to shut down. She only has a little time left; I am so very sorry, James."

Doctor Lightfoot's prognosis was brutal, "Karen told me she had no family except Adam, and he is too young to understand what is happening," she then informed James that Karen had left instructions on what to do when she passes.

"Yes, we found the letter that Karen left, it was addressed to me," James assured her. "It was a shock. Everything is happening so quickly, and I don't have a clue what to do."

"We can do our best to control her pain, and then we wait. It won't be long."

James sat beside Anthony, his tone apologetic, "I'm so pathetic, Anthony. I had no right to bring you into a situation like this. There's nothing to be done." He took a moment to breathe, "I have to wait for her to die. I will not abandon Adam; he's a great kid who has no one in his young life, not one known relative, nobody!" James sobbed.

"He has you, James. If you'll allow me to help, he has me too. We will jump the hurdles, and together, we'll take care of Adam." Then Anthony remembered Karen's letter and suggested they contact Eric Gould.

James told Anthony that Karen's lawyer would see them anytime. He suggested they wait until next week; that way, they would be familiar with the situation. Karen left a very precise Will, containing a codicil that stipulates quality of life and not quantity.

Karen opened her eyes for a few seconds. Adam was trying to wake her. The poor little man didn't understand that his whole world was about to change. "Mommy, it's me. Mommy! Wake up, please." His sad eyes tore through the men. "She isn't going to wake up. I want to tell her that I had you guys for a sleepover."

Anthony sat Adam on his lap. "Your mommy is very sick, and she has in lots of pain. The nurse is coming again to give your mommy some more medication." It felt like a long time for a five-year-old to sit and wait, but he did so quietly. Anthony eventually offered him some juice from the vending machine.

Adam whispered, "I'm always quiet when my mommy has a headache."

"James, I am going to take Adam for a small treat. I will try to find something for him to do to pass the time."

The nurse came in and had just finished making her patient comfortable. "It won't be long now. She's not breathing on her own." James thanked her. "If you need any help finding a babysitter, I know some very caring folk," she said as she gave James her number.

James left Karen's bedside, as he was feeling overwhelmed with hearing the news that she was about to pass away. And as he paced outside her room, he heard a pinging noise and watched the nurse go back into her room and he knew that she had died.

"It's over. She's gone," the nurse spoke gently, "God love her. James, when you tell Adam, he won't understand or be able to grasp the concept that his mommy is no longer with him. It will be difficult to explain this to a five-year-old. I don't envy your task." She closed the curtains around Karen's bed. "I'll tidy around her, and when Adam comes, you should tell him. I am sorry for your loss, young man."

"Thank you," was all James could say to the nurse. "We're very grateful for all that you've done for Karen. It all happened so suddenly and it's a dreadful blow. I know Adam won't be able to understand what's happening, but I'll do my best to explain everything to him." A few moments later, Anthony and Adam showed up.

Without the life support wires, Karen looked asleep. "James, how about I take a picture of Karen?" Anthony asked after a few moments of silence. He explained that he didn't see any photos of her at the apartment, so he set the camera and took a couple of photos of her resting peacefully. "I will get these photos done," he stated.

"Adam, I need you to be a brave boy. Your mommy has gone to live with the angels; come and say goodbye to your mommy, and tell her you love her." Anthony was holding Adam's hand.

The little man was stood still, he had no idea that his mom had gone forever. He touched his mom's hand and he started to shout. "Mommy wake up, please wake up." Tears were flowing freely, "Tell my Mommy I want to go home now, she has to get up now." so Anthony took him out of the room.

James stayed at Karen's bedside, sobbing his heart out. "I promise you Karen, I will keep Adam safe, I will keep him with me, and I will do whatever it takes to make sure he has a good life, you can rest in peace." He stood and kissed her forehead. "Goodbye my friend." He went to find Anthony.

Anthony also said goodbye to Karen before they left the hospital. He promised her that he will help care for Adam and James, he will be a guiding light for them and he will provide a home full of love for both of them. We will raise your son to be a man you will be proud of. We won't let you down."

"Goodbye Karen."

"James, we need to talk. Were you serious about keeping Adam?" James was nodding and still crying. "We will do this together, and when we go to see Eric Gould we'll be as one in all decisions. We both want what is best for the little man."

8

When Anthony, James and Adam arrived at the lawyer's office, it was busy, but they were seen almost immediately. Eric Gould introduced himself then got right down to business. "I must ask you if Adam will be put into care, or did Karen offer an alternative arrangement?"

"I'll be taking care of Adam with help from Anthony. Everything happened so quickly, and we haven't decided on all of the details, but we will readily take responsibility for him. Karen's letter to me stated she wanted me to oversee Adam's welfare."

"How do you feel about this arrangement, Anthony?" Eric inquired.

"James and I will share the responsibility for Adam because we don't want him put into care. At the moment, I can take some time off of work, but down the road, we know we'll need a nanny. We'll keep him safe."

"Do either of you need some time to reflect on making such a huge commitment?" Anthony and James stared at the desk. Then firmly, they both told Eric their circumstances and that they wanted to be Adam's caregivers. They told Eric about the letter Karen wrote to James.

"I need a copy of the letter, and then we must have a conversation without little ears. There are lots of things to cover, but for now,

I need to know you are both of the same mindset." Eric continued, "I am legally bound to notify the authorities of Karen's passing, and at the same time, I can apply to the courts, on your behalf, for temporary custody of Adam until all the details are sorted."

James and Anthony readily agreed to this. Eric informed them of Karen's Will, which would be read one month after her death. Eric explained this was to give James time to assess if he was capable of the trials and tribulations of bringing up a five-year-old and, most importantly, that he wanted to give a home to her son. "If you have any doubts or difficulties in meeting the criteria," Eric stated, "Adam will be placed into foster care."

"I don't know if she told you, but she doesn't want to be buried. She firmly stated that she wants a cremation with no ceremony." Eric looked at the two men. "I have the funds ready that will pay for her remains to go to a funeral home. She has chosen one, and I will do as she requested." It was a lot to digest.

Once Anthony and James took care of all the legal aspects, they decided to grab a snack, and have a talk with Adam when they arrived back at Karen's apartment.

"Adam, do you know what happens when someone dies?" Adam stared at James. He didn't move a muscle.

"Today, your mommy was in terrible pain; her head hurt. The doctor said she wouldn't get better, so your mommy has gone to heaven." Anthony waited for some reaction, "Your mommy told James that she wants you to be a tough little boy, and stay with James and me, where you will be safe."

"Can I go to heaven to see Mommy?" he didn't understand.

"Adam, your mommy wanted James and me to take care of you." Anthony was in a quandary on how to explain this as Adam cried. "We will be your new family."

James and Anthony sat beside him and cried with him.

Yet, Adam constantly asked, "When is my mommy coming home?" until he finally fell asleep on James' knee.

James hired a babysitter to keep Adam safe and entertained. They could not stay at Karen's apartment—it was tiny—so they packed all of Adam's belongings, including his candy packets car. "We can stay at my apartment until we figure everything out. I have one and a half bedrooms and a comfy sofa." So they decided to move into James' apartment, and look for a rental property.

"James, how about I cover Karen's lease for one month? That should give us plenty of time to come back on the weekends. What do you think?"

"Honestly, I can't face doing this tonight, and our priority is to make sure Adam is settled.

They had not located Karen's lease agreement, so they had to go through all of Karen's boxes, cupboards, and drawers before completely vacating the suite.

James was pent up; he gave a half-laugh, "What the hell are we doing?" He continued laughing through his tears, "We met two months ago. We liked one another, and I know we both felt the chemistry. We were arranging to go to the coast for a swim, and now we have gained a son between us. We have to empty an apartment. We must find a home. Our friend died today. Oh, Anthony, I'm scared to death." James' tears flowed as Anthony held him, letting James cry on his shoulder.

"We'll take everything one day at a time. We'll do what we can when we can." He didn't feel convincing, but he wanted James to know they were a team. "We need some help. So, the very first thing we should do is find a small house. The second thing we should do is find a nanny." James nodded in agreement.

"We need to see that lawyer again soon. I will be able to take one week off for vacation, which will allow us to start building a home. How does that sound?" Anthony asked.

"I love you, Anthony. How does that sound?"

"I will tell you tomorrow!" That started a cushion fight, but they were both too tired to prolong the fight, and they sat together as Anthony caressed James' neck and shoulders. He noticed James' comments, and was ecstatic that the 'we' included him.

Going through boxes and old suitcases took time. Trying to find what they needed was upsetting. Anthony went through and shredded old bills that, he assumed, had been paid. He filled three large black garbage bags with shredded bills. Adam was in his element, helping with the shredding.

"James, are you on the schedule tomorrow?"

"I don't have a choice. I need to work; we'll need my wages too."

"I forgot to mention that we may need to pay the outstanding bills for utilities. I went through the drawer, but there were no bills. We should run this by Eric. We need him to go over Karen's bank information to see how she stands financially. I haven't found any legal documents, like Adam's birth certificate or anything important."

They had made an appointment to meet Eric Gould again, as they needed his help to begin their new lives—especially because they wanted Adam to stay with them—and they needed some answers. Did Karen enrol Adam in a school? Which school did she choose? There was so much the men didn't know, but they were committed to Adam's welfare. He was now an orphan. After their last appointment with him, they believed Eric would have the information they needed, including Karen's financial situation.

Anthony stayed at the tiny apartment when he was in Nanaimo. He spent lots of time there, going through boxes and making keepsakes for Adam. He found a few photos of Adam Leon Greene, senior. He expected to find a wedding photo of Karen's, and he searched high and low, but he only found a high school photo of her. He wrapped it carefully and put it in a tote.

There were so few keepsakes, almost enough to fill a shoebox, that would be kept safe and given to Adam to put in his new bedroom. There were several stuffed animals and a superman lamp. Three totes were full of kids' books, and several boxes were packed full of toys.

Opening Karen's closet, Anthony had an idea of what to do with some of her items. He picked out a grey toque, scarf, and mittens to give to Adam. He also picked out a couple of pretty dresses to make pillows to put on Adam's new bed. He packed everything he could in the Jeep and headed for a storage unit to store the possessions until they found a home.

The amount of energy it took to empty the apartment, and working on his new stores, and occupying the sofa, Anthony was forming a plan. They will be moving as soon as possible, they need a bigger apartment.

Meanwhile, out of the blue, a wonderful thought came to him, "I think it's about time we went on a little trip. Let's go north for a three-day break. We can go swimming in the ocean, and we can get binoculars and spot the eagles.

The beaches are sandy, and we can visit my old friend Sammy Keel. He has a house on the beach where we can swim and play." James was grinning from ear to ear, but not a sound came from Adam.

James replied, "Count me in. I love the beach, and we can build sandcastles."

They both looked at Adam. "James, it'll only be fun if kids come too. Where can we find a kid who wants to play on a beach?"

"I can't go to the beach. I need to stay here in case my mommy comes back from heaven." Adam was bewildered. He found it hard to understand why his mommy went away and left him. He didn't know where she was or why she hadn't come back for him.

"Last time we talked to your mommy, she told us to take care of you and to take you to the beach, to the park, and for ice cream. She wanted you to have all these things," Anthony was sincere. "We can hire a boat and go looking for whales in the ocean."

"I'll come too!" Adam didn't want to miss the fun.

James and Anthony had grown to love their little charge and couldn't wait for their next appointment with Eric to find out if they could adopt Adam. It was tough for the two men waiting for any news on the fostering process. They couldn't promise Adam a home until they took care of the legal aspects of Karen's passing.

Company policy frowns on romantic relationships with co-workers, so Anthony needed to tell Alexis the news of his developing relationship with James. He was worried how it would affect his position with the company, yet after a lengthy discussion with Alexis they were able to fine-tune the company policy, allowing Anthony and James to continue their relationship in public.

The month was almost over, and they were both on edge. Anthony called Sophie and explained why James needed a couple of days off. She understood their dilemma and was amazed to see Anthony and James so happy together; a match made in heaven. Anthony needed his passionate, funny, crazy James, and James needed Anthony's matter-of-fact way of handling situations, his stability, and the romance he encapsulated.

Anthony was blissfully happy he had found James. He had fallen in love and was scared stiff to admit it. He loved James' easy-going ways. He was so comforting, yet his spontaneity was infectious; he liked pillow fights and making funny face pancakes.

Before they could dash away for a quick holiday, Anthony assessed his work agenda. He needed to handle any outstanding issues so he could take time off without worrying about the company. He was relieved that Bruce Chow was firmly settled in the new store in Port Alberni thanks to Alexis, who helped pick up some of the slack. She was happy to help Anthony and James any way she could. With her on board, it was a huge relief for the guys, who always sought to do an excellent job.

James knew the sacrifices Anthony had made to get his degree and how he had worked so hard to get to this point in his career. James didn't want anything to jeopardize it, and he was relieved that Alexis had his back.

He also worried about his own financial situation and wondered how he was going to get a job that would help with all of the expenses. "Why do I wish money would grow on trees?" James spoke aloud.

With a road trip imminent, they went shopping for Adam. He needed new shoes, swimwear, sweaters, shorts, a snugly blanket for the car, and, if possible, fuzzy pyjamas. It was often cold and windy on the northern shores of the Island, and his new clothes would suit him well. Adam was pleased when the men fixed his car seat in the Jeep; now, he was high enough to see out of the windows!

A willingness to mix work with pleasure was expected when Anthony visited Port Hardy. He looked forward to seeing Jade Carter, and he intended to do her store evaluation while they were in town. She told him the weather should be warmer and that she was looking forward to meeting James and Adam. She wondered what they were like, how they met, how they fit into Anthony's life, and how they got along with Imelda.

Imelda was always on edge, especially when Anthony called. She wanted him to come home, but apparently, it was not part of his ridiculous master plan. "Why don't you get over yourself and come home? I hate being in this house all alone. Get rid of your stupid master plan; you don't have a love life."

"I warned you time and again that I would leave. You resentfully made my life hell. It would be impossible for me to live there ever again." She said nothing. "You are needy and manipulating, and where Dad was concerned, pathetic. I do feel sorry for you, Mom, but I will not return to that house, so save your breath."

However, he did want to tell her about his ready-made family. He had put off telling her he was gay, but now it didn't matter if she approved or not; he was in a relationship and was very happy. She called him again about the bills and how she would like him to help a little. He immediately e-transferred her some funds, and while she was on the phone, he told her he was heading north to Port Hardy with his friends for the long weekend. Before he finished his call he told her he would visit her when he returned to Victoria.

Adam was chipper! He had the whole back seat of the Jeep to himself, with his blanket, a colouring book, and a small bag of gummy bears. They saw lots of wild animals: a moose, two bears, several deer, and even a wild turkey. When they arrived at their destination, he saw all the bald eagles Anthony had told him about. James was having fun, too, listening to Adam as he continued his chatterbox banter for most of the trip. James had packed their swimwear and an extra snorkel for Adam, although he doubted Adam would stop chatting long enough to use it.

"James, we'll be arriving around supper time. I can't believe how relaxed I feel," Anthony asked Adam if he needed anything. "We are almost there, little man. Is anyone hungry?"

"I didn't realize this place was on the coast. What awesome views," James replied. The Jeep turned into the hotel car park, and James thought Anthony had chosen well. "Is this where you usually stay?"

"Yep, it's very pretty here," Anthony reflected, "it's a home away from home, and some of the islands that you see from here are havens for several species of seals. We can take a boat trip, as early spring is the best time of year to see the whales." He pointed to the harbour and continued, "I love walking around the boats. The smell of the sea grabs me every time."

James carried a sleepy Adam into the suite while whispering, "I think he needs to go to bed now." Anthony agreed. "Did I see a small kitchen on the way in?" James asked.

Anthony smiled and shook his head, "The word small is an oversized word for this kitchen."

"I called Jade and told her we would be here for three days for the long weekend. I have to do my usual store inspection, which takes about four hours. If you like, I will take you to meet Sammy Keel, and Adam can play on the beach there. If you prefer to wait until I've finished work, I'll come back and collect you." Anthony was reluctant to leave them. "Have fun with Adam. I won't be long—and oh! There is something I wanted to discuss with you that are not meant for little ears."

"What is it, Anthony?" James asked.

"Eric, the lawyer, contacted me. Our next appointment has been arranged for Tuesday, and when we go to this meeting, Eric will be reading Karen's Will."

A month has passed already, I can't believe it. Eric said he's been working diligently on the foster care plan and believes Adam will be better off with us. He also has a friend who is willing to help take care of Adam. Everything is going to work out, you'll see."

"Sure. Are we to take Adam with us?"

"He didn't say not to," Anthony assured him.

"What if they take him away from us?" James was apprehensive. "The courts may not favour our request for foster care because we have no experience. Hopefully, they will be sympathetic towards Karen's wishes."

"James, how committed are you to becoming a father?" Anthony realized they hadn't discussed the finer details. "Don't forget, we are in this together. We should make a pact that we will take care of Adam until he has grown up."

"Oh, Anthony, I'm worried that you'll feel trapped. You're taking most of the responsibility for this little fellow. Seriously, what if you decide that you don't want to become a Dad?"

"James, listen very carefully, I don't feel trapped. I'm positive, absolutely positive, that I want to be part of this deal and this family. Adam is a wonderful kid, and if we commit to fostering, or better still, adopting, I'll be so happy as long as we're in it for the long haul." Anthony felt the need to add, "Just mull over everything we have already done and what the expectations are if the court grants us Adam." James yawned, nodding his head.

"Which bed are you having window or door?" Anthony asked, changing the subject. They tossed a quarter to decide. "Sleep well and stop worrying." Anthony said.

Morning came too soon. "I prefer to wait for you before going to Sammy's," James said while making hot chocolate in the minuscule kitchen as Adam slept soundly snuggled up with his stuffed toys and blanket.

As the time to leave approached, Anthony grabbed his laptop and was ready to tackle Jade's store audit. He walked to the door, very close to James, who batted his long eyelashes and smiled at Anthony, which led to a super-strong hug that felt grand.

"I won't be long," Anthony sighed.

He arrived at the store to hear Jade's usual greeting, "Good morning, gorgeous. I've done as much as I can to make this easier for you. Did you bring James and Adam with you?" He confirmed that they were waiting at the hotel and eager to meet her. Jade wondered what kind of man would be able to steal Anthony's heart, and she couldn't wait to find out. She was also curious how a five-year-old boy fit into the equation.

Anthony did his audit as quickly as he could. It helped that Jade made several cups of coffee. He told her all about James and went into detail about their application to Child Services to become foster parents. Jade was afraid to ask how Imelda was handling any of this. She made a safe bet with herself that Anthony hadn't told his mom.

"You really want this child, don't you?" Jade couldn't wait to meet these two new men in his life.

Anthony nodded, "It was in the early days of our relationship, when we both decided it would be great to foster a kid, but we were both certain, it's what we want for Adam. Before she died, Karen wrote a letter to James asking him to oversee Adam's welfare. We're hoping to adopt the little man; I can't wait for you to meet them."

"I fell for James; hook, line, and sinker." She could see he was happily content. "We'll make great parents. We are so emotionally involved that James and I are looking to buy a house and get a full-time nanny. Then Adam can go to school."

"You have thought this out! Good for you guys; I am so happy for you!" she was impressed.

Somehow, Anthony anticipated the next question.

"What did your mom say about this situation?" she looked at him. "You haven't told her yet, have you? Oh, Anthony, you are creating complications in your own mind! You need to tell her."

"I moved out. I couldn't live with her, and I was hoping she would see sense and sell the mausoleum. Not a chance, though. She phoned me for money to pay the bills, but not once did she ask me if I was okay. She simply whined about the house being too big and that she needed me home.

"When I got home, after being here in Port Hardy, I found a stack of mail on the counter, addressed to me, and she opened every one of my letters. I had to get a postal box."

Jade reacted to his comment, "I can't believe she would open your mail, no wonder you left."

"She left ten messages on my phone in one day. She moans about living alone. I found myself butting my head on the wall; I was so frustrated."

He changed the subject, "It's time for you to come and meet James and Adam. We've been invited to Sammy's for a barbeque this afternoon. Jade, please come with us and forget about my mom for now. James and I go to the lawyer's office on Tuesday, and afterwards, I think that will be a good time to tell her."

"There's never going to be a good time to tell her. Get that through your big brain!" Jade was pulling out all the punches.

"Damn it, woman, you're like a dog with a bone! Cease and desist! I know what I must do, and I will tell her, soon."

On the drive to pick up James and Adam, it was very quiet between them. "Jade, I know how much you care, and I love you for that, but for now we need a truce, okay?" She nodded.

They stopped at the hotel, where James and Adam were waiting outside. "Jade," Anthony motioned to Adam, "let me introduce you to Adam." He walked over to Anthony, smiling. "Adam, this is Jade, my friend." Jade kept Adam's attention by handing him a chocolate chip cookie.

"Oh, thank you, Jade! My favourite! How did you know?" Adam whispered.

James was excited to meet Jade. He knew how much she meant to Anthony; he felt like he already knew her, and he agreed with Anthony that she was a very special person. Although she was a store manager, and they shared everything about the business, Jade and Anthony's rapport was like brother and sister. It was obvious they shared confidences.

They arrived at Sammy's carrying a couple of pies and an extra batch of chocolate chip cookies. Jade and Adam went looking for Sammy.

"What do you think of this place? It would be a haven to hide away in when everything gets too much. James?" Anthony asked quizzically, "What's wrong?"

"It's nothing." Anthony's brow tilted as he waited for a better explanation. "Do you think that Adam and I will be too much for you? Because if that's the case . . .?

"Oh, James, I've found that special harmony with you. We are soul-mates who have that close emotional connection. Right now, I'm finding it very difficult to get closer to you because I want you." There was no misconception of those three words. "If, for any reason, you have changed your mind about us, please tell me now."

"I don't deserve you. What if you get tired of me? I have no money, and I'm painfully aware that you are footing all the bills. I can only work one job if I want to spend time with you and Adam. There are much better prospects out there for you."

Anthony put a hand on James' shoulder. "Look at me!" James turned to face him. "I have fallen so hard for you; I don't want prospects, and I don't want things any different. We can have our dreams. Dreams cost nothing. James, you are everything to me; can't you see how much I love you?"

Anthony moved to face James. He placed his lips on James', and the world was at peace between them. "Honestly, I don't want to have this conversation ever again."

"Let's get back to the others." They walked one of the pathways back to the bungalow where the smell of ribs enticed them. They walked up to the fire pit and offered their help. Sammy asked them to grab some drinks as Jade already had the coffee pot on.

"Young Jade here has done a salad, and Adam washed all the veggies in the sink. We are making a banquet." Sammy was manoeuvring an oversized log that was too heavy, but he insisted that he could move it.

"Let me do that," Anthony interceded. Sammy had over-stretched himself. "I'm going to put a cold compress on that muscle, and you'll feel better in no time," James was fussing like a medic. "If you get any pain after a good night's sleep, Sammy, you need to go to the hospital."

"Stop fussing, James. We northerners are a hardy bunch; it'll be better by tomorrow." Sammy settled into a deck chair. "Adam, lad, how would you like to live on a beach?"

"I can't stay too long in case my mommy comes back from heaven," Adam was deadly serious. "She won't know where to look for me. Can we go home now?" James was there to appease him.

"Adam, come with me; let's take a walk. Take off your shoes, and we can play in the sea." As they strolled along the beach, they threw water at each other, making them giggle, but James knew he had to talk about Karen. "You can see the seals from here. Anthony wants to take us out on a boat to see them close up, and we can look out for the whales. They are so huge; they're even bigger than this house!"

James looked at Adam as he stared out to the sea. "You know, Adam, your mommy loved you so much, but she lives with the angels now, in heaven. She has no pain and she's very happy there and if you want to see her, just close your eyes. Close them now, and tell me if you can see your mommy."

"I can see her face, but she only smiles; she can't talk to me." Adam wasn't happy that she couldn't talk to him.

"If you close your eyes and see your mommy, then you can talk to her. She can hear you from heaven, and she can see you." As he watched Adam, he realized he would have to change the way he talked about Karen's death to help Adam understand what had happened.

"Your mommy had to go to heaven so she can see your daddy. She was too sick to stay here, and heaven can make her headaches better."

"I want to go to heaven to see my mommy," Adam's tears flowed.

Then James remembered the photos that Anthony had framed. "We have made pictures of your mommy and your daddy. You can put them on the wall when we find a new home. When you grow up, you will look like your daddy; you will be very handsome, and I bet all the girls will want to be with you."

"Let's head back to Sammy's. I know he has a gift for you. Come on, Adam, let's go and check it out!"

Adam was distracted by Sammy's gift. It was a kite kit. "All the kids up north fly kites," he said as he gave Adam the gift. Sammy got up to accompany Adam. "We need some wind. Come on, Adam, let's climb up the hill." At the top, they sat on the grass, and Sammy helped Adam build the kite. With a bit of direction, he was flying his kite.

"James told me that Anthony was going to take us to see the seals and whales," Adam said. "Please, will you come too, Sammy? Please?" Sammy didn't commit.

"Let's see what the guys have in mind. It might get rough with high waves, and I hurt my back a little when I pulled that log. I think I am too old to be chasing whales." He patted Adam's head. "It's almost your bedtime young man, so let's put the kite away until next time you come for a visit." The pair headed back to the bungalow.

"Anthony," Adam ran to him as the duo returned, "I asked Sammy to come with us to see the seals and whales. Can he come with us?" Anthony said he would call Sammy tomorrow to see how he felt. "Jade can come too if you ask her? We can all go! I would like that."

As it was getting quite late, the four said goodbye to Sammy and walked to the Jeep. After settling in, Jade asked Adam, "So, how was your first day in Port Hardy? Where did you go with Sammy?"

Adam started to tell them about the windy hill but began to yawn. Although he was falling asleep, he still managed to answer, "We put the kite up and flew it off the top of the big hill. It was fun." They continued small chit-chat, and when they dropped Jade off, Adam was fast asleep.

They drove back to the hotel in a comforting silence.

Putting Adam to bed, Anthony asked, "Does he like baths or showers? It's too late to worry about that now, but he can get one in the morning." He pulled the bed sheets over him to snuggle him in and put his three stuffy toys next to him. "He looks so peaceful when he's asleep."

Anthony and James sat side by side on the huge sofa. "Do you want a drink? I can always go to the liquor store for a few beers or anything else you would like." James said he was okay with Coke; he was reluctant to drink alcohol after seeing what it does to his dad.

The two turned on the television. "What shows do you like? We need to know each other's preferences. We'll be staying home lots while taking care of Adam." They flipped through the channels. *17 Again* was advertised. "Have you seen it?" James asked.

Anthony said he hadn't, "Okay, let's give it a try," he said, "I don't particularly like romantic comedies; are you're sure there's not too many soppy bits?"

"It's a comedy, but it's very funny, and I like Zac Efron. Let's try it?" James replied. They relaxed as they watched the movie—and it was a good idea since they were too tired to do much else.

"That was fantastic," Anthony said while brushing his teeth. "I truly enjoyed it. It was not at all what I expected," he was still laughing. "That crazy guy was funny. His peacocking behaviour was so over the top."

James was getting tired. "This sea air knocks me out for the count. I am going to bed now."

"Are you enjoying being here?" Anthony asked.

"I couldn't be happier," James replied with a yawn before he asked, "What do you think the outcome will be when we see the lawyer? What if they decide to put him in the system? Will we be able to appeal it?"

"If I kiss you, James, will you shut up and go to sleep?"

"Mm . . . maybe," Anthony leaned in to kiss him, and James wanted more, but it was still the early days of their relationship. "Good night," James said.

As soon as Anthony's head hit the pillow, he was asleep.

Morning came, and Adam wanted pancakes and orange juice. James was sound asleep, so Anthony put a kid's show on television and gave Adam his juice.

Anthony's phone rang. It was Imelda. He didn't want to wake James, so he decided to call her back when he had settled Adam with some breakfast. As he watched his phone ring, he listened to the tiny coffee pot brew, but Anthony didn't like black coffee and he was not a fan of coffee whitener either. He needed to remember to get some milk.

9

A loud banging on the door was enough to wake the dead. Adam was frightened when a woman's voice yelled like a fish wife, and he jumped on James' bed.

"Anthony! Anthony! Open this door now!"

He put on a robe and went to open the door.

"What on earth are you doing here? Who told you where I was?" She tried to push past him, but he stopped her in her tracks. "We weren't expecting you." He was thoroughly embarrassed and more than a little disgusted that she arrived unexpectedly and uninvited.

"I'll get dressed and meet you downstairs in five minutes," he calmly told her. She started to argue. "I said in five minutes. I don't need you to dress me. Wait for me in the lobby. You had better have a good reason for this invasion of my privacy." Anthony was livid as he closed the door.

"James, you are not going to believe it, but my mother arrived, unannounced, at this hotel. It's more than I can handle."

"Just tell her," James realized what kind of person she was when he heard her yelling out his name. He tried to be supportive, "She is your mom."

"Here goes nothing. If I don't come back in ten minutes, call for search and rescue."

As soon as she saw Anthony in the lobby, she started yelling at him again. He held her elbow firmly, and steered her outside and away from the other patrons. "Let's go outside so you don't wake the whole hotel."

"I had to drive all this way to talk to you." She wanted attention.

"Has something serious happened? Please stop yelling or I'll not talk to you. We need to have an adult discussion; although, I'm finding it difficult to have any sensible conversations with you." He tried to sound menacing, "What do you want?"

Before she could answer, he warned her again, "Keep your voice down and don't shout; you are mortifying me." Anthony continued to manoeuvre her further away from the hotel. He was able to break her stubborn stance, and led her outside to a bench.

"You are behaving like a child, we need to put this behind us, and you need to come home with me." Anthony couldn't believe what he was hearing.

"You're making a spectacle of yourself," Anthony hissed, "you are out of control, an embarrassment."

"You left me with no options, you cannot keep ignoring me. I have driven all this way to see you." Imelda was irate.

"Who are you hiding up there?" Imelda pounded the words out even louder. "I shouldn't have to drive all this way to see my son. What's gotten into you?" His nerves were frayed.

"You are right; you shouldn't have come all this way. I don't want you here, and that's why I didn't invite you." She was a nightmare.

Her yelling was awful and persistent. "First, let me say this," Anthony said in whispered tones, "You had no business coming here, uninvited. I don't want you here. Secondly, you don't have the right to hound me this way, so stay away from me. I already told you to back off and keep your nose out of my business."

"I have every right! I'm your mother," She shrieked.

Anthony insisted she calm down, "Keep out of my business! I'm warning you."

"I want you to come home, you promised to take care of me." She yelled even louder, "I have rights!"

"I doubt that," he answered. She threw her hands down and stamped her feet, finally breaking from the stubborn stance she was in. Anthony took this opportunity to gently lead her further away from the hotel before she began yelling again.

"You will refrain from yelling or screaming like a child. Sit down and listen, please."

Imelda sat on the bench, "I'm listening," she spat out.

Very calmly, Anthony told his mother, "I'm gay. I don't know if you understand, but it's because I'm gay that I have difficulty talking to you." She glared at him as he stated, "This is me! It's who I am."

"My partner, James, who, I will introduce to you later, is the reason why I needed my privacy." Imelda was shocked as she glared at him wide-eyed. "I have a difficult time talking to you, especially about relationships, since I'm gay. I felt so uncomfortable when you would throw women at me. I asked you multiple times to stop making dates for me. I can choose my own partner, and I certainly didn't need any help from you with finding James."

"Anthony, you are my son; you can't be gay. It's impossible!" she yelled.

Anthony stood bewildered by her attitude, "I assure you I am gay."

"Your father would be ashamed of you." Imelda screeched.

"My father's opinion of me is irrelevant, as is yours!" He could not understand why she was so angry about his sexuality.

He was not shocked by his mother's attack; it was one of the reasons why he didn't want to tell her—he knew she would explode.

"Your father said that he didn't want to be around you—that he thought you were gay. You ruined my marriage," Imelda had gone too far with her accusation. This was a side of her he hadn't seen before; he didn't care how she hurt him. She was menacing.

"Stop with the mudslinging," he replied. He desperately wanted to get away from her.

"George told me I coddled you, and that's why you were gay. I didn't believe him." This woman was not his mom; he had never met this person before.

"My family comes first," Anthony replied, "so, on second thoughts, I will not be introducing you to my partner."

"You will regret this, Anthony. You are no son of mine."

"Well, that's a relief. That's the nicest thing you've said all year. You're not my mother, and I don't want you anywhere near me." His parting words were blunt, "I never want to see you again. Unless you have a more enlightened aspect of gay people, please don't call or contact me again." He stood to have the last word, "There is nothing left to say." He walked away from her and didn't look back.

He ran up the stairs to their room, the door was open. James said nothing.

"She's gone. I'll tell you all about it on our drive back tomorrow. Let's take off to the harbour and find a tour boat. I'm sorry, James, but I have to get out of here."

James collected their coats and some snacks. Out at sea and away from the mainland, the wind could be blustery so it was better to be prepared. "Come on, Adam, if we wait too much longer, the whales will be asleep."

"Anthony, was that a wicked witch? She scared me." Out of the mouth of babes!

"You are safe; I sent her away. She was being a nuisance. She won't come again."

"I was shopping with my mommy and a lady came over to yell that my mommy had hit her car in the car park. We didn't have a car, so my mommy told her to go away, and the lady shouted louder. My mommy said she was an old witch."

"We won't let anything happen to you, Adam." James was holding him. "We are two very big men. You are safe with us," he assured him. "Witches are not real, but it's just a name we call noisy old ladies."

James was aware of Anthony's argument with his mother, but it wasn't a subject to talk about with little ears listening. It was, however, a subject to be discussed later that night. James wanted Anthony to know how much he supports and respects him with everything he had done for his mom.

The boat was swaying. James was looking out to sea over Anthony's shoulder. He was thinking about their future and came to the happy conclusion that they were destined to be a family of three.

He thought they would be the best parents; Adam would be happy and would benefit the most from a loving and caring home, just as Karen had obviously thought.

So much time had elapsed while waiting for the results of their foster application, which was proving to be nerve-wracking. Even though Eric was pushing hard for a decision, he had told the men that Karen's last wish was for Adam to be with James and that Karen's wish would be considered at decision time.

James commented, "There's nothing like sailing for blowing away the cobwebs." Anthony was conscious of the silence, and told James he was sorry his mom put the mockers on a wonderful weekend. He had been looking forward to spending quality time with them.

"Look, James! Look, Anthony! Look at what I see!" Adam was excited when he saw a small island full of seals, and from this distance, the whole island looked like moving grey rocks. "Can we take pictures?" It was hard not to be thrilled with Adam's reaction.

"Adam, you can use my phone. Put this wrist band on tightly," Anthony showed him, "and hold the phone tight, take lots of pictures, and we can choose one to go on your bedroom wall."

Adam handed the phone back to Anthony. "James, can I have a photo of you and Adam for my wallet?"

"Yes, if I can have one with all three of us." James was joining in the fun.

"I forgot the binoculars, but if you look in the distance, can you see a whale blowing water through his spout. I think it's a humpback." Anthony began taking pictures and a video of the whale. He needed to remember to put his binoculars in his backpack so he'd have them for future trips. He whispered to James, "For our next trip, we should get Adam his own pair of binoculars."

The trio was worn out when the boat arrived back at Port Hardy harbour. It was an enjoyable trip and watching Adam's excitement was time well spent. Seeing Anthony relaxed was an even bigger bonus for James. "Let's go out for supper tonight. What should we have?"

James suggested, "Take-out."

Adam suggested, "Burgers."

"I agree. Let's take a detour, decide what you want, and I'm going through the drive-thru."

"James, if you can talk to my mommy, will you tell her that I eat all my food before I get a treat? She told me all the time . . . real food first!" He sounded so grown up.

"Remember what I told you," James smiled at Adam, "when you go to bed tonight, close your eyes and see your mommy's face. You can tell her that you eat your food all up, and if she smiles at you, she knows that what you told her was true."

They ate supper, and Adam went to sleep so quickly.

"I have arranged for Jade to come round tomorrow. She's bringing me some product to take back to the office, and she's also bringing Brett."

"Who's Brett?" James looked in wonder.

"He's Jade's new bodyguard. He's a bright kid in his late teens, and he has dyslexia. Jade is working with him by using colour codes and numbers. He can't read words, but he does try to memorize things when he can, and all the clerks are happy to support him. When I first met Brett, he was helping Jade clean up the cooler, and as soon as he saw me go through to the office, he followed me and asked me politely to leave the store. Jade believes he's getting a chance to be like everyone else."

"Wow, that's neat. He sounds like a pretty special young man," James replied before jumping into it. "Anthony, we can tango all night, or we can stop dancing around the problem, you had with your mom." Anthony was quiet. "We need to solve your problem before it eats away at either of you."

Anthony's mind chose to ignore his mom's outburst. He had never imagined that she could be so mean, narrow-minded, and just a bully. He had not seen this side of her.

When she chose to blame him for her marriage breaking up, he was so upset, and still she continued to berate him. He decided to be totally honest with James and told him what had transpired. Imelda was convinced Anthony was to blame for her marriage break up; Imelda accused him of driving his father away. Those accusations were heavy burdens for anyone to have lashed at them.

James allowed him to talk uninterrupted, a luxury he had not allowed himself until tonight.

"I should have told her when I was a teen," Anthony tried to find excuses to correct the situation. "I had very few friends growing up, so I didn't realize that I was different." Anthony need not explain, as James already knows how he felt. "When I left for university, I had my freedom. I had a couple of casual acquaintances that didn't last more than three dates. I thought I was too picky or too busy working on my degree."

Anthony continued. "I got a degree in Business Management which included Marketing and Merchandising; and I also took Computing Sciences during summer vacations and got a diploma." James wanted to be a good listener, for Anthony's sake. He was especially interested in how quickly Anthony went through the ranks.

"My dad gave me spending money every month and always told me not to tell mom. I also had my job with Quick & Easy, so I never struggled for funds. It was a huge shock when I found out my dad had walked out on her."

James asked what his life was like growing up, and how different his mom was compared to now. After he listened, he strongly offered his recommendation, "She needs to see a professional analyst who can help, and who can steer her back to normal. She has major anger management issues that are directed at you. This needs to be addressed, and the only way forward is for her to see her family doctor and ask for a referral to see a specialist. My best approach would be to take her to her family doctor, to ask for a psychological assessment."

"You are the first person I feel comfortable talking to about this. Thank you for sharing some of your stories with me. I know now that you understood me. It has been about three months since we've been together. I know now, James, and I'm more certain than ever, that I want you as a part of my life. I know you and Adam come as a package, and I'm honoured to be part of that package."

"I feel that sometimes I am living in a whirlwind," James replied in a serious tone. "You always bring things back into perspective. If I panic, you stay calm, and I know I can rely on you." He admitted, "Most importantly, if it weren't for you, we wouldn't have been able to keep Adam. When we get back to Nanaimo, I still need to work, as I can't afford to live if I don't work, we need to consider that Adam will need lots of things this summer and school supplies as he starts school in September. Grade 1 is in for a pleasant surprise when they meet Adam." They laughed together.

"Is your phone handy?" Anthony asked as James nodded. "Look up Johnny Mathis. The songs I would sing to you are "Love Story" and "If We Only Have Love." I listen to him all the time."

James played "Love Story" and his eyes filled with tears. Then he played "If We Only Have Love" and James asked where he found these two songs.

"He's my favourite singer of all time. No one else sings like him. He's elderly now, but he still sings from his heart. Another song that makes me feel wonderful is, "A Time for Us." Listen carefully to the words, they were written especially for you and me. He sings that song to the love of his life. He worked avidly for Gay Rights and when you hear his songs, you will be able to relate; he's an incredible human being. My favourite songs are all golden oldies that tell stories," he added, "modern music, well, I don't mind some of it."

James moved closer to Anthony. "I think you are an incredible human being. I can't believe I have you in my life." James meant every word. Then he said, "I want you, too."

"I was going to say let's get some sleep. It's going to be a long drive tomorrow." They hugged, which went beyond what either could have imagined. They finally said goodnight.

James was still waiting for Anthony to tell him what was going to happen with his mom, but there was always tomorrow. James was not tired, and he started to worry about how they were going to be able to afford a larger apartment or a small house.

He then started thinking about his own problems with his dad. It was so hard for James to forgive him but for his mom's sake, he always tried to be pleasant. Karen gave James an opportunity to take care of Adam, and he wanted to make sure he didn't follow in his dads footsteps. He had so many things to think about and a million 'what if's' raced through his mind until he finally fell asleep.

It's Sunday, and if the guys wanted a lazy morning in bed, there was no chance. Adam got up and was ready for breakfast, and he was not so quiet. He turned on the television. "When will Brett, my new friend, be coming?" Adam was excited. "Jade said she would bring Brett, and we can message each other on Jade's phone when I get back home."

James first reaction was to keep the noise down. Adam climbed on his bed and whispered in his ear, "It's time to get up, James. Please get up, Jade is coming."

James bolted out of bed.

"What time is it? What time did she say she was coming here?" Anthony laughed heartily as he was watched James panic and rush in the shower. "We are meeting her for pancakes at ten. No need to rush."

Brett and Adam were best buddies by the time breakfast was over.

"Adam, grab your bag and start filling it with clothes first, then your stuffed toys. Put what you want to play with, in the car on the top of your bag." Again, Anthony was wearing his forever organizer hat.

"James, I need to include you on my car insurance policy. I'll do that tomorrow. Please remind me." They got back into the Jeep, and headed south, on their journey home, Anthony was an avid organizer.

James asked, "Why would I do that when I don't have a car?" Anthony told him that he will be expected to drive on long trips. "It'll be easier with two drivers."

"I've only driven my mom's old Fiesta. I can't drive this Jeep; I would be scared of having an accident."

"I always drive like I'm scared of having an accident. It keeps me alert, which makes me a better driver," Anthony said with confidence.

"Are you sure?" James didn't completely believe Anthony, but he didn't feel the need to argue.

They arrived at James' apartment and unloaded the car. "Let's walk to the playground, and Adam can have a run around. It may help him sleep," James suggested. A couple of kids around Adam's age were racing around the sandbox too.

Anthony checked his phone for messages. Eric Gould had left an email confirming their appointment for Tuesday. When he reminded James, it caused a slight problem as James forgot he had a shift. "I will be off at four. Can we reschedule for later? I need to be with you for this meeting." Anthony did as he asked, and Eric was okay with five o'clock.

James contacted their babysitter and made arrangements for the next day. They both wondered how Eric was getting along with the fostering process.

"The sooner we get to know that everything is settled, the sooner I can get a big enough bed and lose this sofa. If you have any worries at this juncture, you must tell me. Please, don't let things fester. I don't know how you feel, James, but I feel optimistic. We have to go through all the steps it takes to get Adam, and there are legal implications that need to be addressed. The courts will want to see that we can provide for him, give him a home, and keep him safe." Anthony was used to dealing with more critical situations, and he felt, in his heart of hearts, that they were well-prepared for being daddies.

When James walked into work, Sophie asked him lots of questions. Because of the circumstances of James fostering Adam, Sophie offered her help too. She was pleased to hear that the guys had already applied to adopt him. She could not imagine putting little Adam in the care of people he didn't know. Sophie didn't want to ask James if he was keeping up his studies, it's going to be so hard on him financially.

"Anthony asked me to look out for reasonably priced properties, so here's a list. They're all online, and these are still available. I don't know all the areas advertised, but I'm sure you guys will go through them carefully." James thanked Sophie, who then remarked, "Anthony said you would like to be settled before the little guy goes to school. If you need my help with anything, you just need to ask."

"Thanks for all of your help, Sophie, you're a wonderful friend. The last few weeks have been nerve-wracking. This weekend, Anthony drove us north to the Port Hardy store. I met his friend Jade, and we all went to Sammy's, for the best ribs I ever had, and we had a blast. We're also getting to know each other better. At five o'clock this afternoon we have to go see the lawyer, but don't worry, I can work my whole shift."

"If you need a reference, I would be glad to provide one," she said. Sophie was a gem.

The two men walked into their meeting with Eric Gould, not knowing what to expect. Eric's office was austere with an oversized desk in the middle of the room and about ten huge sets of beautifully leather-bound books on a set of bookshelves. It looked impressive. James had Karen's letter with him and handed it to Eric to put on file.

"The letter you just gave me will certainly quicken the adoption process," Eric felt confident. "Take a seat, gentlemen. We have some documents for you to sign. But first of all, I have received the papers from Child Services. You have been granted fostering rights."

"What's next if we want permanent rights?" James was already way ahead of the process.

"In the near future, I'm confident you will get full custody of Adam. The domestic adoption process has had a complete overhaul and the wait times have been considerably reduced unless you want to adopt from abroad, then that takes forever." Eric was pleased with their reactions and had no doubts that Adam was in good hands.

Eric showed them the Letter of Authority, allowing them custody of Adam.

"Now, I need you both to pay attention to what I'm going to tell you. When we met a month ago, you both made an obligation to take care of Adam. You have taken on this charge, and for your commitment, Karen has left everything to you, James, in her Will. This is what I need to go over with you today. Karen's Will is extraordinary in its content."

The three men were sitting at the circular table. "You both need to brace yourselves for what I have to say; it may come as a shock." Eric opened the file.

"Karen has set aside fifty percent of her money, which will be given to Adam on his twentieth birthday. If you should need to use any of this money for Adam's well-being, you need to call me. I am the executor, and I will assess if the request is appropriate and submit the funds you need."

Eric looked closely at the two men. They did not understand or comprehend his intentions. "The other fifty percent has been handed over to you, James. This will be a time of adjustment for you both. Karen stated in her Will that James and his future spouse, partner, and/or childcare providers would have access to half of the fifty percent to set up a home. The other half of the money will be paid to both of you when Adam reaches fifteen years old. If anything happens and you are unable to give Adam a home, I have the authority to withdraw all funds deemed appropriate."

Eric waited, letting the information he gave them sink in. "In a nutshell, you will immediately receive one-quarter of Karen's assets. When Adam is fifteen, you will receive the second quarter. The other fifty percent is to be kept and invested by me until Adam is twenty years old."

"Eric, does this mean we can get a larger apartment, and we can hire a nanny because we both have to work?" James asked.

"Neither of you asked how much," Eric replied. "Why?"

"We have no worries. Together, James and I can afford whatever he needs," Anthony stated. "My father signed over his half of his house, which is worth quite a sum," Anthony mentioned his salary, and James offered his paycheque, saying that he was working hard and trying for a promotion as soon as he could.

"Gentlemen, pay attention please, when you sign this document, and commit to taking care of Adam, you will get—" Eric was cut short.

"We don't need any of Karen's money," James was adamant as he told Eric they have enough earnings to take care of Adam. "We have it covered."

"Gentlemen, if you choose to use Karen's money, you can buy a house in a very nice neighbourhood. Karen also told me that you must use some of the money for your education, James." Eric raised his voice to garner their attention. "She said I was to ensure you would have enough funds to go to university, even if you are unable to take care of Adam. She said you had your heart set on a medical profession, a doctor? You now have that opportunity."

"Please, sign on the appropriate lines," Eric waited.

"I am going to give you the complete Will that has details of the dollar amounts." Eric was amazed that neither of them asked how much he was talking about. He was going to astound them. "Go to the bottom of page two," he offered them a beverage, "Do either of you want a coffee or water?"

"There has been a mistake. This doesn't make any sense," Anthony told Eric. "Karen was very frugal. We both cleared out her old apartment, and honestly, Eric, she had nothing of any value."

Eric put the record straight. "This money came from the insurance settlement that was paid to her when her husband died in a car accident. She was going to refuse the money, but I told her that one day Adam would be a grown man, and he deserved something for not having his dad around. She told me to invest it. I did."

"I'm making the same offer to you guys. If there's a chunk of money that you don't need, I'll invest it for you into secured markets."

"Go over all the information and make some decisions. This will be a life-changer for both of you. Adam has his own independent funds."

They thanked Eric and left his office.

They didn't say a word until they got into the Jeep.

Anthony was the first to pass a comment, "James, this will allow you to become a doctor of whatever you choose." He looked at James' face, and the windfall had not sunk in, "I hope you don't waste this opportunity." He was so happy for his partner! He deserved the chance to become a doctor as he has the brains to achieve whatever he set his mind to.

"Was this correct? We can afford a nice place to live in? Oh, Anthony! It includes a nanny?" James was flabbergasted. "I need you to tell me I am not dreaming." He was quiet for a few seconds before saying, "I think I should still work for a year to pay for my first-year courses."

"Karen insisted you have all the money you need to pay for your university. Why would you choose to wait? There are no better plans than going to school to become a doctor. We can get a place here in Victoria. You can attend UVic and be home every night."

"What about you, Anthony? What would you like?"

"What would make me the happiest man alive is for you to follow your dreams!" he smiled. "We need to tell Adam, tomorrow."

10

Alexis was sorting through some filing when the phone rang. "Hello, Alexis speaking. How may I help you?"

"You can tell Anthony that I have some news for him. He refuses to answer his phone. What I have to tell him is very important. Please pass this message on to him."

"Sorry, I didn't catch your name." Normally, Alexis would have put the phone down on someone so rude. No wonder he refuses to talk to her, she thought. He deserved better.

Alexis sent him a text to call her at the office. "Your mom's been calling you, and you're not replying to her messages. She has something very important to tell you." Anthony had already told Alexis about his mom's erratic behaviour and that he had severed all ties with her.

"Thanks for the message, Alexis. I'll call her and tell her not to call here again. She needs to understand that I can't have her ruining my life. I haven't told her about Adam. He doesn't need to hear her disgusting bile and verbal abuse. She lacks self-control." Anthony made her laugh, "Adam asked me if she was a witch. He said he was scared of her because she screamed so loud."

"If you were my son, Anthony, I would adore the ground you walked on. I will leave it with you." At that moment in time, he wished Alexis was his mom.

He had a bad feeling about calling his mom, and his gut was churning; he wanted to get this over with.

"Hello," Anthony said when his mother picked up, "what's your problem now?" He didn't know what to expect; an apology would have been nice, but that didn't happen.

"Your dad has died. His new wife asked for his half of the house. That was what I needed to tell you."

"Well, she can't have my half of the house."

"She wants half of the house, and she also wants his pensions. She said he promised them to her, before he died." Imelda was sobbing.

"I'm on my way; wait until I get there," Anthony asked that she get out all the legal documents regarding her house.

He arrived and walked in to find Imelda going through some drawers, looking for the papers he requested. "My lawyer will not be available for consultation until he arrives back in the city on Wednesday. Delia will have to wait. I have far more important matters to deal with."

"If I lose my home, it will be your fault," she flung the words at him.

"You need to take responsibility for your own lack of good judgment." He didn't want to listen to her blaming everyone else. "I tried everything in my power to have you sell this mausoleum and make a fresh start. You were too stubborn to take heed of my advice, and since you created this problem, you, and only you, need to fix it!"

"It's not my fault. You went away without telling me where you were going," Again, she blamed her son. "You wanted to be with your so-called friends," she almost spat the words out, "I had no idea where you had gone or when you would be home."

"This property is not a home; I have a new home, filled with love and laughter. I want you out of my life! Where I go, and who I go with, is none of your business." He shot back at her, "Your possessiveness and controlling behaviour drove me crazy. I hated going back to your house, and I was sick to death of arguing with you.

"The main reason I left was to regain my independence, and I abhor your insensitive manipulation." Imelda glared at him. "The fact that you felt justified in opening my mail." He made it clear, "your conversation is crude, undignified, demeaning, and humiliating. I find your overall behaviour nauseating." His trouncing comments rolled like water off of a duck's back.

You need help; let me help you, please!"

"Anthony, I was so disappointed in you. You refused to take my calls. What can I do when you walk away without leaving a forwarding address?"

Anthony was determined to keep his cool. "What documents did she produce that provide or establish ownership of the house? Does Delia have a Will that proves Dad left everything to her?" Anthony wanted his mom to leave him alone. He knew what would happen if he didn't come up with a solution now—his mother would hound him.

"I don't know what proof she has. I told her to go away and not to bother me again," she cried.

"Do not contact Delia. If you do, I will abandon you completely. You will never see me again. Tell me you understand." Imelda had no alternative but to concede.

"When my father handed me half of your house, he registered the transfer of ownership with the Land Titles Office. I paid a one-time insurance payment to ensure that no one could change the title deeds without my consent," Anthony waited for her to say something.

Then Anthony had second thoughts. If he dealt directly with Delia, his mom needn't be involved. She needed to stay away from him and Delia. Though he had a high stress tolerance, she kept escalating it.

"If that was all you wanted, you will have to wait because I have some urgent family matters to take care of. They take precedence over your imaginary problems."

"Please give me Delia's number," he said matter-of-factly. "I will call her," he walked away from his mother to call Delia. When she didn't answer, he left a message. He immediately called James.

"My mother called to tell me my dad had died." He went on to tell James about the exchange of opinions and his mother's inability to shoulder any blame regarding Delia asking for half of her house and for requesting his pensions.

"I can't wait to see you. I need you, James. You are my rock."

"I'm here for you." Then James thought they deserved a treat. "Let's take Adam for his favourite kid's meal. Then afterwards, we can ask Katie to babysit, and we can go for a leisurely meal somewhere nice. What do you think?" A couple of weeks ago, Eric had recommended his old friend, Katie Parker, be hired as Adam's nanny. Katie had just started babysitting Adam. She brought with her some great cooking skills and a wide knowledge of crafts and hobbies suited to small kids.

"Count me in. I'm looking forward to it already. Thanks, James."

Adam was in a giggly mood. He laughed at James' mischievous antics of making funny faces, which were a blast. When they arrived at the apartment, Katie had waited to take Adam for a walk while the guys got ready for a date.

Anthony was hoping to solve most of their problems so that James could register at UVic. He also wanted to go house hunting. "We need to find a place where Adam will have the home Karen wanted for him, one that will satisfy the judge."

They ordered a bottle of Beaujolais when they arrived at the restaurant. It felt good being able to relax. Anthony needed to unload his problems, and James was there to listen to what happened when Anthony met his mom. Having James to confide in was a game-changer, and once Anthony started telling James about his mother's problems, he had to tell him the full story of when she began behaving so out of character. They ordered the prime rib dinner; it was the best steak for miles. Neither of them had a sweet tooth, so they waved the dessert tray away.

"What happened about Delia's claim on your house?" James didn't understand after Anthony delved into the demands she made.

"Dad didn't leave a Will that we know of. About two years ago, I received a letter from my dad's lawyer. It was a shock to find he had handed over half the property to me. I legally own half the house, which Dad's lawyer sent to me, this happened over a year before he married Delia."

"Mom owns the other half. There were no pensions in Dad's name, so according to Mom, he didn't have any. Delia wanted to contact a lawyer, so I told her to go ahead."

As house hunting was an important topic they discussed their on-line options, Anthony and James knew it was urgent to begin their search for a suitable home. They were going through the listings that Sophie found, but James had his eye on one property that came up in the listings recently.

They fell in love with the brick house that James found, and they asked Eric to put in an offer immediately.

Anthony and James were enjoying their bottle of wine. They discussed how things are moving quickly, and how they hoped Katie would accept their invitation to move in when the house offer was accepted.

"Did you talk to Eric? Was there any news about the adoption?"

"James you need to stop worrying, Eric knows what he's doing."

Anthony explained that Eric had also come across a couple of properties that would be suitable, although Eric also preferred the one that James had found.

"Did you talk to Eric today about the house?" Anthony asked.

"Eric said their offer on the property will be accepted. The realtor hasn't gotten hold of the owners yet. Eric also said we'll be in a better position to adopt if we own our home; it means stability."

Katie's whole life had changed when Eric called to ask her if she could help out two friends who needed a nanny. Eric explained the situation, and that they were moving to Victoria with their five-year-old son named Adam. Two days later, Katie was introduced to James and Anthony. She knew then that her life was going to improve for the better.

The men found out their offer for the home was accepted, and the first person they called was Katie; who, after a week of babysitting was offered the job on a permanent basis.

Katie accepted their offer and was excited to start this new phase in her life. She was thrilled when they asked her to move in with them. She was over the moon when she saw the plans of the property. She would have her own room next to Adam's. She was very appreciative to be part of their newly-made family. Everything was looking up.

James and Anthony discussed the property and how it would work for them. The two-story brick house had all the things they wanted, especially a good-size yard that was fenced with a play area, which was ideal for Adam and the friends he would make at school. It also had a deck with a barbeque area. They looked at the realtor's house package. It bragged a large modern kitchen with marble counters, most appliances, a large reception room, a study for James with lots of bookshelves, a playroom for Adam, and a utility bathroom on the main floor. Upstairs consists of two bedrooms on either side of the landing. All four bedrooms had an ensuite.

Katie has two grown-up sons. One is a long-distance truck driver, and the other a Customs Officer at Pearson Airport. She rarely saw them, except on her phone. For quite a while, she felt down and lonely as she felt she wasn't getting anything out of life. She found herself staying in, only going shopping for groceries, and she was convinced she had forgotten how to have fun.

She accepted the generous offer the men made. Katie wanted to help this family, who in turn would help Katie start living life to the fullest. She didn't know Karen, but being a mom, Katie could only imagine Adam's mom would want his happiness foremost. She thought he was a wonderful little guy and wanted to help him grow into a man his mom would be proud of.

With Katie on board, and her willingness to move in with the trio, she quickly became an integral part of their family. Her apartment in Parksville was sublet, and her possessions were packed and ready for the move. Life had a whole new meaning. Adam was adorable, and she was thrilled to be spending time with him. She was full of praise knowing how the two men had rearranged their lives to give Adam a home.

Preparing for their move, they had a professional photographer take a few photos of Adam and to have them framed for their walls. Anthony kept his promise to Adam and had framed some photos of Adam senior, Karen, and baby Adam, to put on his bedroom walls.

They intended on letting Adam choose some of his room furnishings prior to the move. When the time came for the shopping expedition, Katie tagged along with the boys and helped with choosing soft furnishings, some wall decals, and a white sheepskin rug. She also pointed to a desk and chair. She chose plenty of kid items as well, including some Spiderman bath towels, and when Adam spotted the Spiderman quilt she made sure they bought it for him.

When Anthony and James finally arrived back at James' apartment, they contemplated how they would make everything work.

They had been together for four months and were very much in love. Feeling overwhelmed and wanting to relax, James played Johnny Mathis while singing his love songs.

A couple of days later, Eric Gould finally called them. "Are you ready to move?"

"Eric, I have you on speaker," James was excited.

"Gentlemen, I have your new house keys, and you can move in anytime. I transferred the amount from the funds you gave me, and you can move in as soon as you sign on the dotted line. Congratulations! James, did you get accepted at UVic?"

"Yes. I was going to surprise Anthony tonight with the news. I am so thrilled! Thank you, Eric, for everything you have done for us. You are very much appreciated." James gave Anthony a beaming smile.

Eric congratulated them again on their new home. He indicated that they wasted no time getting their affairs in order, and within the week they had planned the move into their new home. Their new furniture was delivered, and when it arrived they had fun sorting out what goes where.

James had to give his notice to Sophie, telling her that he wasn't able to commute to the store. He must keep focused. He had to study to become a doctor while being a dad and spending more time at home. All of this would be impossible if he were working a full-time job. Sophie certainly understood; in fact, she had been training Kelly to fill James' shoes.

During late spring, James managed to study some biology courses from home and was applying for relevant courses to take during the summer. It was enough to get his feet wet, and he was thrilled to the max—he was living his dream, as he walked into his office he shouted, "Let the studying begin!"

Katie and Adam were asked not to disturb him if his study door was closed. He was there every day when Anthony got home, and Adam never distracted him while he was studying. Everything was settling down to a more manageable pace. James took a break every day at lunchtime, and Adam was ready to play.

When it was Adam's birthday, the little man was full of excitement; Katie got his birthday cake with five candles and a superman figurine. He had to blow the candles out five times. The guys bought him a battery driven jeep that could seat two small kids, which he rode around the living room yelling for everyone to move. When he received a Lego box from Katie, he challenged himself to build the tallest tower; and with that she produced the sheepskin rug so he could sit in comfort on their hardwood floors. Katie asked him if he was going to become a famous builder. "I want to fly kites!" he replied.

Adam was a wonderful child, so thoughtful and considerate. Katie was happy with her charge; each day brought something new. Her latest challenge was teaching Adam to read. She had a storage chest full of books from Karen's apartment, and Anthony had loads of patience teaching him the alphabet.

As time moved on, Anthony wanted to know from Katie if all was well, and he asked her for her input regarding Adams needs.

"Adam occasionally asks if his mommy might come home, but when he goes to school, he'll be so busy making friends that he will be able to talk about her without crying," Katie told them that she would keep them up to date on Adam's progress.

As they discussed the upcoming plans Katie had for Adam, Anthony became distracted as his phone began to ring. He excused himself to answer it.

Anthony checked his phone to see who was calling. "Hello?" He said, not immediately recognizing the phone number. Yet, once he heard her voice, he knew he didn't really want to have this conversation, although he knew he had to deal with the unpleasant issues.

It was Delia. He couldn't wait to get this conversation over with.

"Anthony. Thanks for calling me."

"I don't know if I can help you. If you are hoping to get a share of my mom's and mine property, it will not happen." He was direct as he explained that George gave up his share of the house to me long before he married you."

"How could he do that?" Delia was not convinced, "George told me that he owned the house, and his pensions were there for my retirement. Where can I find them? Your mother was very rude when I called to ask for them." She insisted that she was entitled to whatever George had previously owned.

Anthony swore he had no knowledge of any pensions, "I wouldn't know where to look for his pensions. If there were any funds or savings then my mom would be entitled to her share of them. Their divorce settlement only covered the house title, which was legally registered in my name before my dad married you. Originally the house was joint ownership, so he couldn't touch mom's half of the property.

"Mom told me, as far as she knew, he didn't have a Will, and he had no pensions. Without a Will, we are unable to locate where his pensions could be. Did he tell you where to find them? I have no recollection of there being any retirement funds mentioned on the divorce agreement." Then he asked, "Could you be mistaken?"

She was adamant, "No."

Anthony couldn't help her even if he wanted to. Imelda was the only person who would have known about those particular kinds of documents. "My mom has searched everywhere she could think of, and there are no traces of any RSPs or income supplements.

"What exactly did my father say to you?" He did not believe for one minute that George left any pensions.

She was getting frustrated, "He told me that he had some pensions. He didn't tell me how to find them."

"I can't help you, I'm terribly sorry," Anthony said. He was done with this conversation.

"I am going to get legal advice." Delia believed George was telling the truth.

"Please yourself. That's your prerogative," He thought she was chasing rainbows.

Anthony called his mom to ask again if there were any pensions. He asked her to check her bank statements and to look for a charge for a safety deposit box. Imelda told him they didn't exist and that she couldn't find any documents regarding George's pensions. Anthony then contacted his dad's office to see if he had pensions when he was there. As a last resort, he went to his parent's bank and asked if there were any active or dormant accounts in George Lynwood's name.

The teller asked for his full name. "Anthony Evan Lynwood."

"We have a safety deposit box with your name on it," the teller informed him, "you need a key to open the box."

"I don't have a key. I wasn't aware this box existed; this was the first inkling I've had since my dad passed away." He shook his head. "Why would my dad hide his papers in a safety deposit box? This doesn't make any sense."

"I'm afraid I have no knowledge of the contents of the box. Whatever was stored there was completely confidential."

The teller asked Anthony to wait a moment; she went to get help.

"Are you sure my father set this up for me?" he asked the teller when she returned. "I had no idea that this box existed. My father died recently, and I am trying to track any of his assets." Anthony didn't know the drill. "How can I get into the box?" he asked the teller, "I have no key." He was surprised that his dad even thought of him.

"I need your ID, a driver's license or a credit card." The teller told him that she must verify his identity and that he might be able to access the box without a key. "It depends on the manager, one moment, please."

He waited a few minutes until the manager arrived and she asked him to provide his ID again, which he did. "I have your key here in a sealed envelope with your father's signature across the flap. Your father said he was going to call you to pick up the key."

"How bizarre, why would my father go to all this trouble? It doesn't make any sense. He walked out on my mom, and we had no clue where he was; now I find a box here with my name on it." Anthony was curious to find out what his dad was up to.

"Follow me to the vault. I will give you your key so you can open the drawer and take it to the table to inspect the contents. Your father emphatically requested that you read all the papers enclosed. I will be waiting outside the door. When you access the drawer, you can dispose of the contents as you deem fit." She unlocked the vault door and turned away.

To his surprise, the box he opened was not a huge thing, but there were lots of papers. A long letter addressed to "My Son Anthony Evan Lynwood" was on top. Anthony pulled out all the contents, as he wanted to take these documents home so James could help him go through them all. Anthony had never set eyes on these documents before. In fact, he thought that he might have to talk to Eric to find out if the documents were legal. He was deep in thought as he packed up the papers and indicated to the manager that he was done. He drove straight home with his discovery.

"James, can you spare a little time?" he asked once he arrived home. "I found a safety deposit box in Dad's bank, in my name, and I've brought all the contents home. I didn't go through it at the bank as it would have taken me forever." Anthony pulled out a huge envelope that was jammed full of papers. "Look at how much stuff was in there. The bank manager told me to read through the documents very carefully after I have read the personal sealed letter from my dad, George Lynwood."

James was his usual supportive self and asked, "Were you expecting this? Your dad had a strange way of surprising you, first a half of a house, and secondly these are bank drafts. What can it mean?"

They pulled the rest of the contents from the envelope, and one package contained the Last Will and Testament of George Evan Lynwood. Anthony was shocked, "Should this have gone to his wife, Delia? Or given to my mom?"

James advised him to read his letter first; it may shed some light on the issues."

Dear Son,

I feel I should apologize for deserting you, and I understand why you never replied to any of my letters. I was ashamed of what I did, and I knew it would be hard for you to forgive me. I have a leaky heart valve and A-fib, and a few other things that are wrong. I know that I don't have long. The papers attached to this letter are undated bank drafts. I want you to cash them. You, and only you, can do that. My father, your grandpa, left these to you. His Will states that the contents must be handed over to you when you reach your twenty-fifth birthday. He didn't want your mother to have access to this money, as you will read in his Will. This was where Imelda and I could not agree. She wanted to go through your personal mail to find out how you benefitted from my father's Will; I hid everything in a bank box so she couldn't access it. She made my life hell with her bullying, and for quite a while, she tried forcing me to give her the keys. The contents are legally yours and only yours. I promised my father that I would not tell her or give her access to your legacy.

She had, over time, forged my signature on my pensions and was merrily spending our future retirement savings. I left her; I had no choice. I didn't imagine, for one minute, that you would move back home. If I had given you this key, and she found out, she would have stolen the money. Your grandpa loved you so much, but your mom banned him from seeing you. This was the only way I was sure to keep your inheritance safe. None of your grandpa's money will go to Delia, either, as she kept asking me for more money that I didn't have.

I love you with all my heart, Anthony, and I want you to live comfortably with a partner who deserves you. We never discussed you being gay, which made no odds to me. You are a wonderful man, and you will have a good start with this money.

If you can forgive me, I would love to keep in touch with you. I am proud to be your dad. I tried to get your mom to see a doctor, as her issues were erratic and sometimes, she scared me. She always refused help. My guess was she has very bad depression or mental issues, maybe Alzheimer's disease.

If I had known you were coming back home, I would not have left.

Enjoy your inheritance! I love you, my son.

Dad

"This explains a lot. My dad didn't abandon me. She drove him away," he added, "what happened to Mom to make her behave this way?"

"She had no right to accuse you of ruining her marriage, but why did she lie about the pensions? She obviously knew where the money had gone," James was trying hard to figure out why Imelda was shrouded in lies.

"My dad kept quiet about my grandpa. Until now, I never understood why my grandparents fell off the edge of the earth. Mom told me they died when I was a teenager. My grandpa insistently forbade her any access to his money. It was categorically stated in his Will. Dad said she guessed about the money, but grandpa was cautious. Dad denied that his father had left a Will to him, which was true because he bypassed dad and left everything to me. When I went back home, he had arranged to keep everything in a safety deposit box. The bank manager had the key in an envelope that Dad had left there for safekeeping and with strict instructions to give the contents only to me."

"This was very cloak and dagger. Anthony, your dad sounds like a real nice guy, who loved you and made sure Imelda didn't get her hands on your grandpa's Will." James replied. "I think that Imelda has had a mental breakdown. Was her behaviour ever erratic as it is now?"

Anthony shook his head. He was struggling to understand his mom's crazy antics.

"The pensions did exist, but she stole them by falsifying dad's signature and unwisely spent all of his retirement money. Delia will be upset if she finds out why they don't exist." Anthony was thinking clearly now. "I would have given my mom the money if she needed it, and this was the reason why she was hounding me to move back home."

Anthony handed his copy of his grandpa's Will to James, "What a lot of money! Grandpa liquidated his property and sold his business. I feel guilty—not about the money—but I really loved spending time with him. He had oodles of patience, and we had lots of fun; he played all my games with me and had the same passion for the swimming pool. He was special. How could she tell me he was dead?"

"Were you the only grandchild?" Anthony nodded yes. James helped sort all of the papers into neat little piles. "You've inherited a huge sum. If you want my advice, keep the money in the bank until we unravel all of the paperwork, and don't mention it to anyone until you have run it by Eric."

"Okay, that sounds good to me." Anthony would concur with his dad's wishes.

James started to read through all of the papers, "Wow," he stated, "I have counted it again; it's a pretty large sum."

"At the beginning of his letter he said he had written to me, he wanted to keep in touch. On several occasions I have argued with mom about her opening my mail. I bet she tore up his letters so I would never know about the pension money. She has turned into a monster who intentionally kept my dad and me apart."

"Let's take a break," Anthony was overwhelmed. "On second thoughts," he said, "let's go to bed."

11

Anthony was off to work. He needed to pay Jade a visit.

Before a long trip, he liked to fill up with gas at the local 7-11 and grab an extra-large coffee. The Port Hardy store was struggling with their ordering, and it seemed they were not rotating the products. Jade had just returned from a one-week vacation to find her store in turmoil. Alice, the assistant manager, was well-trained, and she should have called him immediately when she noticed something was wrong.

Although he was driving through small villages lined with colourful hanging flower baskets—enhancing the beautiful scenery he always admired—he could think of little else than Jade. It was incomprehensible that neither Jade nor Alice had called him for help sooner.

James knew Anthony would be gone for a couple of days, at least. But Adam knew he was going away, and he was very quiet, almost sulky. Katie couldn't get him to talk about it.

"What happens if he doesn't come back?" Adam asked James, revealing why he was sad. "What if he goes to heaven, and I can't see him?"

"Remember a few weeks ago, when Anthony drove us up north to see Jade and Sammy and Brett? That's where Anthony works sometimes. Let's call him, okay?"

131

Anthony's phone rang. "Hi, James, is everything okay?"

"It will be in a few seconds. Adam has been having a tough time since you left; he thinks you are going to heaven, and he won't see you again." James called for Adam, "Quick, can you guess who is on the phone?"

"You are not in heaven?" Adam yelled at Anthony and then, in a much quieter tone, said, "If you go to heaven, I will never see you again. Please, don't go to heaven."

Anthony knew how to talk to Adam, although it was sometimes difficult to rationalize death for a five year old to understand.

"Adam, this is my job. It's what I have to do when I go to work."

"Why can I not go with you? I want to see Jade and Sammy."

"I will be back as soon as I can, but you can call me, or I will call you every evening when I'm done work. Is that a deal?"

Then Anthony thought it was appropriate to mention Karen. "Your mommy was very sick, and the doctors gave her some medicine, but it didn't make her better, so your mommy died. Adam, I'm not sick; in fact, since you came to live with James and me, I feel great. James goes to school some days, and he always comes home to us. Because we have to work to pay for all your treats, Katie is there with you, and in the summertime, when you start school, you will come home every afternoon, just like James and me." Adam handed the phone to James and ran away to look for Katie.

"You are so good with him. I didn't know how to get it through to him that you are coming back in a couple of days." James then added, "What kind of doctor will I be if I can't sort out our son?"

"The best doctor ever, James Prescott, M.D." Anthony laughed. "Adam's in a very good place right now. He's learning to cope, thanks to you. Without you, his life doesn't bear thinking about."

"That goes for me, too. I don't ever want to be without you. Love you!"

"Love you too," Anthony added.

When Anthony got to Courtney, he drove past the future location of a new Quick & Easy Foods. It was situated in the Comox Valley area, which was a beautiful place to visit. This was a lesser populated place than Campbell River, but in the summer time, there were so many people travelling around the Island. This charming spot, though set back from the sea, had outstanding views from its numerous campsites that are full for the whole summer season, which he noted was good for business.

He drove around the area, got a coffee from a gas bar, and continued his journey. He was thinking of proposing to James. Although his mind was focused on the business, he couldn't help but think back over the last few months with James and how he knew James was his soul-mate. The first thing he decided was to keep it a secret; he planned on getting Katie involved to make this a special occasion.

Campbell River was selected for future consideration. Anthony couldn't drive through without assessing the demographics of this area. It was an ideal place for a new store. There was lots of potential and a steadily growing community—a great place—but he must concentrate on the problems at Port Hardy. He took note to revisit this area on his return to Victoria.

How did everything go haywire? He was thinking of Jade; she didn't call him with problems, she fixed problems and she always recommended solutions. She should have called him.

Knowing how Adam was upset, he didn't want to stay away for too long. He thought about inviting them for the trip, they could board a ferry from Victoria to Port Hardy. He wanted to suggest that James and Adam travel the most scenic route; they would like that. It all depended on Jade's store issues.

The hotel was close by, so he took his luggage, signed in, only to find the hotel was full to the gills. He needed a good night's sleep and tomorrow would be a better time to tackle his problems. He sent a text to Jade, telling her not to tell the staff that he was in town, and that he would be at the store early tomorrow morning.

That morning, he went through the drive-thru for a breakfast muffin and coffee, and when he arrived at the store, he walked in quietly. He needed to see the staff's reactions as they arrived. Alice was already there. When she saw Anthony, she greeted him in her usual way, "Good to see you again, Anthony. I'm sorry everything is in turmoil."

Brett was just as happy to see him. Billy arrived and had no adverse reaction when he saw a boss from head office.

"Don't worry about it; I'll help you sort it, one step at a time. We will start with the coolers. Your first job is to bag the empty cartons and Brett you can do a special job of cleaning the shelves."

Jade arrived. "Hi, Anthony, I think I know what happened," she admitted, "it was my fault." Anthony raised his brows and followed her to her office, closing the door.

"I am so sorry I didn't tell you when it happened, but I left my car parked behind our store and I walked to work. Some inconsiderate ass broke into it. They jimmied the trunk and got into my vehicle on the passenger side. I didn't notice straight away, but they took my wallet and my personal phone from under the seat. I kept the store's security keypad numbers in there. I thought they were safe. My car alarm was pretty loud, but if it was parked at the front of the store, it would have been easier to spot. No one heard the alarm."

"I hope they nab the culprit. Do you have any clues as to who did it?" Anthony was more concerned about Jade's safety than the store's turmoil. "You know you must call me immediately! For you, I would have flown up here ASAP."

"I called the cops, and they kept telling me that no-one had broken into the premises, to humour me, they did the fingerprints, etc., and I called the insurance company."

"What happened next?" He wanted to know the whole story.

"That was when I found my wallet, spare keys, and my personal phone were missing," Jade was in tears. She felt responsible because the store's security information was taken.

"What about the in-store cameras? Did you check?"

Jade had a blank look, Anthony explained that the store is also equipped with outdoor cameras, monitoring the front and back of the store. "Did you view these?"

Jade had no idea the security cameras existed, "Oh Anthony, where can I find them?"

"We have a contract with the alarm company," Anthony assumed she knew.

"First, we need to lock the store. Here, Jade, I need your help, let's stick this notice on the window." Anthony was looking around assessing the amount of damage. "I'll also be speaking to the police and to Greg about the alarms."

"Now, my dear Jade, it's time we go for lunch. Let's try to work out who did this by going through the sequence of events from when they came through the store using the footage." He asked her to detail even the slightest suspicion. After what had happened in the store, lunch was doggy bagged due to lack of appetites. "Was there any cash missing?"

Jade told Anthony that the cash-out envelopes from the night before were in the safe. She also pointed out that they didn't seem to locate the safe.

Anthony contacted the alarm company and explained what happened, asking Greg for any footage of the break in.

"But Anthony, the alarm was never tripped, whoever did this had the pass-codes," Greg, the security specialist, didn't like to admit that the alarm didn't go off. This was not good.

Anthony assured Greg that the person who got into the store had broken into the manager's car and stole everything: her phone, purse, and wallet, which contained the store passwords, and a spare set of keys. Everything was hidden under the car seat, and she was parked at the back door of the store." He also explained that Jade wasn't using her car and that she thought it was safe parked at the back of the store.

"Anthony, the police assured me there was no break-in, and that no locks were tampered with. I felt awful, I didn't understand what had happened."

She explained that when she entered the premises nothing stuck out that there had been a break in. As she opened the freezer door she came face to face with the destruction. Initially she thought one of the clerks had an accident and she started to clean up the mess. She then went to her office and everything was a shambles, and that's when she realized something was out of kilter. That's when she called the police, to report a break-in.

The officer that came asked how they broke in, as none of the doors were damaged, and the alarm didn't go off. The officer asked that they touch nothing until they have gathered finger prints and evidence.

"I'm going through the footage from the back door camera as we speak. Are you coming over here to see it?" Greg was on it, and if there was a face or any kind of recognizable content, he would hold it for Anthony.

"I'm in Port Hardy now, so can you send it to my laptop?" Anthony asked; as he stayed on the phone with Greg, Anthony caught the attention of Jade. "Jade, the footage will be sent to my laptop. Let's wait until we receive it." He told her it wouldn't be long as Greg was very good at his job.

"My treat, do you guys want pizza?" He handed Alice the money and told them to take a break.

Anthony guided Jade around the store, pointing to the security cameras. He assured her the cameras were also motion detectors and that a regular camera was set up near the rear exit. They could access everything through the laptop. "Do you have your laptop?" he asked her.

"No, I don't have it, but I wouldn't know how to access the information." Jade was in tears.

He went into the file cabinet to see if their hard copies were taken and was surprised to find Jade's laptop, which may be evidence.

He explained how everything worked on his laptop, "When you use the keypad, the doors lock and are alarmed. You can access the cameras on your laptop by logging into our security site."

Greg's email came in with footage from the outside rear camera. It showed three people walking to her car. One of the individuals got into the car, and the first thing they did was locate the keys and a cell phone from under the passenger seat, as though they knew where to look. They wore hoods and kept their heads down.

"Greg," Anthony called him once he received his email, "you are wonderful. I have Jade Carter, the manager, here with me, and we are going through the footage now." Greg said he was happy to oblige. "Thanks again," Anthony said.

"Before we view more footage," Jade said, "I went into the store that morning, and the first thing I did was start cleaning up the mess. I didn't know about any protocol regarding break-ins, and I actually thought Alice had a problem as she was the last one to leave. It was a hell of a shock when I opened the storeroom door." Jade wanted Anthony to know what she did, so no one else was blamed. She also reminded Anthony that her own personal cell-phone was not password protected.

He gave her his full attention before moving back to the video. "Here it goes, there are three in-store cameras that run 24-7, so we should have some footage to give to the police." They were glued to the screen. "Look carefully, in case you recognize anyone." At first, Anthony had it on play, but after about ten minutes, he had it on fast forward and slowed the footage when they saw two people enter the backdoor. One keyed in the alarm pass-code, and it worked. Greg continued running the footage.

Anthony was looking for any obvious clues, "Have you ever seen these guys before?" Jade was certain she had never seen them. "We must pass this on to the police so they can search for them. Come on, Jade let's take this to the station. Let's proves it wasn't an inside job."

"Hi, I'm Anthony Lynwood with Quick & Easy Foods. Can I speak to the officer regarding the break-in at the store two days ago? I have his card."

"One moment, sir, I'll see if he's in. Please, take a seat."

"This is Jade Carter, the store manager. We were able to access the footage of the store's robbery. It's on this stick." Anthony gave it to the officer, along with Jade's laptop. "This was found in the filing cabinet, in case you want to fingerprint it. The intruders didn't wear gloves."

"I'll get my officers to watch it and get back to you," Anthony gave them his business card and the store phone number.

"Our security service guy, Greg will send you more videos when he has them." They left the station.

"Were they watching me, do you think?" Jade asked once they got back into Anthony's Jeep. He didn't want to scare her. "I was on vacation, but I stayed home. Oh, Anthony, I hope the other clerks are okay."

"Jade, please stop blaming yourself. These criminals are at the top of their game. They know who to watch, and they probably know your every move." Jade closed her eyes and shook her head slightly.

"My concern at this moment is for the safety of you and your staff. It's a traumatic experience, especially when you don't know why you were targeted. All the clerks must be feeling uneasy, so I'll talk to them and address any issues." The hardest part was waiting to see if the cops recognize these three."

Anthony stuck the blurry mug shots on the cooler door and told the staff to call 911 if they recognized them. He then addressed their questions. "There was a high possibility they 'cased the joint,' as the Yanks say. Before we start second-guessing ourselves, we need to wait until the police get back to us."

"There's one more thing I need from all of you. No-one can discuss the details of this break-in because, at this moment, we can only speculate, so please don't be tempted to spread gossip. We don't want the thieves to know we have cameras in the store."

"In future, I'll wait in the parking lot until another staff member arrives, and I will go inside with them," Jade was feeling sick.

"If that will make you feel better, sure," Anthony agreed. "You could also have your laptop with you, and check the store before going in." He finished the meeting, hoping he helped ease the mind of some of Jade's staff.

He contacted Alexis to update her, and she told him that Greg had already called her, and she was very busy changing the passwords in case the thieves targeted another store.

"Let's get back into the storage area so I can look behind the cooler. I want to look around again. Okay, Anthony?" Jade wanted to check if the safe was tampered with. Fortunately, the safe was untouched as it was in the concrete floor.

He also wanted to take a good look around. They began walking to the back door together when Anthony noticed many people hovering outside the store. It was a newsworthy headline, and as par for the course, Anthony dealt with the nosey folks.

He apologised for any inconvenience but due to a recent break-in the store will be closed until the police have done their job.

His phone was vibrating, "I need to take this." It was Alexis, asking if she could help. "Let me know if the cops figure out who is responsible," Alexis had a store that was robbed, and she knew what Jade was going through. "If I can help from this end, let me know what you need." Anthony told Alexis that Greg was trying to get hold of him on another line and that he would call her back.

Greg imparted his findings, "We have some enhanced footage on its way to you. Did the cops get anything from the initial footage?"

"Honestly, I think the culprits were well shielded from the cameras." Anthony did not hold out much hope of nabbing them.

"Au contraire, my man, we have full face pictures of two of them. The third is a girl who was sitting outside the store as a lookout. Check your email; I sent you the photos." Anthony opened his email while still on the phone with Greg. He couldn't wait for the store to get back to normal.

"Wow, the images are very clear," Anthony told him. "I'm afraid I don't recognize them, but Jade might know them. Wait a moment, Greg." Anthony walked back into the store to find Jade. "Have you seen him before? Maybe you've seen this one? And there's the girl."

"I have never set eyes on any of them," Jade stared at the screen. "We need to show these to the cops, and we need to replace the pictures at the cooler."

Greg piped in, "I've already sent the whole footage to the RCMP. Our lawmen don't recognize these guys, but they might be dangerous, as the break-in looked professional." Greg expected the cops to circulate the mug shots. "They were looking for the safe, but they didn't find it."

Anthony's phone was humming a tune, "Sorry, Greg, I have to let you go. Thanks for your hard work! We'll talk soon."

Anthony hung up only to move to his next call. "Hi, this is Anthony speaking," the person on the other end was young, with a giggle in his voice.

"When are you coming home?" Anthony couldn't help but feel surrounded by a warm fuzzy feeling. A six-foot-two guy with muscles to spare, and the word 'home' made him shiver in a good way, of course.

Anthony walked away from Jade and tried to answer, "I'm still at Jade's store. We need a couple of days to sort out the mess."

"Did you hear that, James? He has to sort a mess!" Adam was curious. "Is Brett there helping you? Can we come to help you?" he handed the phone to James.

"I'll be home as soon as I can. Please, let me have a word with Katie?"

James stayed on the phone and listened to Anthony's short version of the break-in while Adam hunted down Katie. "How's Jade coping? This must be a very stressful time for her."

"Jade is doing fine. We actually got three mug shots; the film is very clear." Anthony told him some of the problems the intruders had caused, "All the security was compromised, so we need a completely new system. Greg is working on it as we speak."

"Katie here; what can I do for you?"

"I want to ask you a favour. Don't make James suspicious. I'm going to propose this weekend. Can you make a cake for us?"

"I sure can," Katie gave the phone back to Adam. They all shouted their goodbyes at the same time.

"I heard that. I'm so happy for you." Jade asked if she could fly down and be there for this happy occasion.

"I prefer to do this part on my own. You are welcome to come to the wedding; in fact, we can invite Sammy and Sophie from Nanaimo, and a few close friends. Keep it for the select few." He was scared, and as usual, he shared his feelings with Jade and had asked for her opinion, "What happens if he says no? I keep thinking we should wait until he has finished UVic. I will be in threads if he says no."

"You mean shreds, Anthony. Stop thinking like that. James loves you, and you know that, so it's time to take the next step."

"My master plan is working, I found James, we have our own home, James is living his dream of becoming a doctor, we have a son, it really is a dream come true." Jade was so happy for him. "If he says yes to my proposal, then I'll have it all."

"I asked Katie to make a cake for us. She'll make James' favourite tiramisu; I just know it. It's the best dessert ever."

"He's lucky to have you. You are so handsome; I wanted you all to myself," she confessed, "but that couldn't happen." She wanted him to know how special he was.

Jade was ready to get the store up and running, "It's time to start recreating new passwords and making this store secure again. If we stay focused, we can get this job done today."

Anthony laughed, "Those should have been my words!"

They worked diligently and went for a late supper, and he told her, "Remember to ask all the staff if they have seen any of those monsters lurking around the store. Jade, please keep me informed, and if anyone recognizes any of them, call the cops immediately and then call me."

Anthony handed Jade a box, "The cops have your laptop, so I'm going to give you this new one. What I need you to do is reload everything from this stick. It will have to work until I get the product information to make sense. Until then, your stock numbers will be out of sync. Don't worry about that. I trust your instinct, so order accordingly."

She was relieved to hear he had kept faith in her, he still believed she could cope, and after everything that went wrong, he still wanted to keep her there. That's when the tears started. She was relieved; he was so special, the most wonderful colleague and friend. He gave his shoulder for her to cry on, and he held her until her tears subsided.

"The stress level of all your staff goes through the roof when something bad happens," he handed her another tissue, "Let your staff know they can talk to me, if need be." She nodded.

The next day, Anthony woke early. The insurance company representative came and took photos of everything, reminding Jade to change all the passwords. They provided a locksmith to come and replace the locks, and her new pass-codes for the alarm came from Greg, who explained, in great detail, what changes she had to make. Greg also reminded her to call her car insurance agent as she is probably covered to have it fixed, but if she had a problem to call him, and he would send the video to clarify her claim.

Anthony reminded her why she was to notify him if anything looked amiss, "Call me immediately, please Jade don't forget."

Before Anthony left for Victoria, he went to visit Sammy. "How's my friend doing today?" Sammy spun round. "I just called in for a cup of tea with you and to see how you are doing. Then I'll be driving back to Victoria today."

Sammy was thrilled to see Anthony, "How are the boys?" he pulled out the teabag, added milk, and handed the cup to Anthony.

He explained to Sammy that Adam was feeling insecure, that his problem was Anthony working away from home, "He thought I was going to heaven, and he was afraid I wouldn't come back."

"It must be tough, how did you cope?" Anthony told Sammy that Adam could call him every evening, and so far, he was getting used to him working away from home. "I told Adam I was due back tonight. You can bet your bottom dollar that he waits up for me."

"How are things at the store?"

"It's tense, I admit, but Jade's a wonderful person who copes very well, but what can I say?" Anthony was full of praise, "She doesn't deserve to be targeted like this."

He explained to Sammy that the police had mug shots of those who broke in, and all the security measures were back in place. Jade was feeling better, and she was having a staff meeting today to give updates. They would open the store tomorrow, business-as-usual. "She had no control over the situation."

"Keep my phone number handy. If there was ever a repeat performance, I'd be there like a shot," Sammy offered, "If I saw anything bad happen, I'd call the cops. I'm too old to be a hero, but I can be there for the lass."

"I have a long drive back to Victoria today, so I can't stay much longer." He thanked Sammy and told him he will pass the message on to Jade, and he told Sammy that she has become very skittish. "If you call in the store Sammy, keep your eye on her, Jade is like the sister I never had, and I care about her."

Before he left, Sammy asked, "How's James doing with his studies?" Anthony was very happy to share James' success, "He works hard, and he tells me it will pay off when he graduates in three years instead of four."

Anthony was going to share with Sammy his intention to propose to James, but he didn't want to jinx it.

12

Jade has never actually seen Greg—she'd only spoken to him on the phone. The next morning, after Anthony left Port Hardy, a man walked into the store and asked for the manager. Greg actually went to the store to examine all the security equipment himself, to make sure everything was coded correctly.

"You want to see me?" He was stood staring at Jade, she was nothing like he imagined. "How can I help you?" She gave him a welcoming smile.

"Hi, I'm Greg; I need to check out your security system. There were too many problems that needed changing and I felt it necessary to come and check it all out, so you and your staff will be safe."

"I need to call my boss, to see if he arranged this?" Jade was not sure, after the break-in she was being overly cautious. "Anthony I have a man here who wants to check the security. Did you send him?"

Anthony told her it was Greg Fenton, the guy who sent us the footage of the creeps; he's there to ensure everything is working properly."

The highway was pretty clear up north, but it became much busier as Anthony got further south to Campbell River. He was too excited about the proposal to stop for long; he wanted to make it home before James went to bed.

He found himself looking at the time. It was getting late, and he wasn't sure if he would propose today, but he wanted to know how James was feeling, and he wanted to be home. The last three days had taken their toll, and he was more preoccupied than usual. His brain was processing the situation as his mind's eye was mulching over the footage, remembering the thieves' faces and trying to make sense of it all. As he drove into the driveway, he felt exhausted but he decided to pop the question that night.

He got out of the car, and James was waiting for him on the front doorstep with a smile that looked so mischievous. Anthony stood still, waiting for James to tell him why he was grinning like a Cheshire cat.

"What are you up to?" he asked suspiciously, but James' smile was infectious.

"Come, let's put on some music and relax," James entered the house first and warned Anthony, "We need to talk. The little man is fast asleep, and I have something to tell you."

Anthony followed James, and that's when he spotted an old-fashioned record player and a package beside it with a card. Anthony knelt on the floor and opened the card while staring at the package wrapped in bubble wrap. The card was set aside. "It's not my birthday, James."

"I needed a way of telling you how much you mean to me and how much I love you. When I saw the record player, I had to raid a few second-hand stores to find those," James pointed to the package of vinyl records. "Open it!"

"Wow." Anthony couldn't believe his eyes, "Why did you get these for me? I feel so special, thank you." He began playing his favourite Johnny Mathis songs on vinyl, no less.

A couple of weeks ago Anthony couldn't resist the temptation to swing into an electronic store and purchase a special gift for James, a gaming laptop. "Let me get my briefcase from the car."

He handed James a gift. "I wanted to surprise you, so I left it in my car," Anthony told him to open it. The screensaver of an Elf Hunter and a Mage gave a huge clue to the type of laptop it was. "I was hoping you were still interested in playing *World of Warcraft*. We can have fun playing together sometime. The whole game is loaded for you."

James was excited and grinned at his mate, "Wow! I'm so happy, thank you! I'm going to love playing computer games with you!" Their laughter died down.

"That isn't all," Anthony needed to pop the question now before he lost his nerve. "James, you know how I feel about you." James wasn't giving an inch, so he stayed very quiet as Anthony continued, "If you feel the same way I do, I want to . . . James, I'm scared. I want to . . ."

James was giddy, and teased Anthony, "Do you want to marry me?"

"Yes, I want to ask you to marry me," he got the words out at last.

"What took you so long?" James teased, "I could be tripping over my beard waiting for you to propose." They laughed.

"James, you have a way with words that is second to none."

They both knew how each felt about one another. James was sneakily storing this interlude to memory so he could tease Anthony down the road.

"Was that a yes?" Anthony looked serious, and James nodded. "It's yes for me too," he smiled.

Anthony stood in disbelief and finally jumped with joy—he couldn't believe the music to his ears! In a matter of months, he had gained the family he had always wanted—and now he was engaged to his soul-mate.

"I'm exhausted, I drove for hours intending to ask you tonight, and I had my usual, 'tomorrow is another day,' moment. What if you said no?" Anthony was excited, "I can't understand how we both knew this was the time for a major commitment. This is our very own 'now and forever' moment."

"When you called to speak to Katie, we were close by, and I could hear your voice," James admitted, "If you don't tell Katie, I'll share my tiramisu," he laughed.

"We need to plan, or I think you need to plan—you're older than me, so it's easier if you plan," James wanted an answer right now, as he was excited and anxious he asked, "When is the best time?"

"James, you are incorrigible. Stick to the 'we' and 'we' could both plan everything together," Anthony was in high spirits, "but I'm off to bed."

"What about me?" Anthony couldn't stop laughing at James' expressions. It was too late for a cushion fight.

Adam was the first person up in the morning. He went downstairs, where he saw the record player that James bought for Anthony, and he gave out a howling squeal.

He went to tell Katie that the guys wanted breakfast. He knew that breakfast was always delicious when Katie made it. "But it's Saturday. Adam, don't wake the boys. They were very late going to bed."

"Katie, it's okay," Anthony said as he made his way downstairs, "he already made enough noise to wake the dead." As Anthony finished speaking, he caught himself and lowered his head, but it was too late.

"Did my mommy wake up?" Adam was unsure of Anthony's phrase. He was getting used to his mommy only appearing in his dreams.

Anthony had to say something, but he struggled for the right words. James came to the rescue, "Your mommy's an angel who lives in heaven all the time. Close your eyes, Adam. Now, can you see your mommy?" Adam nodded. "She's still awake and can smile at you. Next time you see her, tell her that we all love her, and we all miss her." Adam confirmed that he had told her and that Karen was smiling.

"Does anyone want pancakes? Today we have strawberries or peaches."

"Katie, I owe you big time," James said, and Katie laughed.

"How was your trip? Was the weather nice up there? I would love to see the place that Adam keeps talking about. He gives me a moment-by-moment recollection of his trip north. I asked him to draw some of the wildlife he saw from your trip." He drew a picture of Katie, on an island, holding a baby seal. "He is quite a talented young artist."

"Jade was stressed," Anthony explained. "Greg is staying close by in case they come back. It would be awesome if I could call to tell her that we are going to Port Hardy for a few days of vacation.

"We need to plan a trip. The four of us can go when James' courses ease up. Or, better still, James could sit out in the sun all day while he studies." Anthony was forming another plan; he wondered if James would like to get married on the beach at Sammy's place, and he decided to bring up the subject when the time was right. He thought that tiny bit of beach was the most romantic place on earth.

"James, how about inviting your family here, and I can get to know them?" Anthony was forming a plan, but James had to be on board too.

"I need you to listen to me," He asked, "How old are your siblings?"

"My oldest sister Sagan will be eighteen at the end of this year. Why do you ask?"

"You remember all that money my grandpa left me?" James nodded. "I have a plan, and I need your permission. I thought we could contribute some money to pay for Sagan's tuition at UVic?

We can put the same amounts in trust funds for Kaitlen and Nick." James was dumbfounded. "James, tell me what you think. Can we do that?"

"Anthony, are you sure you want to do that? It's a wonderful thought. Sagan would have to struggle with a full-time job and pay for courses when she could afford it. This would make all the difference in the world to her."

"It's pathetic to leave all that money in the bank, and I know my grandpa would approve of sharing it for the greater good." James was speechless. "I'm positive he would approve, so they can all benefit. Let's invite your family to a meal next weekend, and we can talk to Sagan. Her funds will be secure with us. Does she have any plans or a career in mind?"

James had the broadest grin, "I was talking to her a few days ago, and she asked what the tuition was for becoming a medical doctor." He told Anthony that Sagan had told him that her studies would have to wait as she intended to work full-time and take the courses when she could afford them. "Can we tell her together? I want to see her smile. My mom isn't going to believe it." James had another thought, "She could use my books."

James told Anthony that she will graduate high school next spring, and she could do the same thing James was doing; she could enrol in courses for the summer instead of getting a job.

"Let's plan for Saturday. You can ask Katie to bake a cake, and let's do up some ribs. We can try the Cajun red pepper and the Korean honey glaze. I'm going to make asparagus with chocolate drizzle and sea salt. Yummy!" Then they made more suggestions, "How about stuffed peppers?" They started an extensive shopping list.

Anthony offered to pick up the groceries. "I have to call in the Victoria store to give a promotion to Hayden. He has so much potential, and I don't want him to think I forgot about him." James asked if he was still involved in the Indigenous creative arts, and Anthony ran some of Hayden's ideas by James, who thought they were marvellous.

James offered to accompany Anthony, and Katie, who was making a jigsaw puzzle with Adam, offered her help too.

The weather on the Island was usually sunny in the spring and summer, and the nights were terrific for barbequing. Adam loved hot dogs, especially when Katie made them. She cooked wieners and used four plastic toothpicks for legs and four blobs of cheese for ears, a nose, and a tail.

When it wasn't rainy, they all liked to play croquet, but none of them were any good at it. Another pastime was trivia. Anthony would invent a quiz from one of Adam's storybooks, and when he asked questions, James invariably called out his answer first, and Adam would roll around the floor giggling. Adam would correct him, and they all laughed; the little man loved the weekends.

They were all lazing around on the deck while Adam practiced his alphabet. Anthony asked, "Who was the orange and white striped fish who got lost at sea?"

"I know! It's Ginger!" Adam was laughing as usual since James was wrong again.

"It's Nemo, and he was looking for his dad," Adam laughed. Anthony got up and went into the living room. "You need to watch this." He handed the DVD to James, and that action started a pillow fight.

Katie called out, "Boys, we have a visitor!" She already showed the woman the backyard where they watched the tom-foolery from the kitchen window.

"I'm Kimberly West. I'm with Child Welfare," she explained it was her job to pay random visits to families to see if the child was happy and not having social problems. She wanted to know how

Adam was coping with Karen's demise, and she needed to ensure that he would be ready for school in September.

"Basically, I have to know that all his needs are being met."

Anthony and James welcomed this visitor and introduced her to Katie. They explained that Katie was their live-in nanny who assumed responsibility for Adam when the men were working and at school. Katie wanted Kimberly to know how happy she was since moving in with the family and how wonderful it was to know the guys are pushing hard for adoption.

"I hope this isn't a bad time. Although my visits are random, I don't want to be here mid-mealtimes."

"Come in and take a seat," Anthony said and invited her to join them.

Kimberly sat across from Adam. "Which one of you gentlemen is Adam?"

"I'm Adam, that's James, and that's Anthony. Oh! And there's Katie. She makes the best pancakes in the whole world."

"I'm here to see if you are all happy and to make sure everything is going well." Kimberly was admiring their home. "Can I see your room Adam?" He grabbed her hand and led the way.

"My room has photos of my mommy and daddy." He opened his closet and she was amazed how many books he had. "This is a great room." She suggested they go back to sit with the guys and Adam showed the way.

"Generally, how are you all coping?" James answered that everything was going exceptionally well, and Anthony agreed.

"You have a beautiful home." Kimberley was impressed, as she turned to Katie. "So? Is everything going well with you, Katie?"

Before she could say a word, Adam answered for her. "She fixes up a mess. Anthony fixes the mess too." Adam was a treasure, a chatter box.

"So Adam, what do you do here?" Kimberly was trying very hard not to laugh. "Are you getting ready to start school in Grade 1?" She watched his little face light up.

"I can say the alp-abet. I'm learning to read. When we play in the yard, I get to tell Anthony about things. He asks me about an orange fish. James got it wrong; it was Nemo. James always gets the answers wrong. He said it was Ginger."

"Are you looking forward to making new friends?" Kimberly smiled.

Adam nodded, "I'm going to the beach again to Sammy's and last time I went, I saw a whale. We are going again, and we are taking Katie because she didn't see them before. Do you want to come too?"

Kimberly was amazed. By the time she stood to leave, she told the duo, "Adam's a great kid. You both must be so proud; you're doing an amazing job." Then she added, "If I had one wish, it would be that all my kids could live here with you two. You're both awesome."

James followed her to the door. "How long will we have to wait to adopt Adam?" he asked.

She couldn't say exactly, but she pointed out, "Everything is progressing nicely, and it shouldn't be too much longer. Eric Gould informed the court that you were financially secure to care for Adam, and the judge positively recognized this factor. You have a beautiful home in every sense of the word; and my evaluation will be positive and in your favour."

"Here's my card. If you're going to the beach, can you send me an email? I will call when you are home." Kimberly waved goodbye to Adam and left.

Katie took Adam for his bath, and James read him a story about kites. When James came downstairs, he joined Anthony in the kitchen, where Anthony was making hot chocolate.

Anne Beatson

"Did you call your mom and invite the family over for a bar-beque?" Anthony asked. He was ready to organize the day, and he was especially looking forward to meeting James' family.

Anthony also needed to talk about his dad, and he wanted James' opinion of the letter. He went into the legal stuff regarding his grandpa's Will, and he didn't understand why his dad didn't want to meet him so they could discuss the problems George was having with Imelda. As he finished stirring the hot chocolate, he thought of how to approach the topic.

James had lived through something very similar when his dad stole every penny of his education fund. He knew what George had gone through, why he couldn't cope, and how he looked out for Anthony.

"After your mom's surgery, would you have believed him? I think not. You need to get your head around the situation. You said yourself, you would have happily handed over the money to your mom, and that would have been against your grandpa's wish." James was trying to explain that something had happened to George to force him to abandon his son, and it was obviously because of Imelda's outlandish behaviour. What crazy notion did she have when she stole their retirement money?"

"I feel that I let my dad down somehow. I would have found it mind-boggling that my mom would have stolen his pensions. She certainly had me brainwashed. She told me that my grand-parents had died, and I didn't think to question it. She told me so many lies."

"Have you figured out what she did with the pensions? She could have spent the money on house repairs, holidays, gambling, or supporting a charity."

Anthony was adamant that his mom never bought anything of any value for as long as he could remember. "Where did all of my dad's pension money go? She was always frugal, but we enjoyed good food . . . although, not a patch on Katie's cooking. The house was huge, but I can't recall her ever re-furnishing or redecorating." The missing money was a mystery.

James gave him more food for thought. "Does she have it in the bank, I wonder?" And they laughed. "It could be hidden in plain sight." Then James added, "Maybe she became obsessed that she had to live alone, and she was scared of being broke."

Anthony and James sipped on their hot chocolate. "I remember my grandpa very well. He would be over the moon to know we are using his money for the kids' education." Anthony laughed, "It could mean a whole family of doctors!"

"What have you decided regarding your mom?" James asked. "Are you going to confront her or just let it go?" Anthony said he didn't know, and he would have to give it some thought, but what he did know was that he would never trust her again.

"My next question is: what did your dad mean about Delia?"

"James, you read the letter. He emphatically stated that Delia had no claim on anything in the safety deposit box as the funds were willed directly to me from my granddad, and he was resolute that she receives nothing."

"James, is your dad still drinking? The reason I'm asking is we can help your mom with everyday stuff, you know, groceries, school fees, anything for the kids?"

"She sticks by him. There's one consolation, though. He's a very passive drunk, and he has never physically hurt my mom." James felt that Anthony was doing enough, "You are paying for my sibling's educations. You have already helped my family more than you could imagine." James knew, if need be, Anthony would go to the ends of the earth to provide for him.

"James, the money is ours. We decide what we do with our money, okay?"

A few days later, Kimberly paid another visit to see Adam. "I wanted to come myself to share the good news. The adoption is going forward as we speak, and I will let you know when we have the paperwork to sign. We can meet in Eric Gould's office. You'll be expected to see the judge, who will finalize the process. I'm so happy for you all. You make a wonderful family."

"Adam, you are a lucky boy, James and Anthony will take care of you, until you are a grown man. What do you think?" Kimberly saw the raw excitement on Adam's face.

"I think we should go to Sammy's and see the whales and the seals. Sammy lets me fly my kite and swim in the sea." She watched the trio plan their trip. Adam was the centre of their world, and Kimberly couldn't be happier.

"You all amaze me. Adam is a lucky kid to have a family like this. Take care, and if you need some help or information, don't hesitate to call me."

As soon as she left, they were in action mode.

"With this kind of news, I agree, we should finally go away for a few days," Anthony asked, "How about you, James? Fancy a trip up north?"

"You can't go without me," he said and then looked around. "Let's ask Katie, what do you think?"

"This kid wants to come too!" Adam yelled; he didn't want to miss the fun. He was over the moon!

"Let's sort this weekend out first with your family," Anthony couldn't wait to go to the wild and wonderful north. "I'll put my planning cap on and see what hotels are available for our next trip."

He turned to James, "Make sure you get all your study paraphernalia together. You'll have no distractions there."

"Why? Are you staying home?" James teased him again. The pillow fight started just as Katie headed back to the kitchen, shaking her head.

"Call your mom," Anthony told James, "and ask how they're getting here. Are they coming on the ferry or flying? We can book them in a hotel on the harbour front for a couple of nights. I bet you have lots of catching up to do." Anthony has his organizer hat on. "It gives me a chance to get to know them. How do you think they'll take the news of our wedding?"

James hadn't a clue, "The subject has never come up before." This caused a bout of belly laughs. "If everything goes well this weekend, we should have two ring bearers: Adam and Nick."

"I would love that; let's keep our fingers crossed that this weekend goes well." Anthony was excited to meet James' family, and James' family was just as excited to meet Anthony and Adam.

"What are you smiling at?" James asked.

"Do you realize that Adam is going to meet his grandma and grandpa?"

"Do you realize that they are your in-laws?" James said a matter-of-factly.

"Now you have gone and done it! I'm a nervous wreck," Anthony was trying to hide his grin from James as he asked, "Are we telling Sagan what we intend to do? Or do you want to tell her yourself?"

"Ah, my favourite word is 'we,' so we will do it together on Saturday."

Katie loved working for Anthony and James; she quickly settled into the household and when they told her about the barbeque she started preparations for cooking up a storm.

She sometimes wondered, though, if she would be kept around when Adam grew up. She couldn't imagine her life without these three guys.

The little man was devastated when his mom died, and these two men didn't hesitate to do everything possible to keep him safe. Anthony's company had offered every kind of assistance. Their circumstances had evolved so much that, if they took the time to look back, they would see how their lives are so much better. They both made time for Adam even with their busy schedules.

Katie heard Adam giggling. The little man's laughter was so comical that Katie wished she could bottle it and sell it for a mint of money.

She sat looking out of the window while drinking tea. Her mind was doing hoops. If Sagan wants to live here, they may need her room. The thought of having to move back to her lonely apartment was not an easy pill to swallow.

James had phoned his mom, and she told him they would be driving to the ferry. James had rented a Pacifica to pick them up at the ferry since they were a family of five. Their time of arrival was noon. Anthony, Adam, and Katie would wait at the house.

13

When the Prescott family arrived, they all seemed to be talking at once. Upon entering the house, they did their introductions. "Mom, Dad, I would like you to meet Anthony, my partner and this is Adam, our son, and, another important addition to our family, Mom and Dad, meet Katie. She also lives with us and takes care of Adam and us when we are working, and even when we are not working."

The introductions went well. Nick was the first to mention he was excited to meet Adam, "Show me your room and let's see what kind of games you have." Anthony thought he saw a young James as Nick was so much like his big brother. Adam latched onto him as soon as they met.

Katie put the kettle on, to brew a teapot of tea, "Maria, can I make you a hot or cold drink?"

"Yes, please, I will take tea with you. Can I help?" Maria was very friendly, and she reminded Katie of James from the first moment they met. He favoured his mom with his black hair, tanned complexion, and dark brown eyes fanned with thick lashes. To complete his description, he was a handsome man with a most beautiful smile.

"What about Ray?" Katie had been told a little about Ray's drinking problem.

"Ray, will you take tea?" Maria was sure he would. He nodded and walked over to the counter to stand by his wife.

"This is a beautiful home, and I love the yard. Can I carry a tray outside? It's far too nice to stay in," he was eager to help.

James turned to see Ray with a cup of tea in his hand, and James thought it was for him, but his dad told him very quietly, "I am over six months clean, son. I went to get help, and my only regret was that I hadn't done it sooner."

"Wow, Dad. I am so proud of you." This was music to James' ears.

"I'll try to pay you some money back. I am so ashamed. I hated myself, and when I felt so low, I kept thinking about you and how I had hurt you. That shame gave me the incentive to quit drinking, and your mom gave me all the support she possibly could. Your siblings suggested we could go for walks. They were all so happy to help take my mind off of it."

"I don't want any money from you. Honestly, Dad, since I've been with Anthony, my world has changed so much. He's a wonderful man, and we are a very happy family."

"Anyone living in this house must be happy. I can see you're doing well, and I'm overjoyed to know you're studying again. I'm still the monster who stole your dream."

"Dad, you must forget about it. Let it go. Come outside and play croquet with the kids; let's have some fun."

"Maria is very happy now, and I'm so grateful that she never gave up on me," Ray told James.

The whole evening was catch-up stories. James told Anthony that his dad was six months sober. Anthony brought up the wedding, and James' whole family wanted to come.

"Maria, how did it feel to meet your grandson?"

"Oh, I'm a grandma. I'm a grandma!" She yelled, "He's a perfect child, and Ray, you're his grandpa!"

"Adam, you have a grandma and a grandpa," Maria hugged him. "He is our first grandchild!" Adam didn't understand why they liked him so much, and he was certainly being fussed over. What kid wouldn't respond gleefully?

Anthony loved James' family from the start. He enjoyed watching their interactions.

They sat on the deck, and Katie had a full tray: a pitcher of lemonade, a fresh pot of tea, and a jug of hot chocolate. She asked Maria for help to get the desserts with the plates and forks. Ray was helpful in handing out the tiramisu. Maria thanked Katie, and told her how much she enjoyed every morsel of food.

There was a lull in conversation as everyone enjoyed the treats, and Anthony was ready to broach the subject of Sagan. James stood beside his partner.

"James is at UVic's medical faculty, where he's studying hard to pass every subject. He will, no doubt, become the best doctor in his field," Anthony gushed. They all applauded, and James took a bow.

"We have invited you here today because we have something very special to announce." Together, James and Anthony handed Sagan a syllabus for the University of Victoria, Medical faculty. "We decided that one doctor in the family isn't enough, and next year, after graduation, we want Sagan to go to UVic and get her degree. We can make her dream come true."

Sagan was amazed, "You guys are crazy!" She didn't believe what she was hearing. "There's no way I could afford this. Although I have not, and will not, give up my goal, my sights are set that I will be a doctor one day. Meanwhile, I will take some courses while I work."

"Sagan, how much do you want your dream to come true?" Anthony was trying to force an answer from her.

"It's my ultimate dream, but I can't do it yet. Eventually, I'd like to be in cardiology. It takes about ten years, but in my case, it may take a little longer."

James told her, "Look through the literature very carefully, and you may find a way to catch your dream. Sis, Anthony and I will do what we can to make it happen." Sagan didn't understand what he meant until she delved into the stack of papers. She saw the cheque for her tuition, made out to UVic. She was overcome with joy. "Anthony wants you to attend full-time university. Will you do that?"

At first, she thought it was a joke, but the expressions on James and Anthony's faces were serious. "Where will I live?" She was thinking things through, her demeanour reflecting her excitement. "I'll find a place," She muttered to herself as she looked at the bank drafts. "The first bank draft is for tuition, and the second one is for a dorm; is this for real?"

Maria was shocked but in the best way possible. Ray was openly crying. He would never be able to pay for that tuition if he did five jobs.

After receiving the gift, Sagan went through the package, and she talked to Anthony, "I didn't expect this opportunity. I have no idea how to thank you. I'm afraid I'll wake up, and this will be just a dream."

His advice was to study hard and reach her goal, and if she needed help to let him know.

It was getting late, and Adam was pestering Nick to have a sleepover.

"We're coming to your hotel for breakfast around ten. We can bring Nick with us tomorrow," Anthony told Maria.

Katie was getting to know Maria, and enjoyed their visit. "I hope I can come too."

Anthony grinned at her, "There's always room for you, Katie."

James went outside to start the Pacifica. It was a short drive to their hotel, and he parked while he went with them to book in—they were booked into the Empress Hotel on the harbour front.

"Are you sure? This is the Empress," Ray was amazed, "we could have . . ."

"Dad, go and enjoy your suite. See you all tomorrow at ten," James said goodbye and left.

Everything went smoothly. James couldn't get over his dad getting help and staying sober for six months. His family was so happy, and Sagan, she was still in shock.

Anthony was fast asleep on the sofa when James walked in. Katie was making a hot chocolate in the kitchen. She handed James his drink—including a few marshmallows—just how he liked it.

"Your family is very nice. You shocked even me when you gave Sagan her chance to become a doctor like you." Katie was preparing for the time when they no longer needed her. "When she's out of dorms, I think that's two years down the road, I'll move out so that she can stay here with you."

"Katie, I thought you were happy here? Have you changed your mind? Do you really want to move out of here?" James was visibly upset that she believed they would ask her to leave.

"I have never been as happy as I am now, but Sagan is your family," Katie added graciously.

"You are our family, too. You will never be asked to leave. We love having you here, and we have also planned for our future with you in it. We bought this house so you would know how welcome you are here. This is your home. Anthony asked me if there was something wrong . . . I think you need to talk to me, Katie."

"I was worried about Adam. When he reaches his teens, he won't want me around, and the last thing I want is to be a burden to you guys."

"Katie, you are not now, and never will be, a burden. We were hoping you would continue to live here with us. We love having you around. We hoped you would do a bit of housework and cook tiramisu for us. We all want to have you around for as long as you can put up with us."

"Thank you, James," Katie's relief was obvious, "I love being here."

"Anthony and I haven't had any practice setting up a home, and we have been looking at more furnishings. Katie, we were hoping you had some ideas, mainly to help us make this place more comfortable and welcoming." James was saying all the right things, and to put the icing on the cake, he added, "I heard you talking to Mom about a storage unit. You should have all of your possessions here. We have space in the basement for any spare boxes you want to store, and if we did need more space we can have the basement finished, there is already the plumbing done for a bathroom.

"One of our priorities was to get some more furniture. Adam needs shelves, and Anthony needs bookshelves and an armchair for the office. All of these rooms could benefit from a little TLC, a little bit of colour, and some personality to make it ours. When Adam goes to school, you could take on the project, if you like. Hire some decorators and work at your own pace. When you moved here, you had some beautiful teapots that resided in a box. Why not plan to put up a shelf to display them?"

After hearing of James' ideas, Katie was ecstatic. She went to bed light-hearted and ready to fall into a peaceful sleep—it had been a busy day.

James was tempted to get an icy cold washcloth to help Anthony wake up, but he was too late; Anthony woke up when Katie called, "See you in the morning."

"You are a very lucky man, James." Anthony was pleased as they made their way to their room. "It was wonderful to meet your family, and you must be proud of your mom, having the patience and love to stand by your dad. Alcoholism can be a tough addiction to kick."

James grinned as he fluffed back the comforter on their bed, "It's amazing about my dad staying sober. I'm so proud of him, but I was so worried about Katie when she met my family. It seemed like something was off, and she went very quiet. I'm glad I talked to her tonight and that she wants to stay with us. She needs to realize that we love having her around; she fits in perfectly with our lifestyle."

Anthony smiled when he got into bed, "She does, and we just have to keep reminding her of that."

James decided to keep an eye on Katie; he smiled to himself, he was thinking about breakfast at the Empress, what a treat this was for his whole family; thanks to Anthony.

Katie and the four guys arrived for breakfast at the Empress. It was a great meal, and they planned to spend the day together. The IMAX had a turtles show on that the two boys wanted to see, so they all went to see it. They spent the afternoon walking along Douglas Street, enjoying the shops, taking a horse and buggy ride through Beacon Hill Children's park, and seeing the goat races, and leisurely strolling around the harbour. It was almost supper time, and they couldn't decide where to eat. Maria and Katie talked about fish when Adam suggested the iconic Barb's Fish and Chips, so they all boarded a water taxi and crossed the harbour to their favourite eatery.

After a fantastic meal, James took them back to the hotel, letting them know that he would come by tomorrow to drive them back to the Swartz Bay ferry terminal. They shared hugs and spoke of the wonderful weekend they spent with James, and how happy they were to welcome Anthony and Adam into the family.

Maria wanted James to thank Katie for the welcome they felt. She told her son what a wonderful caring person Katie was and she was a gem the way she took care of Adam.

That weekend went well, now I need to knuckle down and do some work. I have to do some store visits soon. I have a wonderful job, and I would like to keep it," Anthony said as he was trying to convince James to go with him. "We can do what we did last month when I booked the hotel for the three of us. I have to call in and see the progress in Comox, and I need to see how the shop-fitters are getting along. I need to go to Nanaimo store, I have been neglecting them." Anthony laid out his itinerary and explained, "If you don't want to come, James, I understand."

James was reticent, "I do want to come, but I need to run something by you, something that doesn't involve work, and I reckon this is as good a time as any. We want to marry, more than anything, so I'm wondering if you'd give some thought to a service, on the beach, at Sammy's cottage." James waited for an answer, "If you want a big wedding in a hotel, I understand." Anthony's silence was a little unnerving. "It was just a thought. Please, say something."

"James, my love, I was wondering the exact same thing, and I was hesitant to talk to you about it. When do you have in mind?"

"Truthfully?" James looked serious as he answered, "Tomorrow." They laughed their socks off.

"I had the same uncanny idea as you. Tomorrow it is, and now that it's settled, I have one more thing to say to you." They went from silly to serious, "I adore you, James. You fill my life with love and meaning, and I can't imagine my life without you."

"Ditto . . . "

"I didn't expect that!" Anthony offered, "I can help you with words, if you need me to."

"Anthony, I have the words. You are the most beautiful man I have ever met, but it's time I show you how much I love you. Come."

Realistically, they had made a joint decision, and the date of their nuptials was the last week of August when the weather was mid-summer hot with occasional showers. They settled a further decision to ask Sammy for the loan of his garden. They both love Sammy's place, especially with the ocean as a backdrop. Nothing on earth could be more beautiful.

"The icing on the cake for us will be our son, Adam, who will be a ring bearer with my brother Nick. We have four weeks before Adam starts school, and that should give us enough time to plan everything."

"Katie will take care of Adam, so we'll get some alone time. We have our whole lives ahead of us to celebrate. We need to invite your family and our closest friends, will that be okay?" Anthony was still a little unsure of any arrangements, and he continued, "Everything must be a 'we' decision."

"That's better than okay," James agreed. "I was having a problem trying to figure out how we could plan a wedding with Adam starting school, since we decided not to interrupt his classes. I start at UVic in September, and I don't want to wait one day longer to get married. I love you," James then pointed out to Anthony that if they didn't do it now, they would have to wait for the good weather next spring. "Please tell me you agree with me, Anthony."

"I am so happy, James. We're almost certain to get the adoption papers signed. We can plan everything, and with Jade's help, I'm confident she'll find us the legal eagles we need for the ceremony. We can fly your family in for the celebration and fly them out again afterwards."

"Have you thought about inviting your mom?"

"Why? She would ruin everything. You heard her yelling at me."

"Think about it," James advised, as his head tilted.

"I don't want her there in case she kicks off; I won't let her ruin our special day. I do need to see her about Dad's pensions, so I won't officially decide until I have talked to her. It was painful and embarrassing watching her behave as she did. I honestly don't want her there."

"If your answer is no, I'll not ask you again. I'll support your decision."

They hugged. "So, Anthony, are we going to wear a tux?"

"Of course, why would we not? If that's what you would like, I will wear one too. The photos may look more ceremonious," Anthony laughed. "Is that a real word?"

"Can I book us to go visit Sammy next week? We can make all the arrangements when we get there. We can ask the hotel if they can deliver our food to Sammy's. Jade, Katie, Maria, Sophie, Sagan, and Kaitlen can all lend a hand. I will call Alexis and arrange for time off for our wedding.

"Next week, I must do an audit in Port Hardy. I haven't done one since the break-in. On the way, I also want to go to the Nanaimo store to do Sophie's store evaluation.

"It's a long drive, and you can get a few hours studying done. It's time I put my manager hat on again. I enjoy my job, and I don't want to jeopardize it."

"About the wedding," James said, "Anthony, forgive me, I know I'm being selfish, but I need you to help solve a small problem. Will we wear shoes with our tuxes?" James certainly had Anthony's attention. They began laughing uproariously. "I take it the answer is no?" and they laughed even more.

"We will go with shoes . . . optional. What do you think?" James nodded, "Problem solved." Anthony had hit every one of James's funny bones.

Their doorbell rang, and James went to the front door where a delivery man asked him to sign for a letter. He came back with the mail, and waving the envelope in the air, he called, "Anthony, we must do this together."

Anthony opened the letter. It was a formality; they had to appear in court on August 23rd, and they must take Adam. They have their son! "Wow, perfect timing!" James exclaimed.

Katie was the first person they shared their news with. "You know boys, I had no doubts. Adam is a very lucky kid. Have you told him yet?"

"We have to take him to the courthouse. We can tell him then; we'll see his face light up the whole room! Katie, we would love for you to be there with us. Please say you'll come."

Katie promised to be there. She loved being included. Adam still asked her several times about his daddy and his mommy. He had difficulty understanding why she was in heaven. In the care of Anthony and James, Katie was sure he would continue being a super kid. His role models were the most charismatic men she had ever met—compared to her two sons, who were both rough and ready. Still, her boys were loveable, kind, and she missed them terribly.

14

"James, I need to go to the Port Alberni store today. My last visit was cut short, and I need to know that Bruce has got the ordering under control." James opted to stay home and study while Anthony went to visit the store.

"I'll be home for supper. On second thoughts, let's go out for dinner. We all deserve a treat, especially Katie; she needs a break. Ask her if she has a favourite. Call me, and I'll meet you there."

James said he would call and let him know where they decided to eat, and to find out if Anthony was finished at the store.

"This is a celebration," James stated as Anthony started the car. "If you get delayed, call me, and we'll bring you a doggie bag. How does that sound?"

"It sounds great. I should have no problem meeting you."

Port Alberni was high in the hills north of Victoria. The views were incredible. Bruce Chow was busy rotating the products so the freshest went to the back. "Hi, Anthony, it's so good to see you. Have a look around and see how it's going." Bruce was proud his store was doing great.

"I came today because I had to leave in a hurry on my last visit. I'm here to let you know that your store will be representing some of the local First Nations Arts and Crafts. I'll be back in a couple of weeks with the artist we chose for this store, and they will bring their wares. We will need a few feet of space." Anthony walked to the end-cap in the second aisle. "This is an ideal spot. I'll call you before my next visit in case we need to move some products around.

"We are trying to support our First Nations, and all the artists have agreed to price each piece individually. Their artwork is unique. I have made the initial arrangements so you can keep in touch with the artist, and be able to have extra facings, replenish stock, and rotate pieces."

"Indigenous artists have a unique way of expressing their artistic skills, which are passed down from their Elders." Anthony continued, "We have been diligent in making sure the artwork is true and authentic. Every store will have a different display, and we need you to promote and support the program."

"Anthony, I will do my best," Bruce was sincere. "My teenage daughters love the turquoise jewellery."

"So, Bruce, how do you like the work here?" Anthony asked, changing the subject. "If you have any ideas that might make your store function better, please let me know."

"I can cope with this store. I like the products, and I can promote the combinations of foods. Last week, my wife made some interesting dishes—small shrimp pastries. I took photos of them in different stages and made small handouts of the recipe; I posted them near the freezer. This week, my wife made stuffed garlic and parsley mushrooms. The recipes always go so quick."

"What a great idea! I'm so glad your wife is supporting you; she sounds like a very nice lady." Anthony was thrilled that Bruce had family support.

"She is very nice. These recipes, with veggies, are what we have for our meals. It was no trouble to make." Bruce, and his wife, had come up with a great idea.

Anthony then asked, "How many bags of shrimp did you sell?"

"All of them!" Bruce grinned from ear to ear, as he looked at Anthony over the top of his glasses.

The store was getting ready to close, so Anthony said his good-byes and left.

James had great timing and had called Anthony, asking if he would be back in time to meet them at the restaurant—Spaghetti Spinner.

Anthony said he had one call to make then he was heading back to Victoria.

"Hello, Alexis, I've been at Bruce's store for most of the day, and he came up with a super idea. I will send it to your phone. His wife does all the prep for this idea, and he is very successful in displaying the foods." He sent her the text.

"I just got your text, Anthony, and I love it. What a concept! Now, on to other important things—how are you and James?"

"James and I couldn't be happier. I proposed to him, did I tell you?"

Alexis was thrilled, "You did! When is the great day and where?"

"It will be during this summer holiday because Adam is going to Grade 1 in September—we don't want him to miss school. You are invited, and, of course, we would love for you and your husband to be there. We're having a small ceremony at Sammy Keel's bungalow on the beach at Port Hardy." Then he thought to mention, "It's a secret, we want to have the ceremony on the beach there, but we haven't asked Sammy yet."

Alexis laughed at the thoughts of a beach wedding. "How are you guys going to arrange a wedding in less than four weeks?"

"You'll like Sammy. He's a great guy, and apart from James' dad Ray, Sammy is Adam's grandpa, he adopted Adam the first time they met. You won't believe how close they are."

Their conversation naturally began to discuss the logistics of the wedding. Anthony explained that there are early morning flights and return flights around supper time. Alexis assured him that she would try to get a flight. "We will send out invitations in the next few days," Anthony said, "please, try to make it."

Anthony was almost at the restaurant, and he was nursing some hunger pains. When he entered, James waved to him, and he walked up to the table, announcing, "I could eat a horse!"

Adam told him in no uncertain terms, "They don't sell horses. We don't eat horses. I'm having a kid's meal with spaghetti and meatballs."

Anthony ordered a salad, followed by a meat lasagne—with no horse meat.

After they ate, Katie quietly sipped on a glass of water. "Here is a little something I made for you both," she said as she gave them a small package each.

They opened the packets that contained a tiny collage of photos of Adam, miniatures that fit on key rings. The men were pleasantly surprised. Anthony's had James in his frame, and James had Anthony in his. They were great little gifts, and the guys loved them.

"Katie, you spoil us, thank you!" James paid the tab. "I think it's time to go. This little man has had a big day today, and it is way past his bedtime."

On the way home, the duo was discussing buffet food for a wedding luncheon. Katie wanted to lend a hand and she offered, "I can help with setting up a couple of classy tables, with a wine bar, a dessert platter, or anything your huge hearts' desire," Katie said.

"James, what kind of deserts would you like?" Amazing, all four passengers simultaneously called out, "Tiramisu!"

While Adam was preparing for bed, James asked him to go say goodnight to his daddy. He went downstairs and quietly crept up close to Anthony. "Night-nights, Daddy." Anthony chased him up to his room, where James was waiting to tuck him in.

The next morning, Anthony decided to call Sammy to let him know that they were coming for a visit next weekend. He told Sammy that they needed to run a few things by him, but he'll wait until they get there. They had settled on a date, and Adam was so excited that he had convinced Katie to come and see the whales.

Anthony explained to Sammy that Katie was Adam's nanny, and she was coming for a visit too. "You'll like her, Sammy, she's so much fun."

"Will I be able to fly my kite with Sammy?" Adam asked. He knew it was always fun to be around Sammy. "When we get there, can I play on the beach?" Adam took a quick breath, "Can I go to see Brett and Jade?"

"You'll be able to see everyone as we're going to sort out where and what we need to book so that we can get married."

"We're going to make a quick call on Sophie because she mentioned she wanted me to see a new idea she's been working on." Anthony planned ahead, and booked the hotel in Port Hardy, for their trip.

The four of them were busy packing to be ready for the trip up north to see Sammy the next day. While driving, Anthony mentioned to Katie about getting a car; he wanted her to think about it.

Anthony knew Sophie was ready to be promoted to the new district manager's position. He was looking forward to this next store visit. She worked so hard for James and gave him the hours that he could manage to deal with Adam's adoption. Kelly, James' replacement, was now in a good place to assume a manager's position.

Anthony had gone from being a loner—not much dating and lots of studying while doing a job he excelled at—to becoming a social butterfly. He couldn't believe how much his life had changed. He knew he still had to have a conversation with his mom, but he was in no hurry to confront her.

He adored James and treasured every minute since he came into Anthony's life, filling it with promise and love. What could be better? James has the opportunity to resume his studies, become a doctor, and fulfill his dreams. Together they have purchased a house, and with Katie's help they have created a loving home for a child. In the interim, Katie had made the family complete. Anthony loved his life.

Katie pointed out that Adam would be starting Grade school next month, and the excitement was boiling over when the little man talked about school and making friends. She was planning a shopping trip for his school supplies.

James broached the subject of a car for Katie. "Katie, what kind of car would you like? Jeeps are pretty good when handling Canadian winters. They manoeuvre very well through snow and slush, or would you prefer a smaller car?" James waited for an answer. "We want you to weigh your options, or would you prefer to shop for a car yourself?"

"I would love an Audi R8 Spyder," Katie was poker-faced, "I always wanted a convertible sports car, and this one is very elegant—a white one with black trim. Why do you ask?"

James gulped, as he quickly had his phone out and Googled the car. "Wow, I think the Audi is stunning, beautiful, and elegant, but I think we need a vehicle that is more child-friendly." Katie started giggling, and James was in shock. He was imagining Katie revving the snot out of the very fast car.

"I was weighing up the distance from the house to the school; it makes sense for me to drive." Katie was actually thinking of getting a car someday, not a sports car. She was teasing them and owned that she would opt for a kid-friendly car. She was thinking of a small car. She had considered buying one, well, it had crossed her mind. Katie was sensible to their needs.

Anthony cottoned on to the humour in Katie's choice of car. "Katie, I'm getting a new Jeep this month. We have the option of buying out the lease on this one. What do you think of that idea?" He was offering her his car, "If you prefer a different vehicle, we can help you choose one. It's up to you to decide."

"I would love this Jeep. I need to know how much the buy-out is going to cost. I have some savings," she knew she could afford it.

James was impressed with Katie. She was willing to buy a car so Adam could benefit. "We haven't discussed the Jeep option yet. Anthony only found out yesterday that his company is updating his car. It makes no difference to us. If you prefer a new car, then we're open to whatever model you feel good about, so think about it."

"I think this Jeep is a super choice! It fits so much shopping in the back. I just need to know how much it's going to cost," she was thrilled at the idea of having transport again.

Anthony laid it out flat, "We are getting you a vehicle of your choice; we'll foot the purchase price, including: insurance, plates, services, oil changes, the works!" He gave her a few seconds to think and digest his offer, but she remained quiet. "We want you to be happy with your choice."

"You can't buy me a Jeep!" Their offer was unbelievable to Katie, and she told them again that she had some savings. She could only imagine herself driving a Jeep; their generosity was way over the top. "Why would you just give me a vehicle?"

"It is a perk of the job, Katie. We are committed to keeping you forever. Please, say you'll accept it because Anthony has to call Alexis and tell her we want to keep the Jeep."

"I insist that I pay for it," she didn't want to take advantage of these men. She loved them and wanted to stay with them. "I already live rent-free. This is too much."

"Katie, please say you accept," Anthony was pleading for a "yes" answer, "We need you to be on-call all the time when we're not home. If you need something urgent, or you need to pick up Adam from school and I am too far away to get to you . . . it's important that you have a vehicle and you are not stressed going from point A to B safely. Accept the Jeep; it's part of the job."

"What can I say?" she was almost in tears. "Thank you both."

"We are getting close to Sophie's store." Anthony was entering the car park. "This is where Adam first met James, they became friends, and now James is his daddy."

Adam started chatting as he remembered the car made of candy boxes that was in his room, on his dresser, taking pride of place.

"Good morning, everyone!" Anthony's chipper greeting always made Sophie smile; she had called for a quick employee meeting to greet Anthony. All employees were invited to hear his updates; they were also there for free pizza. "We are dropping in to see you, as our destination is way north. Let me introduce you to . . . Katie, where did she go?" he saw Katie with Adam, "I'll introduce you to them in a few minutes.

"Sophie, as the ex-manager of this store, how do you feel?" he quickly realized she had no clue as to what he was talking about. "Your promotion to district manager is imminent; it's awaiting your acceptance, and all I need is your signature to seal the deal. You look shocked." Sophie stared at Anthony; she didn't say a word. "I take it you didn't get my text and the job expectations? Oh, I sent a collection of funny stories of being on the road?"

"Oh, I didn't check my messages. I'm so sorry, Anthony. We have been busy all day." Sophie pulled up her email. "Wow, oh, wow. I never expected this. I was hoping I might be considered for a promotion sometime down the road. Thank you, Anthony."

"Where did Kelly go?" Sophie asked as she looked up from her phone.

"She was over by the First Nation Arts display, talking to James and Adam." Sophie began walking towards them. "Kelly, Anthony needs to talk to you. You can use my office."

"Kelly already knows; she answered my text, that's why I assumed you knew." Anthony was smiling, and his phone was ringing, so he walked out of the store to take the call.

"Anthony, it's Hayden here," Anthony knew what was coming next. "Thank you so much! I couldn't believe it when your memo mentioned that several stores have their Indigenous Arts and Crafts area set up. My duties have changed, so now I work thirty hours in the store and eight hours coordinating with the artists. I am over the moon with the cheque you sent me! I won't let you down, and I love my job. Thank you!" Anthony had made sure Hayden got the recognition he deserved.

"I have a new schedule for you. One six-hour day per week, you will visit one store in the Victoria area: Port Alberni, Nanaimo, and Victoria, for now. You will spend the whole day working with the local artist and the store manager to troubleshoot any problems and learning new duties. You can grab a cab, for now. As this is a new position, we'll have to work out the details together in September; we'll decide on the other official duties, okay?" Hayden was thrilled. "We intend on opening three more outlets this year, and I want you to be creative and help with marketing, but I'll go into more detail when we meet."

James went to congratulate Sophie and he told her that she deserved the promotion. "Since I left you and went to live in Victoria, my life has done a three-sixty. I've enrolled in UVic's medical program and I've been doing home studies to give me a head start. I am now living in paradise with a wonderful man, a son, and Katie."

James went ahead and introduced Sophie to Katie. "This special lady is the glue that holds us all together, and she makes the best tiramisu in Canada." They laughed at James, who only ever requested tiramisu. "Last week, we invited my family over for a barbeque. Sophie, you won't believe it, my dad has stopped drinking. I haven't seen my mom this happy in years. Anthony and I have arranged for my sister, Sagan, to go into the medical program at UVic. She was ecstatic; it has always been her ambition to become a cardiologist."

James was curious. "Did Anthony really shock you with the district manager's position?"

Sophie was giddy with the news of her promotion, "I honestly didn't have a clue. I had no idea, and when he called me his ex-manager, I thought I was fired. It took a few seconds before I realized what he was talking about," Sophie was shaking her head with disbelief.

"When Anthony hired you, he already knew you were going to be his district manager. He intended to promote me to store manager. We were a sure thing—the chosen ones—and that makes us special, eh?"

Anthony got down to business with Sophie. They discussed her new position, the benefits, perks, change of hours (working some weekends), and making the company look good. The list was huge. He also wanted her to teach a Customer Service Excellence program to all new employees.

"The company will lease a Jeep for you as they are a very reliable vehicle on our Canadian roads, especially in winter. You will also be given a credit card for your gas." She was hanging on to his every word. "Welcome to our corporate environment; you will fit right in. Congratulations, Sophie!" He then explained that she would report directly to him.

"When Alexis came for her annual store visit, she was here to assess you, and she needed to believe in you. You aced it, as her visit was a great success. Please take a few days to go over everything with Kelly."

"We need to leave now, or we'll be driving in the dark. I'll be calling in on my way back to Victoria to do your evaluation. James will help, and Kelly will do the evaluation with us since she will take over the store."

Anthony checked the time, it was time to head north on the second leg of their journey. He rounded up his family along with some snacks and they promptly left for Port Hardy.

"James, I think it's going to be a while before it sinks into Sophie's mind. She was the intended district manager from the start. She was so happy." Adam was sleeping on Katie's arm. "Sophie wants to come to our wedding so Katie, keep in touch with her if you can. She offered to help if we need her, so you can keep her in the loop."

"She's a very nice young lady; being calm and collected are great traits to have. I will certainly keep in touch," Katie assured him.

The rest of the journey passed quickly. The roads had little traffic travelling north. As they pulled into the hotel, Adam was still fast asleep. James gently carried him and tucked him into bed after removing his shoes. "Anthony, say goodnight to your son."

Anthony was talking to Katie, "I can take Adam if you want to sleep in tomorrow?" she asked; she was always so thoughtful.

"It's supposed to be a break for you too. Honestly, Katie, he will be fine, and you can have a lie-in. There's no kitchen here, so we'll have to go out for fast food. It's a treat for Adam," he explained that tomorrow they were also going to Sammy's for lunch.

"Sammy is looking forward to meeting you, Katie."

"Jade has also been invited tomorrow; she'll be coming along too. She's also looking forward to meeting you Katie."

"I'm looking forward to meeting Jade and Sammy. Adam talks about them all the time. He told me that Sammy makes the best ribs and Jade makes melting chocolate chip cookies."

Katie said goodnight. She headed to her room as she heard her phone.

"Hi, Mom, I'm in Victoria; I thought I could come over and see you. It would be nice to meet the family that you talk about all the time."

"Jason Wade Parker! What a surprise, I haven't seen you in months." Katie was missing her sons. "How's the job at Pearson?"

"It's okay, well, better than okay. I have some nice friends and a very special one is with me right now. When will you be home?" Jason asked, "Where are you, Mom?"

"I am at Port Hardy, way up north. We drove here to organize a wedding. I don't know if I can fly down to see you. How long are you staying?" Katie wished he had called her earlier so she could have been there to welcome him and his girlfriend.

Jason wanted to tell her his news face to face. He wanted to see her reaction. "I told you about Sabella, the girl I've been dating. We are now engaged. We have flown here to tell you personally that we are getting married. It's time you met my fiancé."

"How long are you staying on the Island? When do you fly back?" Katie didn't want to miss out on their visit. "You should have called me sooner, and I could have been there to greet you. Tell Sabella that I am looking forward to meeting her!"

"We're flying south tomorrow to Seattle; Sabella's parents live there," Jason told her, "We wanted you to know in case you had problems getting time off."

"How long are you on vacation for? Am I going to see you?" Katie was thinking of asking the guys if she could fly south tomorrow.

"We are going to Seattle for four days, and then we'll be back in Victoria for four days. Sabella wants to see all the sights." He couldn't wait to show off his new fiancé. "You'll love her, Mom."

"That is perfect timing! We leave here in three days, and I we will be back in Victoria around suppertime. So Jason, which hotel shall I book you into for the four days? Pick a place."

Jason said he could only remember the Empress.

"Good choice, I'll book you into the Empress. It will be my engagement gift to you both," she was so excited. "It faces the harbour and has oceans of stuff going on there, especially with the warmer weather."

They said their goodbyes. She sat for a while on her bed, wondering why she hadn't asked what date they would be getting married or where they intended to get married. "I wonder if he called Ethan," she asked herself.

She was debating if she could ask for a few days off, but she believed it wouldn't be a problem if she could take Adam with her. She decided to tell the guys tomorrow.

15

Adam was awake, and he believed it was his job to wake everyone else. "Daddy, if you don't get up, it will be night-time again!" When this didn't work, he started to sing, "The Wheels on the Bus" with an extensive chorus of "going round, and round, and round!"

James looked at the clock and whispered, "It's still night-time; it's only six o'clock."

"I want to see Sammy, fly my kite, walk on the beach, see the whales, and go for ice cream. I can't find Katie."

"Katie must be fast asleep. Go get dressed—quietly—and we'll walk around the harbour until breakfast."

They left Anthony in bed sleeping soundly. "Let's look at some of the boats in the harbour," he said as he pointed out a beautiful yacht. "This boat is called a yacht, and do you know how you can tell it's a yacht?" Adam shook his head. "I'll give you a clue. A yacht has a mast. See the long pole that's fixed to the middle of the boat?" Adam nodded yes. "The sails are attached to the mast. When the wind blows, the sails fill with the wind, and the yacht glides through the water."

"Can we get a yacht?" Adam asked.

"Yacht's cost a lot of money. You might want one now, but that isn't possible. You need to be twenty-one years old to get a boat license. If you still want a yacht by then, you'll only have fifteen years to wait."

It was time to change the subject, so James pointed out a docked ferry. Adam wasn't interested until James told him, "You can drive your car onto this ferry and walk around the ship until the ferry docks. You get back into your car and drive back onto the Island," Adam was paying attention as he was trying to imagine what James was telling him.

"Can we do that, Dad . . . please?" Adam was making a puppy plea.

"Not this trip, but sometime soon, I hope. We'll ask Anthony if it's possible."

For now, Adam was content with that answer. James' next suggestion took Adam's mind off the ferries. "Let's go wake up the others so we can have breakfast, okay?"

Anthony was still in bed. "Wake up, sleepyhead," James was feeling hungry. "If you don't hurry, we are going to breakfast without you!" It was an idle threat, but Adam laughed as James hit Anthony with a pillow. At that moment, Katie knocked on the door.

"Am I late for breakfast? I missed my hugga-bear this morning."

"I'm here!" Adam called from the bathroom.

"He woke up very early, so we decided to take a walk around the harbour." James then confessed, "I've got a huge appetite with all that fresh air."

"Let's go. We are expected for pancakes at Sammy's around ten o'clock," Anthony replied. He was excited to start arranging their nuptials. "Jade will be meeting us there."

After breakfast, the drive to Sammy's was an eye-opener for the guys. They were driving along the coast road with the ocean as a backdrop. Adam was looking through his binoculars and yelled to Katie to see the eagles.

Katie had made up her mind to tell the guys that her son, Jason, called her last night with news that he was engaged to be married. "They are going to Seattle for four days to meet Sabella's parents, and they'll call on us when they arrive back here in Victoria. "Jason wants to meet you three! I tell him everything since I have you guys to talk about."

"Sammy!" Adam yelled as they drove up, "I've come to see you again. Can we fly the kite now?" Sammy was waiting for them to arrive.

He told Jade that one of the first words out of Adam's mouth was sure to include kite.

Adam ran to him and hugged him hard. "Can we, please?"

"In a few minutes, meanwhile, you get the kite and make sure there are no knots in the string," Sammy sat by Adam in the kitchen. James was introducing Katie to Jade and then to Sammy.

"We will have to prepare some pancakes first, though," said Sammy. "So, Adam, can you remember how to mix the batter?" Adam was right on it. Katie had the fixings prepared, and Sammy had the barbeque hot and ready. He was sneaking glances at Katie, admiring her smile and the sound of her voice. He thought she was quite a woman.

"When we take the kite out, we can ask Katie if she wants to see it. What do you think?" Sammy asked Adam. Katie overheard him and was already gathering her running shoes to climb up the hill.

"Be very careful, Katie. The strong wind can blow you over!" Adam repeated what Sammy had told him when they first went kiting.

Once they arrived at the top of the hill, Katie was in awe of the scenery. "Sammy, this spot is heavenly. The views are exceptional. The guys said they might take us whale watching." Katie told him, "I've never seen a real live whale," Katie shared. She was interested in all the things Sammy pointed out. "Adam is so at home here, and he's happy here too. He talks about you all the time, and I noticed you have him prepping the batter and cleaning the veggies for later." she smiled. She felt comfortable chatting with this gentle man, and willingly shared her thoughts with Sammy.

"I've known Anthony and James for six months or more. You know, these two men had no qualms giving up what was needed to provide Adam with a permanent home. He's a very lucky little guy. I bet you enjoy taking care of him, and from what I can see, he has adjusted marvellously after losing his mom." Sammy was all praise, "Adam talks about you all the time, Katie, lassie. I feel like I know you already."

Adam was playing with some of the local kids, and every now and again, he proved he's adept when working his vocal cords. His laughter was so loud. Sammy stood close to Adam, "Come on, Adam, it's time to leave."

The little man looked sad. "Don't get upset young man, Jade's coming with Brett to see you. They'll be waiting for us," Sammy had oodles of patience with Adam. The little man gathered the kite and started winding the string. Adam beat him back to the house, and sure enough, Jade had arrived with his young friend Brett.

"Brett's mom will pick him up after supper; it's his grandma's birthday today, so Adam, he can only stay for a little while because he has to visit her." Jade started clearing off the picnic table to prepare for lunch.

James, who was relaxing on the beach, got up from the sand and gathered up his towel. Anthony knew James needed a break, so they quietly walked to the water. "We need to discuss our nuptials with Sammy. We don't have much time, as we also need to go to the hotel and arrange for food deliveries."

"Let's talk about it over supper. We'll open up the conversation for any ideas. We know the date we want, so it might just work," James was all set to ask Sammy.

It soon became evident that Sammy and Katie had a lot of things in common. It showed in their body language, eye contact, and their quiet, giggly, tidbits of conversation.

Katie told everyone about her oldest son Jason, a customs officer from Pearson Airport, in Toronto. He proposed to a wonderful girl called Sabella, whose family were from Seattle, and that they were visiting her parents and coming back to Victoria in a few days. Her story helped break the ice for Anthony and James' question for Sammy.

"We are here, James and I, to ask a huge favour from all of you. Firstly, Sammy, we were hoping that you would be kind enough to . . . I mean . . . that is . . . um, we need a venue for our wedding. We were wondering if we can impose and have our wedding here, on the beach by the ocean," Anthony asked.

"Sammy, we are so happy here. When we first came for a visit, this place was all we talked about, it's what Anthony and I dreamed of." James agreed.

Sammy smiled, he wanted confirmation, "You want the actual service here, on this beach?" The two men were nodding in assent. "I don't believe it! I would be delighted to host your service at my beach cottage. I may need a little help," he directed his conversation to Katie. "I'm rusty when it comes to entertaining."

"We want to make sure we include all our friends, Sammy. Will you be a witness?" Anthony smiled, "Jade, will you be a witness too? James' family will be coming, and his brother, Nick, and Adam will carry the rings for us. Katie, your help will make the ceremony complete. We want you to walk us down to the beach as it would be symbolic of a family member giving their loved one away." There was complete silence. "What do you think?"

Katie was almost in tears, but was quick to agree, "I will love that." She added, "It's going to happen this August, during school holidays, no school for the next few weeks. It's an honour. Thanks, you guys!"

"Jade, we'll need some of your expertise. Anthony said you were the best organizer he knows. Sophie, from Nanaimo, will be here two days before the wedding, and she has a bucket load of ideas. Together, we can make this happen."

Katie's excitement was overflowing, "All you two need to do is show up on the day!" Their friends laughed heartily.

Sammy's favourite story must be shared as he tells everyone how proud he was of Anthony, who he considers is the son he always wanted. He respectfully added, "The heavens shone down on me the day I met you, Anthony." He related his story of Anthony going to see him in the hospital, "He came to help me. He took me home, and his friend, Jade, helped me too. They were complete strangers who quickly became my closest friends. I only found out several weeks later that Anthony's partner, James, was equally special, and now I have adopted the boys. I'm very proud of you both for working so hard to make sure Adam has a home full of love." Sammy stopped talking as he was emotionally charged.

"When can we go to see the whales?" Adam interrupted. He loved their last trip and was ready for another visit to the ocean. "Can we go tomorrow, please Dad?"

"I'll try to arrange it for tomorrow if I can," Anthony laughed at the disruption, but he wanted everyone to go. "And it's my treat, so no excuses, it will be mega fun!"

James opted to go too, "I need a break from studying."

Katie asked Sammy if he was going. Adam had told Sammy that Katie wanted to go and see the seals too, and that she had been looking forward to this trip, "Can you come too, Sammy, please come?"

"I don't see why not. Of course, I'll come." Sammy caught Katie's eye and winked, "I'm sure Katie will come too, Adam. We can show her the island of seals."

Adam invited Jade, but she had to work.

"Can we go on a yacht?" Adam asked. Anthony's eyes went wide.

"Who has a yacht?" Anthony asked. Adam told everyone that James had walked with him around the harbour, and they saw a yacht and a ferry.

"Adam, how did you know it was a yacht?" Katie was amazed.

"It has a mast. That's a log that holds the sails up. The sails blow in the wind, and it goes fast on the water. Isn't that right, Daddy?"

James said he was correct. "We also saw a ferry, didn't we, Adam?"

"Can we go on a ferry that we can walk on? Can we take the Jeep for a ride on the ferry?" They were all laughing, as Adam was testing the waters.

They assured Adam that they would have a trip on a ferry sometime soon and pointed out that a ferry was too big for whale watching.

"I'm going for a swim," Anthony threw a towel over his shoulder. "What about you, Jade? You love to swim."

Jade opted to walk with him down to the beach.

"We're all alone; what's on your mind?" Anthony knew something was wrong, "Talk to me, Jade."

"It's nothing I can't handle."

"Then tell me," Anthony could see she was upset, and he tucked her under his arm. "If you share your troubles with me, they will go away faster. That's a promise."

"It's not that easy. I did a very foolish thing. I loaned my cousin's wife, Ava, some money because she gave me a sob story about owing four months' rent, having no food, and that she needed me to take her two daughters for a couple of days."

Okay so far. Anthony was waiting for the worst. Jade was the level-headed one of her family and should have seen what was coming. "She left her kids with you?" Jade nodded. "Where is she now?"

"I haven't a clue. This happened two weeks ago. Her daughters don't get up until later in the day. They sit around and make a huge mess. They are hopeless, and I don't know what I can do to fix everything."

"Have you any idea what happened to your cousin?" he also asked, if her friends or family had seen Ava recently?"

"Nobody knows where she went," Jade confirmed that Ava's apartment was not being used. When my cousin Troy walked out on Ava, he told me he tried very hard to get custody of his daughters, when the court refused his plea, Troy left town. He warned me that she was trouble, but he didn't go into detail.

"Has she gone off like this before?" Anthony needed to know.

"She has taken off for a day or two, but two weeks is a long time. The girls are at my apartment, and they swore they haven't heard from her."

"Do you believe them?" Anthony asked.

"No, I don't trust them, and that's why I'm having a bad time."

"Do you want my help?" Anthony asked as she nodded. "We will deal with every issue methodically, one thing at a time." Jade was relieved and agreed to his terms. Anthony never judged. First he finds the problem and then he finds the solution; it felt good to get this burden off her chest. She knew she had done the right thing confiding in him.

"I'll pick you up when we get back from whale watching." She nodded. "I'll come to your place and talk to the girls, and we'll decide from there on what to do next."

"Thanks, Anthony."

"When I talk to the girls, I want you to stay in the background and follow my lead. Don't argue with me, and please stay quiet. I should be able to figure out if they are lying."

"Did your cousin pay her back rent?" Jade shrugged—she didn't know. "Do you have a key to her apartment?" Jade did. "That's a start," Anthony replied.

"Let's join the others, it must be ribs time. What do you think? Are you ready to eat?"

As they got closer to the bungalow, the smell of ribs was heavenly.

With Brett having left a few hours ago, it was close to Adam's bedtime. "It's getting late, it's time to leave." Anthony said as he watched the little man slowly nod off beside James. "We need to be awake for the whales tomorrow!"

Before they left, Sammy chatted with the boys, "I think that Jade has a problem. If she tells you, and I can help, let me know. She seemed very skittish today, not at all like her usual self. I have never seen her like this." Sammy chatted on about everything and anything. He was very sociable, and he simply loved the company, especially since Katie joined the clan.

When they reached their hotel, Katie told the guys to put Adam in with her, she had bags of room. "Wait till Adam remembers it's our whale watching trip!" James said, "We're glad you're coming with us, Katie, it's an amazing experience; Sammy hasn't been out on a boat with us before." She blushed, and James noticed.

Anthony told her, "The last time we went out, we saw a humpback whale. Don't forget to look up and see the eagles! Pack a camera or take your phone; the scenery is stunning. You'll also need warm clothes or a blanket, it gets cold out there."

"I can't wait. Sleep tight," she replied as she went off to bed.

Sure enough, Adam was up early next morning, and he didn't waste time waking everyone, he sang about the wheels on the bus, so loud it worked. He was eager to get to the boat dock.

When they arrived at the harbour, it was blustery, and the winds were persistent all the way to the first islands of seals. As they got closer, the noise got louder, becoming almost deafening. "Is that a bald eagle? Look, everyone!" an excited Katie was thrilled with everything she saw on this trip. "Look, Adam, I see a whale!" Adam was enthralled with the orca, then he realized there was more than one, and the boat slowed enough so they could watch the pod pass by. Their day was full of first experiences, but the company made the trip epic. They had so much fun.

"I've always wanted to see an orca swimming in the ocean," Katie told Sammy, "and now that I have seen a pod, I couldn't be more thrilled."

"They usually travel in this area, and we think it's the best place on earth to see them from late springtime to midsummer. Although some folks brag that Johnstone Strait has almost three hundred resident orcas. Maybe we can take a trip there another time?" The guys heard Sammy invite Katie to join him on another outing.

"I can't wait to tell my sons about this boat trip. Everything was breathtaking, and the company was awe-inspiring—especially with you, Sammy. You have enough knowledge about the area to make the excitement real." She gazed across the ocean, "To see all this in real life is a picture I won't ever forget. Thank you, gentlemen, for that was the experience of a lifetime."

"I told you, Katie," Adam snuggled with her all the way back to the harbour. He decided he wanted to paint a picture of the orcas when he got home.

Katie yawned, "Too much fresh air mixed with wonderful company, what an experience."

16

It was mid-afternoon when they returned to the harbour, where they all helped unload their gear. Anthony phoned Jade, "I'm on my way to your store to collect you now."

"I can be ready in a moment," Jade needed to clear up this chaos quickly.

They parked close to Jade's apartment, and once they entered, they walked slowly into the hallway where the smell of drugs was overpowering. After Jade opened the door, Anthony stood in the doorway, using his large frame to bar either of the girls from leaving the room.

They instantly stood up, staring at him. "Sit down, ladies," his voice boomed. When they didn't sit, he insisted, "It was a command, not a suggestion." Anthony held a no-nonsense stance. "There's an obvious drug problem here. Who gave you permission to do drugs in your aunt's home?" He waited, but neither spoke. "You talk to me, or I'll call the cops who will have social services pick you up and take you into a care facility today."

"You can't do that. We are none of your business," they both replied.

Anthony asked with an authoritative tone, "Where's your mother?" He got the same response.

A knock on the door, Anthony moved so Jade could answer it. Greg coughed to get Jade's attention, and when she turned around to see him he was wearing a janitor's outfit. She asks if he needs to go in, he had his finger over his lips and he whispered to her. "Pretend you don't know me."

"Okay." Jade whispered. Greg put his finger to his lips, again and she realized he was here to help Anthony.

He whispered for her to play along and pretend she didn't recognize him; he was here to help find her cousin. Anthony had contacted Greg after chatting with Jade to get some insight into the situation. Greg felt uneasy, and he wanted to make sure Jade was safe, especially after seeing the thieves on the store video; he had a bad feeling it might all be connected.

"Sorry, ma'am," Greg said, "I need to search for drug paraphernalia. The neighbours are complaining about the stench," he walked past her and Anthony and moved into the suite.

Anthony told Jade to stay by his side while Greg searched for drugs.

One of the girls asked Jade why she had come home so early. The other one stated, "If they find drugs here, you'll get the blame. No one can pin it on us," she smirked. Now Greg and Anthony were certain the drugs were here, somewhere.

"I can," Anthony stated. "I'll ask you again, where is your mother? We need to contact her. We need to know if she abandoned you two."

"You have no right to question us. Our mom isn't here."

"I am asking you to contact your mom. She needs to know what you two are doing. I can't believe she would leave you two here for two weeks unless she knows what you're up to," Anthony wanted to keep them talking for as long as he could.

Greg worked diligently. Not only did he look for drugs, but he was planting cameras throughout the apartment while ensuring it all worked. At the same time he didn't find any drugs.

He assured Anthony that it was obvious the drugs were there somewhere, and he intended to find out where they hid the drugs, it will be on the surveillance footage.

As Greg walked into the living room with Anthony, they continued their fabricated conversation, "I've no doubt there are drugs here, sir and ma'am, but, unfortunately, I couldn't find any. I'll be in contact if there are more complaints from the tenants, and at that time, the cops and their drug-sniffing dogs will be involved and they can smell drugs from a very long way." Greg's parting words did not get the reaction he expected, and then he realized the girls were high.

Greg was again explaining that the tracker dogs are the best way to get to the bottom of this problem. "For now, we can only wait until the neighbours complain." He left them hoping his plot works, and the drug dealers come for a visit unaware of the cameras.

"If your mother contacts you, let us know immediately," Anthony left his number. "Jade, I need you to come with me. I will take you to our hotel tonight because you can't sleep here; this place is disgusting."

Jade followed Anthony, and while they walked away, Anthony warned, "Jade, please don't look up at your apartment. Just get into my car."

She did as he asked because she needed him to explain why Greg was there.

"Do you still have Ava's door key?" He hoped so, as he had arranged to meet Greg at Ava's apartment.

"What are you doing? Where are you taking me?" Jade complained, "Please, take me back. I want to turf those idiot girls out of my apartment. I'm going to call the cops and get them arrested!"

"My first instinct was to go to the police," he told Jade, "but this isn't a great idea, especially after hearing both of them threaten you for whatever they were hiding in your apartment. Jade, you don't deserve this. Greg has a handle on what's happening, and he asked me to get you out of there."

He then explained that Greg had installed pinhead security cameras throughout her apartment to help them hear and see what the girls were doing. "If they know Ava's whereabouts, they may try to warn her. At least, I hope that's what they'll do. We need to do what Greg says, and you, Jade, need to be very careful, which means you can't stay there tonight. We need to know you're safe."

Anthony explained that Greg is also a licensed private investigator who is legally within his limits to help her, if she should request any help. Anthony added, for good measure, "He was so worried for your safety that he dropped what he was working on and came here to be with you."

"I'm a damsel in distress, and he's my knight in shining armour," she laughed. She admitted she was happy to see Greg. "I'm not complaining. Greg is easy on the eyes. We have been texting, then we talked on the phone and he comes to see me when he can. Did he tell you that we kept in touch?" Anthony nodded. "How did he get here so fast from Victoria?" Jade was stunned.

"That isn't pot they are smoking. They're using hard drugs, which makes them dangerous and unpredictable." Anthony filled in the blanks, "Those girls need help. They'll be in danger when the jackass providing the drugs finds out we have contacted the cops. What kind of person is Ava? How could she just abandon them? That boggles my mind!" He shook his head. "She's a lousy role model for a mother, she doesn't deserve kids. She doesn't deserve to be a mom."

"How did you get Greg's help so quickly?" Jade's thoughts were more towards Greg instead of the girls. "He arrived at the perfect moment; I'm impressed!"

"That was easy, he likes you. I mean, he really likes you; you're his main topic of conversation." Anthony grinned.

"Why was Greg here, though? How did he know where my apartment was? I want to know!" Jade tried her best to get answers, but Anthony didn't want to say.

"It's a trade secret," Anthony replied, but Jade wanted an answer, and Anthony finally had to tell her, "I told him, of course!"

"I need to get hold of James," Anthony told Jade. "He will be worried. He needs to know what happened, but he'll have to walk to the harbour so we can talk without little ears."

Anthony dialled, and James was quick to pick up. "We were going to send out the cavalry to look for you two. What happened that took so long?" James was shocked, "From the beginning, eh?"

Anthony told the story about Ava borrowing money from Jade and simply disappearing, leaving her two teenage daughters with Jade. Then he explained that Jade had to move into the hotel because Greg rushed here to fix security cameras in her apartment. He didn't want her to stay there, as he needed to give the girls leeway to continue doing whatever they were doing. He told James about the teens' nasty attitudes, how they threatened Jade, and the disgusting stench in her apartment.

"Greg wants to catch them red-handed, and he has all the equipment and cameras installed. He just needed Jade to stay away."

"How much longer will you be?" James was curious. Anthony told him he was already on his way back to the hotel and that he'd be with James for the whole night. James was pleased and relieved.

Anthony called Sammy and invited him over to their hotel for supper. They had pizza delivered. There were only two chairs in the room, so the guys gathered up the pillows, and Sammy and Katie sat on the chairs. "Drum roll . . ." James had set up a movie to start. He had surprised everyone with the DVD of *Free Willy* and was incredibly happy that Sammy had a DVD player. It was a fun night, and Adam didn't want to miss a moment. Adam fell fast asleep once the movie ended, and Sammy quietly sneaked out to head back home.

The morning came too fast. After yesterday at Jade's, Anthony was preparing himself to deal with whatever came along. "James, I still need to do a store assessment while I'm here."

"Can I help? I was almost a store manager. I know my way around," he offered.

"Will Katie take Adam for the morning, do you think?"

James told him that Katie and Adam had made plans with Sammy to walk around the harbour and to visit some local shops. It was obvious that the attraction between Katie and Sammy was gathering momentum.

"Let's go and help Jade!" James proclaimed, "And then we can focus on Sophie's store, and transfer it to Kelly." Anthony was pleased that James wanted to help. "We assume these dudes are dangerous, so stay alert.

"Greg called to ask if we'd meet with him outside of Jade's place in about half an hour. He said we need to bring Jade."

Jade was up all night. Sleep completely evaded her, and this morning she had a couple of cups of coffee, but she couldn't eat breakfast. She was worried as the three of them drove to her apartment. Greg was waiting outside, and they all piled into his van.

"Brace yourselves. This movie is epic!" Greg warned. "I deserve an Oscar!" You won't believe what you're looking at. Jade, your apartment suite is being used as a crack house. I need you to watch that screen and tell me what you see." Greg was focused on the girls, and he reminded Jade that they swore they had not been out of the apartment. "In the kitchen, we have weigh scales, tiny zipper bags, a cereal packet with white powder, and a bag of flour. Jade, we must take these tapes to the cops, now. See how the two girls are making up bags to sell with the help of this lady," Greg closed in the footage to see who the lady was.

"These peeps are oblivious of our cameras. Look at how the three women have company," said Greg. "Do you recognize any of them?" Jade moved in to see who the individuals were. She recognized them as the two men who broke into the store and damaged her car.

"No, damn it, no! I can't believe what I'm seeing!" Jade watched the girls prepare and bag the drugs in her kitchen while the two men watched on. "I need to move! I will never feel safe there again."

They watched the five individuals move around. "Guess what I see? It's Ava. The extra woman who was helping the girls was on camera. She looks a lot like the woman from the store camera footage." Greg pointed out the obvious, "We need help now. It's time to call for the cavalry. We need to stand back, stay out of their way, and let the cops do their job."

Greg called the RCMP and informed the officers that the pictures from the surveillance cameras in Jade's apartment show a very close resemblance to the guys who broke into Jade's store.

"These guys didn't have a clue they were on camera. I think we need plainclothes cops here too." Greg told the officer on the case, Detective Brooke, to bring lots of evidence bags as it looked like there were several pounds of the substance. Greg confirmed the occupants didn't visibly have firearms, but he wasn't positive.

Detective Brooke thanked Greg for his help. "We won't take any chances. We are on our way. Meet me at the convenience store across the street to the left of the apartment block. We'll get better results if we surprise them."

Greg had all the tapes available, but he turned to talk to Jade. "You need to tell the police that you were very upset and that you requested I put the surveillance cameras in your apartment. Let's wait until the cops do their job," Greg told the group, "and then we'll start to empty your apartment. We can place most of your belongings into the van, but you'll need to store the other items for now."

"Greg, I can't thank you enough. You are my guardian angel." She stared back at the footage of her apartment.

"Anthony mentioned, that when the police officer greeted them, they had backup. They knew that the police were ready to completely take over the situation, while the detective thanked Jade and Greg for the video footage.

"Anthony told me something nasty was going on. I didn't let him finish telling me before I rushed here. Why didn't you confide in me?" Greg was pleading, "Jade, we're more than friends, and we look out for each other."

Jade looked up into Greg's eyes. Her sigh of relief was heavy. "You're safe now," he said as he pulled her into a hug. His sigh of relief was blockbuster as he happily held her close.

"Jade, you must know how I feel about you," he whispered as he gently kissed her on the forehead. She leaned into him and didn't want to move away. She wanted him to hold her close, and as they stood together in silence, she sighed again in relief. He then stood back and spoke, "Let's leave the cops to their evidence collecting, okay honey?"

They both left Greg's van to join the others to find Detective Brooke at the convenience store across the street.

"The cameras made it simple to figure who was doing what, but we need to get out of here. Officer, Jade is stressed, and her anxiety level is soaring. Can we leave now?"

Detective Brooke thanked Greg, "We got them thanks to you and your friends. If any questions come up, I'll be contacting you."

They left the store and went to the hotel where Anthony had arranged for Jade to stay for a couple of weeks. Jade's in good hands, as Greg was staying with her. She was still amazed when Greg told her that he came all this way to look out for her. "As soon as Anthony told me that you had unwelcome visitors, I made it my business to be here to support you. I drove up here overnight."

"Oh, Greg, thank you! I'm glad you did. I know we talked lots about the break- in, and I had hoped we were friends, but I wanted more. I feel the same way you do."

"Jade, are you sure?" he kissed her ardently, and she responded with an "Oh, yes, so sure!" kiss.

Anthony and James were ready to drive south. They drove to the hotel and packed up as quickly as they could, Katie was already packed, and Adam was watching a movie. Sammy came to say goodbye, and waved to them as they set off for Victoria.

On the drive back, Anthony and James talked about the last twenty-four hours, filling Katie in on the events, although their conversation was limited due to little ears.

James teased, "Oh, and Katie, what about you? Did you enjoy the whale watching experience and was today's shopping fun? We noticed you smiled most of the time."

"I didn't expect to see any orcas on this trip. I also saw a humpback whale, and the whole experience was fabulous. We are planning to go whale watching again. Sammy told me they are easier to see in the springtime, from May to June. I'm looking forward to it," Katie told them. She found it difficult to hide her excitement,

"Sammy and his beach hut are magical. You and Anthony went there and left as a couple, and I met Sammy there."

"Another romance blooms because of Anthony," James sang. Katie grinned while looking out at the scenery. "So," James asked Anthony, "how did you know it was the same guys who robbed the store?"

Anthony told them that Greg had a gut feeling, "He had been watching Jade's place most of the night. He was convinced the guys who caused the chaos in Jade's store would be back because the security information was stolen and not discarded." Anthony went on to explain, "The hardest part for Jade was finding out that Ava was involved. She was the store lookout and was responsible for her daughter's drug-dealing activities. I also suspect her of telling the thieves where to find Jade's phone because, on the video, the guy opened the car door and felt under the seat before opening the glove box.

"When I called Greg, he insisted I get Jade out of the apartment immediately and to book her in a hotel." Anthony informed them, "He's exceptionally good at his job. He was a cop for several years, but his biggest incentive was to protect the woman of his dreams."

"I'm looking at the time, and I made a promise to call in the Nanaimo store and do the change over from Sophie to Kelly. If you help me James, we can do it super fast." Anthony also asked Katie to go for some take-out so they could get back on the road and home to Victoria.

The change of manager went well. Anthony had more good news for Sophie, "Your Jeep will be delivered in two days. Please sign all of the insurance forms." Then he remembered, "Don't forget to hold onto the insurance slips. We'll meet on Wednesday, the day after you get your vehicle, at head office at noon, okay, Sophie?" She was so excited.

"We need to get Adam home so he can go to bed," James commented. They left the store, and were back on the road heading south.

"That brings us to you, Katie. You were enjoying every moment with Sammy by your side. What happens if he's the man of your dreams?" James was being nosey, but it was obvious he had hit the nail on the head as he watched her expressions, so he added, "You can't deny it, Katie, this is kismet."

"I hear you playing the oldies of Johnny Mathis, and I'm tempted to sing along too. He has the most beautiful voice I've ever heard." Katie was another fan, and she added, "He doesn't even need music. It's heaven to listen to him." Anthony added that every song tells a story, as he turned on his music in the car and the first song they heard was "You Decorated my Life."

"I can't believe Adam is sleeping through all this noise!"

"My dad used to sing Johnny's songs to my mom. He couldn't make the high notes, no matter how hard he tried, but that didn't stop him." Anthony had allowed a dark cloud to invade his peace. He immediately knew he had run out of options and that he must visit his mom to tell her the news, and soon.

"Hi, Alexis, before I tell you what happened, I want to thank you for all of your help. I owe you big time for covering for me. My job means a great deal to me, and I do value my position. Thank you again for your help." Anthony commented as he ran into his boss at the office. "It was a long drive yesterday, and Adam loves the trips, he calls out "animal" when he sees an animal and we adults have to guess."

He had something on his mind that he wanted to run by her. They headed towards the coffee machine. "Jade didn't know that we had security cameras in the stores, do you think I should tell all the managers? It may save precious time getting the information to the cops." Alexis thought it wise to tell the managers.

"Thanks for being there for Jade, she told me you had talked to her and that you understood what she was feeling."

"You're welcome. It was wonderful that I was able to help," she assured him.

"When Greg and I went to see Jade, her apartment was being used as a drug house. You will never guess who nabbed the troublemakers that wrecked Jade's store and her car."

"Anthony, I know all about it. Jade called me yesterday," she grinned. "Greg also called to let me know he would be staying in Port Hardy; he was reluctant to leave Jade. Is there something going on there?"

"It's not for me to say," Alexis looked at Anthony over her glasses. "Maybe, but its early days yet," Anthony's grin appeased a curious Alexis.

"Greg has been looking out for Jade since the break-in. He actually drove his camper van to Port Hardy to be close to her. He told me that the guys who stole her ID would probably be back. He was right."

"Jade's cousin, Ava, was the lookout woman on the surveillance videos," Alexis replied, "I could hardly believe it. She risked her daughters' lives. Jade also mentioned you played an 'undercover role' when confronting the errant kids. Is that true?" she waited for confirmation. He nodded.

Anthony changed the subject as quickly as he could, "We arranged to have our nuptials at Sammy Keel's bungalow. Now we are all set to make a life-long commitment." Alexis was waiting for a further update. "Katie and Sammy were getting along just fine. He even came whale watching with us, and then invited Katie to go with him next year."

"I got some news of my own, from my doctor a few days ago," Alexis smiled. "Kurt came with me. He was ecstatic! We found out I'm almost four months," she patted her stomach. "My parents will be thrilled. We are taking a few days off to visit them in Calgary. We'll be back in time for your wedding."

"Congratulations! This is great news!"

She talked about parenting and how she didn't feel it was ever going to happen, "Enough of me, though. Let's get back to the business."

They got into a deep discussion of the First Nations Arts and Craft displays. "I was impressed with your ideas, and I think you have a great thing happening. Maybe, now that Hayden is with this project part-time, we should offer the same deal for the month of December, which is ideally a great time to buy for Christmas."

He agreed, "Hayden suggested that we rotate the artists, so the displays vary, and that will keep people interested. He wants to help promote awareness of local artists."

Anthony told Alexis that he promoted Hayden to assistant manager, and he was having a trial run to see how much of his marketing prowess the business could use to promote the arts and crafts.

"Tell me something, Anthony. When you told Sophie about her promotion, how did she react?"

"Alexis, she was having an exceptionally busy day. She hadn't seen her email, so she wasn't aware of the promotion or the information," Anthony told her. "Kelly had read her own email, offering her a promotion to store manager, but she didn't mention it to Sophie." He started laughing, "I asked her how she felt about the offer we made. She didn't believe me at first; she thought I was there to fire her."

"It's time I wasn't here," he said. As he stood up to leave, she asked him about a wedding present. "You are both coming to the ceremony, Alexis. That's the only gift we want."

"We had a meeting in the Vancouver office, and we decided, after your brave performance and dedication to your job, that you get an extra week off," she was happy to relay the message. He was ecstatic.

Anthony left the office and was on his way home, when he decided to make a quick stop. He pulled up outside of Imelda's house. He was trying to pluck up the courage to invite her to the wedding, but he was also aware that she could disrupt everything with little or no provocation.

There was a huge For Sale sign in the garden. He felt like someone had hit him in the guts.

He walked into the house, "What do you think you are doing?"

Imelda was entertaining a younger man, "I don't know what you mean. You walk into my house and ask what I am doing?"

"Why don't you introduce me to your friend?" Anthony calmly asked.

"His name is Charles."

"What are you doing here, Charles?"

"I'm here at Imelda's request. She has just put her property on the market. I have the listing, and I also have several buyers who are interested in this area." Charles was very uncomfortable, "If she wants to sell her house, what does that have to do with you?"

"Let me enlighten you, Charles. I own half of this house, and I'm not selling my half to anyone. When you check with Land Titles, you will find my name is on the deeds."

"How dare you come in here after being away for several months and make an issue of the sale of my property?" Imelda was fuming.

Anthony turned to the realtor and asked him to leave. "Charles, take your sign with you. When you do your homework, and you'll find that I own half of this property."

"I am very sorry, sir. I didn't know. This lady has the deeds in her name. She showed them to me."

"You are leaving me with no choice, Mom, I have to call the police," he had heard enough. "Say goodbye to my mother, Charles, and leave—now!"

Charles knew it was pointless in trying to negotiate further. He was happy to pick up his case and leave.

"I have brought you some papers that my dad left me. He accuses you of being a master manipulator—a cold-hearted thief. Don't look shocked. What did you do with Dad's pensions?"

Imelda did what she did best: she cried, and cried.

"Turn off the waterworks, the tears are as phony as you," he said before calmly asking what she intended to do with his half of the money.

"I was going to give half to you, of course." The tears had stopped. "I couldn't get hold of you to talk to you. What was I to do?" she replied.

"How did you con the bank into allowing you to sell what you don't own?"

Her response was typical, "I just wanted what was mine." She spat.

Anthony fired back, "This house is secure, and you cannot sell this house unless I agree to the sale. You intended to steal my half of the house. I am warning you now, if anything like this ever happens again, I will call the police.

"Did you know that Dad left me a safety deposit box, explaining how you stole his pensions? You forged his signature and spent money that did not belong to you." He was watching her as she shook her shoulders. "My grandpa left a letter for me dated four years after you told me he was dead." She stayed silent. "I did, however, find out the reason you wanted me to live here with you."

"George had money from his dad," she replied. "I knew he had hidden it from me. At that time, as his legal spouse, I should have gotten that money. Your grandpa wanted me to have it," she was getting excited.

"I have a copy of his grandpa's Will. It states emphatically that you are not, under any circumstances, to receive a penny," Anthony stressed emphatically, "Not under any circumstances."

He put a copy of the Will on the table. "Take a good look; read the contents. He warned Dad to get away from you as quickly as he could. The safety deposit key is with my lawyer. Only James, or me, can access the funds.

"It shames me to say this, but I am getting married soon, and I can't offer you an invitation. You embarrassed me the last time I saw you; and that won't ever happen again."

"Who are you marrying?" she asked in a berating tone.

"I'm marrying James, my partner. We have a son, who is wonderful. You must not come near our home, or my son, or James." He stressed forcefully as he was seething, "Stay away from all of us. You need to get professional help, and if you don't get help, I will cut all ties with you. You were a loving and caring mom who was fun to be with. Now you are a monster. I want my mom back, so please, get some help, and go see a doctor."

He was watching her shred all of the safety deposit box copies.

"You have turned into a nightmare. You have no self-control," he said sadly.

"Now you can't prove that I am not the sole owner of this property," She took a childish stance.

Anthony laughed, "I have all the originals in my safety deposit box, and I have all legal documents with my lawyer." He pointed out her limitations, "You have no access to my bank. If, however, you want to sell this house, I will offer you a fair price. We don't need it. We already have a beautiful home. The money from our property will go to our son."

"How can you have a child? It's impossible. How did you get a kid?"

"How can you be a mother?" He thought, feeling helpless.

Anthony calmed himself and replied, "James and I adopted a little orphan. I'm glad we got all that out of the way, Mother. Goodbye."

The situation was a struggle for Anthony. Driving home, he tried to figure out why she had changed so much, what was her obsession about money? Why would she refuse to get help? Her whole demeanour scared him. How far would she actually go to get more money? What did she do with all of his dad's pensions? He simply had no choice; he would disown her. James and Adam were too important to risk her upsetting them again. He felt helpless and miserable as he drove home.

"James, I have something to tell you. I went to see my mother. I know it was long overdue," James rushed out of his study.

"Did it make you feel better? Is she coming to our wedding?" James watched his expressions. "Come, sit with me."

Anthony looked wretched, "I have to tell you this before I burst," he went through a long list of his mother's antics.

"I drove into the crescent on my way home. I couldn't fail to notice a For Sale sign on the lawn. She had a guy with her, a realtor, who was planning an open house, and he had lots of interested parties."

"How could she sell your half of the house?" James asked.

"She couldn't. She faked my signature on the deeds and signed them over to herself. The lies rolled off her tongue like a sixty-five-gallon barrel rolling down Mount Everest." He took a couple of deep breaths. "She told me I had made a mistake and that my grandpa left the money to George, which would go automatically to her when Dad died." Anthony was still seething, "I gave her copies of Dad's and Grandpa's Wills. Then she started shredding the papers I gave her. She told me that I couldn't prove anything. I told her I have a solid arrangement with you and that she cannot access my bank account."

"I mentioned that we have a son, and that didn't move her at all. She didn't care, and she didn't even ask his name."

"We need to warn Katie," James was also upset. "How could she do this to you? What is wrong with her? Maybe we could get her assessed with a psychiatrist?"

They sat quietly, making mental notes on how to keep Adam safe.

"Imagine where I would be right now if my dad hadn't proved that my own mom could be so cold and calculating." James listened. "I need to let you go, James. I don't want you to be a part of this charade. I can't cope with her. I don't know how to deal with this situation, and you deserve so much better than me and all of my baggage."

"I'll pretend you didn't just say that." James sighed. "Stop over-thinking the problem. We need to help her; you can't possibly let her ruin your whole life. We, and I do mean we, need some professional advice. Imelda has a lot of turmoil going on inside her head that's eating away at her. You are a bi-product, a release of her anger."

"I was so embarrassed when she was yelling at me at the hotel. I couldn't get her to stop. I felt the whole guest list could hear every word she yelled."

"You need to ask yourself, what happened to her to make her change so drastically? Why didn't she visit your dad when he was in the hospital? Why did she tell you she still loved him? What did she do with all the money from your dad's pensions? Does she have a gambling problem? Why did she invite women to bear her a grandchild? Most Moms want what is best for their children. If she were thinking straight, she wouldn't have picked up strange women from off the street. That was far from a 'run of the mill' circumstance."

Anthony agreed with him. "She wasn't always like she is now."

"It's just a few suggestions, but it might put some light on her behaviour. You have no answers, and that's why I recommend a professional getting involved. If she has a mental illness, she needs compassion, not blame." James honest opinion was to try to help her, that she needed a psychological assessment.

"Her whole life is out of kilter. Her random acts and ideas are so out of character," Anthony replied.

James had given this problem a lot of thought, "Take me to meet your mom. Please, Anthony, let me talk to her. I think it might help if she realizes we are on her side."

"I want my mom back, and that woman is not my mom. I'm afraid she may become abusive to you. Do you think we should do this? Are you sure?" He began asking James a lot of questions, but James was adamant that her doctor would answer some of the recent changes in his mom. James wanted to get involved.

"What you cannot do is leave me, or turn me away. Anthony, listen to me. We'll get to the bottom of her problems and do whatever we can to help her. So far, we've been working like a well-oiled machine. We are in this together."

"The best word in the dictionary is 'we'!" he thanked James for being there when he needed him the most.

"We are getting married in three weeks' time, okay?" James was serious.

"Only if I can fit you into my busy schedule; so . . . I suppose so!" Anthony condescended, and laughter filled the room, along with pillows.

"Remind me when we go to the store to pick up a bunch more cushions," Anthony laughed again.

James was his comical self, "It's a bunch of grapes, a bunch of flowers, or a bunch of coconuts. I've never heard of a bunch of cushions!"

"A cluster of cushions . . . sounds perfect! Cluster means a small group of things that are closely packed together," Anthony wanted to have the last word, "like you and me."

James came back with a smart remark, "A pile of cushions sounds better, and for your information, I don't want to be a cluster." James was on a roll, "Grab your jacket, and let's go meet your Mom."

"How are you going to do this?" Anthony shrugged his shoulders.

James insisted he wanted some answers, "If she was my mom, I would want a solid explanation of the situation. We need to formulate a plan so she agrees, and we need to keep her in her most amiable state of mind. The professionals know how to manipulate the subject into feeling that everything is copacetic, which should help Imelda and make her want to see the doctor."

Once they arrived and had settled down with Imelda, James chatted generally with her, until he felt it was the right time to ask her if she would agree to see a doctor. He told her, the doctor will give her some pills that would help control the bad feelings that she keeps having. Anthony went to make a cup of tea but hovered close by in case his mom lost control. Imelda was amazed to find that Anthony's partner was a doctor in training and that she liked him. He made her feel at ease.

"I'm not going to the doctor," she sounded resolute. Anthony thought, "Here she goes again."

"Imelda, I want you to take me to your doctor so I can explain why you are so sad, angry, and confused. I want to take care of you so let's go together." James was stroking the back of her hand and she was relaxing again. "Anthony and I are getting married in three weeks, and now that I have met you, I would love for you to come and be a part of our celebration."

James gave her a few seconds to absorb this information. "Your son loves you so much," but before he could say more, she jumped at the chance, as long as James would go with her.

"You will take me? I don't want to go with anyone else. Thank you, James."

17

It was a blustery, chilly day as they drove through the streets to the courthouse. Katie was relieved they had bundled Adam up as light raindrops appeared on the windshield. It was a brisk five-minute walk from the car park to the courthouse, and when they arrived, they were shown into the courtroom. Katie held Adam's hand as she gathered his mittens and toque and removed his coat.

She had her tissues ready in case she was overcome with emotions, but James told her this was only a formality. Kimberly and Eric walked in and sat behind Katie. It was nerve-wracking even though they were guaranteed a positive outcome.

The judge got straight to business, "I am proud to oversee this course of action." He was impressed with these two young men. They were very special, and he knew that not many young people would have taken on this responsibility.

"Thank you, Your Honour," James and Anthony said in unison.

The judge followed them to the desk, where a clerk handed them the adoption papers to be signed. Once completed, they were notarized.

Kimberly, Eric, and Katie sat with Adam until the judge called him over.

"So, Adam, what are you going to do this summer? Do you have any special plans or places you would like to see?" The judge asked. He was very friendly and obviously loved kids.

"My daddies took me up to Port Hardy to see their friends, and we are going again. Sammy lives on the beach, and we fly my kite from up on the hill. We went on a boat to see whales and seals, and we took Katie, and she liked the eagles."

"You were very lucky to see a whale."

"When we go next week, they are going to get rings and play music at Sammy's, and I can carry the rings with Nick, and they are getting nitched."

The judge heartily laughed. "Adam, I think you mean hitched. It means they are getting married." The judge continued speaking to Adam when he sat next to him, "I believe you will be starting school soon? You are going into Grade 1. Work hard, Adam, and make your daddies proud. Okay, young man, have fun."

"It feels like forever when you're waiting to adopt. Be glad the process could be fast-tracked due to Canada's new legislation for adoptions. This process used to take a year or more, but we can acquire our information instantaneously on line, so there were no reasons not to go ahead," The judge congratulated them, and their friends did the same.

"Thanks, Anthony. We wouldn't be here today if it weren't for you," James pointed out.

"Thanks, James, for inviting me to be a part of your life. I am so happy." Anthony's heart was full of love.

James and Anthony had booked a table at a restaurant, and everyone at the courthouse was invited.

"I am officially a Dad!" Anthony laughed as he remembered Adam's comment to the judge. "He told the judge we were getting nitched, and the judge was howling with laughter."

"We all love this little guy. He is super smart, very comical, and now no one can take him from us," James said.

An exciting phone call came from Sophie, congratulating the guys and wishing them all the best for their future. "James, you are a wonderful human being who is smart and caring. Now, what's it like being a Dad?" Sophie often got small texts from James. "I love it," he replied before stating, "We're heading north to make final arrangements for our wedding service, and we want you to come to the wedding. We'll send out our wedding invitations soon."

"I would be honoured to come to see you both nitched! I wouldn't miss it for the world!" Sophie was so happy for them all.

After speaking to Sophie, Alexis called. "How did your court hearing go?" she asked. She had been covering some of Anthony's duties, so he could concentrate on James and Adam.

Greg and Jade had called with their best wishes and conveyed some surprising news. Ava and her two daughters had to appear in court today. They were awaiting trial for the theft and destruction of property, breaking and entering Jade's car, and a long list of drug charges, including possession and dealing drugs.

Greg explained to Jade that the judge intended to opt for a custodial sentence. There was no point in footing the cost of a lawyer, as the video footage was a foregone guilty verdict. Greg's primary concern was Jade, and she told him she felt betrayed.

"That woman has a heart of gold, so Greg it's up to you to make sure she's safe." Anthony offered to help in any way if they needed it, but Greg told him that it's becoming his life's mission to keep her safe.

18

"Katie!" James called out as he approached the kitchen, "Did Jason and Sabella arrive here on time last night?"

"They sure did! They love the hotel." Katie was making a stack of pancakes with her fruit concoction that was displayed deliciously. "I hope you guys are hungry." She was busy as Adam approached, sleepy-eyed for his breakfast. "Don't tell Adam, that I'm making his favourite pancakes, or he will eat them all."

Adam was seated when Katie turned back to the counter, and Anthony was brewing coffee and pouring chocolate milk for Adam.

"When are we going to meet the engaged couple?" Anthony asked.

"I wanted to ask you about that. I booked them into the Empress for three nights. They invited me to go with them tomorrow for a drive along the coast for a little one day shopping trip, and if you don't mind we can come back here for supper. Sabella loves the tiny shops. She also enjoys watching Indigenous People working on their paintings, and carvings, not to mention the metal works."

"Do you want to go with them?" James asked with a wide smile. "Adam is safe with us."

"I would love to go with them, but I should ask you first." Katie had been missing her sons for a while. "They asked me to spend the next day with them in Victoria showing them around. Would

216

you mind if we came back here for supper tomorrow night? I will think of something easy to cook."

James piped up, "Oh no you won't! We'll get supper ready for when you arrive back, you are now officially on vacation, and that is a take it or leave it offer."

"On their third day I hope you don't mind, I have invited them to come over here and just relax."

Katie said she would take it. "Will Adam want to come with me, do you think?"

"No, thank you, though. We've already arranged for him to have snorkelling lessons. He's a strong swimmer and should have no problems. You know Anthony and I love the sport, but we found it was too difficult for us to teach him in the ocean with the waves crashing around and the undercurrents."

Anthony backed up what James had told her. "You need to have a good visit with your family. We simply hoped you were going to bring them here so we could all meet." Anthony made it clear that Katie's family was welcomed to come to the house anytime.

"When you return from your jaunts, Adam will be here. If you are running late at supper time, give us a call, and we will start without you." Anthony smiled, adding, "We are looking forward to meeting Jason and Sabella. You know, Katie, when you have family coming for a visit, we expect you to take time off. So, concentrate on Jason's visit. We have just one rule . . . enjoy yourself!"

"I feel so guilty; asking for time off," she was going to go into a spiel of her duties, but Anthony anticipated her argument.

"As soon as we heard Jason was coming for a visit, we arranged for some daddies and son time. You are off the clock until after the wedding." James and Anthony had plans, "No guilt trips for you, Katie. We appreciate everything you do for us.

"Tomorrow, we have planned a trip to the mainland. We're having lunch with James' parents, but we intend to be back for supper. We are going on a 'f e r r y' trip." James spelt it out. "Adam wants us to buy him one."

It was too late! The little ears could spell out, "F e r r y. That is ferry. Can I come with you?"

"If you are a good kid today, we will think about it," James teased while laughing, "and I should have kept my mouth closed."

The boys went to the pool, where Adam had his first snorkel lesson. He was trying hard. The men were working on some fun time ideas while Katie was away, but to help them think, they went for ice cream after Adam's lesson. He got his favourite hot fudge treat.

As they pulled up at their front door, they noticed a car. "Can we help you?" James asked. Anthony and Adam went to unlock the door. The driver smiled at them.

"I'm Ethan Parker, Katie's youngest son. My mom isn't expecting me. Jason called me, and when he found out that I was close by in Granville Island, he texted me your address. I hope you don't mind me gate crashing, but Mom talks about you both all the time, and honestly, I have received enough texts and stories about you guys that I am tempted to write a book."

Ethan looked around, "This is a gorgeous home. Mom said she was being taken care of, and she loves her young charge. Where is your son, Adam?"

James held out his hand, "I'm James Prescott, and this is Anthony Lynwood. You just missed Adam, has gone next door to play with a couple of kids, until supper." After the introductions, they welcomed Ethan inside.

"We will get a call when they are about a half-hour away. Before they get here, you can hide on the patio. Katie's in for a huge surprise!" James said. "Take a seat."

"Was there anything I can help you with?" Ethan asked and was immediately given the lighter and asked to light the barbeque.

"This home is fantastic! No wonder Mom loves living here. I think it's great that we have a chance to meet."

"Ethan, we also heard lots about you gadding around the country. What kind of long-distance do you drive?" Anthony asked.

"My run, at this moment, is from Williams Lake to Mexico. I work for a good company, and I will continue working long-distance until I find a wife that is more interesting than driving around this beautiful continent." Ethan had their attention, "I'm trucking logs to Mexico, and on my return trips, I bring back canoes and kayaks, and sometimes I bring rugs."

"I hear the phone. James, whatever you do, don't let the cat out of the bag! Katie's going to get the surprise of her life." Anthony laughed. He couldn't wait to see her reaction.

"Look who's walking up the driveway. I don't believe it! Anthony, come see." There was Sammy, walking towards the front door. "This is wonderful! Let him in."

Anthony told Ethan that Sammy was a very special family friend who lives in Port Hardy. "Sammy! What a wonderful surprise! I can't wait until Adam finds out you're here. He'll be over the moon." They walked over to Ethan. "Let me introduce you to Sammy. This is Ethan, Katie's youngest son; Ethan, come and meet Sammy, he's our very close friend."

Sammy looked confused. "Katie told me it was Jason who had come for a visit. She didn't mention you, Ethan."

"She doesn't know I'm here," Ethan laughed. "I took some vacation days so I could come and see Jason, Mom, and Sabella." Ethan was thrilled his big brother was engaged, "I'm so looking forward to seeing the lady who wants to marry the big lug!"

The front door opened, and he could hear Katie as she stood at the door. "I'm starving. I could eat some of Sammy's ribs right now; they are the best ribs I've ever tasted." She began looking for Adam. "Where's Adam?" she asked before stopping in her tracks.

"Ethan!" she yelled. "I didn't know you were coming." She gave her son the biggest hug ever. Jason and Sabella walked over to Ethan, and introductions were made.

Katie remembered she texted Jason and asked when they planned to get married. He confirmed next Christmas time.

"Katie, please check the barbeque. We are having ribs, and we are starving." Anthony couldn't wait. She walked onto the patio and let out a shriek.

"Sammy! Oh, Sammy! I didn't expect to see you here." There was an intentionally long kiss, and Katie was teary-eyed. "Let me introduce you to my sons and future daughter-in-law." They walked towards her sons with their arms looped through each other.

"Sammy, where are you staying?" she asked.

James instantly replied, "Here, of course. Adam will be moving into our spare room. We have lots of room."

Sammy replied, "I won't impose . . . I was thinking of . . .

"Please, stay here with us. Wait until Adam gets home. He won't be happy if you choose a hotel when we have lots of room here." Anthony, James, and Katie's sons had no doubts that Sammy and Katie were more than casual acquaintances, and they couldn't be happier.

Like a whirling dervish, Adam came around to the patio, "Grandpa!" he cried out. "I went to the pool, and I tried to learn to snorkel with my daddies; it was fun. I didn't know you were coming!" Adam crawled up on Sammy's knee. He couldn't be happier until James introduced the guys.

"Adam, meet your uncle Jason and your uncle Ethan." James knew it was a lot to take in for a five-year-old. "These are Katie's sons. Remember, she told you about them." Without hesitation, Adam's tiny hand shot out to offer some handshakes.

"Now that I have uncles, what do I do with them?" Adam was amazed.

"You include them in your growing family." Anthony was proud his son wanted to shake their hands. "They would love to hear your stories," Anthony said before adding, "They are welcome to call here and see us anytime."

The little man met Sabella. "This lady is your aunt Sabella, and she is going to marry your uncle Jason." It was all too much information! Adam went looking for Katie.

"Why are you crying, Katie? Dad said you would be happy to meet everyone." Katie was ecstatic when Adam hugged her.

"Awe-wee my love, I am not sad, I am so happy! These are happy tears. All of us here today are the most important people in my whole life."

"Come on, you two. We have lots of food and some of my ribs, especially for you, Katie." Sammy handed her a plate. Adam was next in line, and with his plate in hand, Sammy doled out some ribs to the hungry young guy, who thought he was given a wonderful treat.

Very quietly, Anthony told Katie that Adam was moving into their spare room, next to them, and that Sammy was staying as her guest for a few days. After everyone had eaten, they sat around the fire pit, and fairy lights lit the deck. Sammy brought a gift for Adam, who tore at the wrapper to find a horseshoe game they could play in the yard.

Adam was talking to Uncle Ethan, who had some great stories of riding his truck through the Rockies. One funny story was about bears, where Ethan had to sit in the truck for a long time before the bears moved out of his way. Ethan told him that he switched the music on as loud as he could, and that was why the bears went away. "I don't think they like loud noises."

"I sing in the morning when my dad's stay in bed. As soon as I start singing, 'The Wheels on the Bus,' really loud, they get up the quickest." Adam had the company in stitches.

Adam was curious about what Uncle Jason did for work. "I work in an airport. It's a place where all the planes land and take off."

"Can you drive your car on a plane?" Jason told him that most of the planes only hold people. He also told him, "Cars are too heavy. When you come to visit us, you will need to fly because it is too far to drive."

Katie asked Sammy if he wanted to go with her to the hotel to drop the boys off. Sammy didn't hesitate, "Sure!"

"Did you hire this Jeep, Mom?" Ethan asked.

"The boys gave it to me as a gift. It will come in handy when Adam is in school. I offered to pay for it, but they told me absolutely no way." Her sons commented on how lucky she was. "They pay for my gas, insurance, everything. I don't pay rent either. They take real good care of me." Katie related the story of James asking her what kind of car she would like and when she asked for an Audi R8 Spyder. James's face was priceless.

"When Adam goes to school," she said, "I get to have a blast! I am going to be in charge of redecorating, picking new furniture, and making this place cozy."

Jason was the first to say, "They are great guys, and Adam is a hoot! They are doing a fantastic job taking care of him. So are you, Mom! He's an amazing little fellow."

Ethan added, "You have a lucky leprechaun watching out for you." And he had to ask, "Do you get any free time, or are you working all the time?"

"Ethan, I don't work here. I live here as one of the family. The guys spend more time taking care of Adam than I do, and we all share the cleaning. They do their own laundry! I have never had it so good."

"I get as much time off as I need. I'm also included in their outings, and that's how I met Sammy. The boys took me to Port Hardy, and we went whale watching. They introduced Sammy to me, and, as you can see, we have become very good friends."

"Apart from a visit with you two kids, I couldn't be happier." She wanted them to be happy for her.

She found Sammy and sat beside him. He was included in their conversation, and he explained, "My wife died over twenty years ago, and I was living like a recluse until Anthony came to my rescue. Then I met James, and they always visit me. They include me in their family circle when they spend time up north. This was my first trip south."

Jason and Ethan included Sammy when planning their next trip. Katie was delighted.

She offered her guests a tour of the house, and showed off what a wonderful home she has, and that she is going to put up a couple of small shelves for her teapots.

When it was time to go to the airport, Katie told Sammy she needed his help. She didn't just want him to be around; she wanted him included. Both sons had accepted her choice. When Jason and Ethan were leaving, she noticed how they hugged Anthony and James. "You're a part of our family now, too. Give us a hug, brother." Katie was all smiles. They told her they intended to be back for Christmas. Now, that was special!

"Anthony, my love, I am so tired I could sleep on a zip line," James sighed.

"I'm glad Adam didn't kick up a fuss with having to move into our spare room," Anthony replied.

"The whole weekend was a blast, and Adam was comical when you introduced his new uncles. He had to ask you what he was going to do with them!" Anthony laughed.

James expanded on the great time they all had, "Katie is taken with Sammy. We should invite him to stay until the wedding."

"Anthony, let's not be here when they arrive back."

"James Prescott, are you feeling romantic?"

19

The next couple of weeks went by so quickly. With help from the hotel, the ladies and Sammy had the food ready for the buffet; and the caterer and waiter from the hotel had everything in hand. Sophie and Sammy had decorated Sammy's beach cottage. Brett was keeping busy aligning the chairs to face the ocean and lots of tables were waiting their floral centerpieces. Sammy was there to greet Katie and Adam as they arrived in her Jeep. Before entering the house, Katie showed Sammy the keepsakes she made for the rings, two tiny cushions in the shape of the men's initials, with rings on each; one ring for Nick to carry and the other for Adam to carry. Their lapel flowers were delivered. Jade and Brett had made assorted party favours and James' family was already there.

Sagan and Kaitlen had borrowed the coffee maker and some pods from Jade's store and were kept busy making beverages. When Sammy was getting dressed, Katie began helping set up outside. Nick and Brett opened more deck chairs and set them around the tables. Everyone was busy setting the scene for the couple getting married. The justice of the peace was sitting in a deck chair facing the ocean, waiting patiently.

Alexis arrived wearing a midnight blue cocktail dress with a back kick-pleat. She was starting to show off her baby bump, and husband Kurt was carrying the table centers, which he handed over to Katie, who stood quite still as she admired Alexis's handy work.

"Katie, you look great. That colour of green suits you," Alexis said as Sammy came out of the house and hovered close to Katie. "You must have been so busy! I can see now why Anthony and James wanted the service here. I'm getting a friendly, welcoming feeling, yet this stretch of coast is so rugged by contrast."

At that moment, Imelda walked into their midst.

"Hello, you must be Imelda? I've seen your photo on Anthony's wall," Sammy introduced himself and added, "We are so glad you could make it. The boys wanted an ocean-side wedding, and this was their perfect venue. There's no shortage of ocean here." Sammy was a great host with a warm, welcoming smile.

"It is so beautiful here," she whispered.

"The service will start soon, Imelda, so how about we find you a seat close to the front, next to my Katie and me."

Imelda was comfortable with Sammy. She whispered again, "I've come to apologize to my son. I was awful to him and I need his forgiveness. I'm here to support him and his partner James." She began to relax, which was a good sign. "I only met James a few weeks ago when he came to see me. He explained why I was feeling sad, angry, and depressed, and that he knew a doctor who was willing to explain about different treatments. James was so supportive; he recommended we both visit a doctor who would make some sense of my condition; he even offered to accompany me. He arranged an appointment and he came with me to see the doctor. He helped me understand my mood swings, and why I kept refusing help."

Sammy listened as Imelda sang James' praises. "James was so certain that if we got the right kind of help I would be able to attend their wedding." James asked Maria, his mom, for help, and she insisted I travel with her family today," Imelda smiled, and continued chatting, "I feel calm because of my medication, but sometimes I feel very tired and I feel like I'm walking round in circles."

"Let me introduce you to Katie." Katie followed his lead and welcomed Imelda to their ocean get-away.

"I came here with the boys and I met Sammy, and found the magic of this cottage, now Sammy and I are much more than friends, isn't that right, my love?" Katie linked her arm through his, "It's time, Sammy. Let's rally the troops and make this happen."

Sammy settled Imelda in the front row next to two empty seats for him and Katie. Everyone began to take their seats, with Brett guiding the way, which gave Sammy the opportunity to take Katie to the house. He waited with her until the boys got dressed and ready.

Anthony was more than a little panicked as he asked Sammy, "She didn't call me, so I wasn't expecting her to come. How did she get here?"

"James asked his mom to look out for her at the airport in case she decided to come, so she flew up here on the same flight as James' family," Sammy informed Anthony. "She'll be returning on the same flight as Maria and Ray tonight. She'll be fine, son. She's on some prescribed medication, so if she tires, I'll take good care of her. She wants to be here. She didn't want to miss your big day."

"Thanks, Sammy. Did you know that James and I were going to try and arrange for a consultation with a psychologist? Her mood swings had escalated, and James thought it was anxiety or another problem. He told me she desperately needed help," Anthony knew what James had achieved and he continued to explain. "It was James who took her to the doctor. He arranged everything for her."

"Anthony, your mother has arrived, and she looks well," Katie whispered, confirming what Sammy had said, and she mentioned that Imelda was sitting in the front row next to her and Sammy.

"She told me she wants to apologize to you for her outburst and the troubles she caused in the past." Katie wanted to see Anthony relax for the ceremony, so she continued with the good news, "She wanted to tell you that she had been seeing a psychiatrist and a psychologist. She's been battling dementia and depression, and for the last four weeks, she was prescribed a strong medication that makes her sleepy."

"Sammy, thank you for everything you have done for us. This whole place is perfect, and we both wanted to get married here. It's magical." Anthony knew Imelda was in good hands and was relaxing, but he felt he should explain her situation. "My mom was trying to cope. She needed help, and we also needed help to understand her problems." Anthony explained his mom's situation, then he heard his cue for the music, and his focus was automatically on his next steps down the sandy aisle.

Katie had both James and Anthony, walking them from the cottage to the ocean, wearing their black tuxedos, with white collarless shirts. Adam and Nick had the rings. The service was amazing as everything was planned with the simplest details, as they said their vows and added their own sentiments.

"James, you are my one love that I have waited for; I want to share my life with you, now and forever."

"Anthony, you are my one love I have waited for; I want to share my life with you, now and forever."

The service was short but beautiful, and the married couple sealed their nuptials with a kiss.

Adam and Nick had done a great job setting up the chairs. The ladies got together and finished the final details of the buffet. Everyone helped to make the ceremony and the service go smoothly.

James was pulled past the buffet by Anthony. "I want to introduce our son to my mom." As they got close to Imelda, "Mom,

James and I have a wonderful surprise for you. There is one more person you should meet." The three of them walked over to Adam. "Adam, he's our son, which makes him your grandson." Imelda smiled, but she couldn't hide the tears that were welling in her eyes. "Say hello to your grandma, Adam."

James was pleased that Imelda had made it to the wedding. At the first opportunity, he told her that she was brave and if she felt anxious or tired to let him know. James had done his magic again by realizing that Imelda was ill and not getting better. He knew she was receding in her mind, and only now had been diagnosed with dementia; she was getting the help she needed.

"Grandma, do you know my mommy went to heaven, and my daddies take care of me now. Oh, and Katie, she looks after me all the time. She makes the best tiramisu. Do you like tiramisu?" he was curious. "Where do you live?"

"I live in Victoria," Imelda told him. "How old are you, Adam?"

"I'm five, and I go to Grade 1. Katie got a car so she can drive me to school."

Adam was a little chatterbox. He told her all about his trips to the ocean, "We saw the whales and seals out at sea on an island. Sammy takes me up that hill so we can fly my kite." Adam also mentioned the eagles, "My daddies bought me binoculars, so I can see the eagles in the sky." Imelda was so taken with this little man.

She was also curious and asked Anthony what had happened to Adam's mom. "He mentioned his mommy was in heaven. Did she die?"

"Yes, Mom, she died of a brain tumour several months ago. The saddest thing of all was Adam's daddy had died on the way to the hospital when Adam was born. He was an orphan. James took responsibility for him, and I wanted to be a part of both their lives. I am so happy, Mom." Imelda gave him a hug.

As the day progressed, Sammy was vigilant regarding Imelda. He noticed she looked a little tired, so he took her into the house and made her some iced tea when Maria came over for a chat. She perked up and had a good conversation with James' mom. The party was in full swing, and everyone was enjoying themselves.

"Imelda, it's time we had a little chat. I want to tell you what a wonderful young man you have there," Sammy said. "He's always made time for me ever since I was in a road accident, and he actually came to the hospital, and he drove me, a complete stranger, home. He made me comfortable and came back the next day with Jade in tow, bringing my car."

"Oh, Sammy, thank you for being so kind to Anthony. I'm seeing a doctor who did lots of tests, and they found that I have dementia. My husband, George, knew something was wrong when I would lose control and yell at him. In a self-piteous way, I would cry or not speak for days. George finally left me. I directed my attention at Anthony in a negative way, and he was just like his dad. He told me I needed psychological help. It felt like a slap in the face," she told him. "This happens to other people, I thought, not to me."

She broached another subject. "Why is Anthony gay? I never understood. When he told me I was mean because I didn't understand."

Sammy explained, "He's the same person, and he hasn't changed. He wasn't given a choice as to how his lifestyle or his sexuality would be. He is gay." Sammy needed this conversation to be simple. "He is attracted to a man, James." Sammy was watching her expressions. "When you fell in love with your husband, do you remember how you felt?" Imelda nodded and smiled. "Anthony and James have those exact same feelings, but for each other.

"What about you, are you getting all the help you need?" Sammy asked, hoping that she was committed to seeing her doctor regularly.

"It was James who helped me. He introduced me to Dr. Owen Waterford, an expert in his field. James makes Anthony's life complete; I see that now." She was very dignified in her demure as she told the story of why she lied to her son. "I know I hurt Anthony, but I couldn't help myself. I would get confused and lash out. It wasn't me. I love him more than anyone or anything in this world. Thanks again, Sammy; you are a great asset to my son's life."

"I spent twenty years living here alone until I met Anthony. He turned my world upside down. He's the son I only dreamt of. He includes me in so many things. One day, he came over with James, and I watched them fall in love. He introduced me to Katie, and I fell in love the instant we met. She will always be the love of my life," he shared some of his recent memories with her.

"I had a vague inkling to steal Katie away, but two things stop me. This area is remote, and the winters are long and very unfriendly. This would be too remote for my Katie, as she's very much a people person, but I imagine us spending summers here with the boys.

"The second and most important reason is that my Katie takes her responsibilities seriously, we all see how she provides excellent care of Adam, and I can't, or I won't, split them apart."

"No wonder Anthony loves it here. It's a unique place where all is well," she had been so comfortable here. "It's tranquil, with splendid views. This just might be the kind of place I should be looking for."

"Thank you again, Sammy, for taking the time to chat. I had unknowingly put myself in a lonely, dark place. My doctor recommended I sell my house and go into some kind of place, like a senior's bungalow, where I can be monitored or get a companion who will help me. I know that was good advice which I will discuss with Anthony and James after their honeymoon."

"I'm glad we had this chat, Imelda, but now I'm going to find my Katie."

Sammy joined the party and found Katie sitting in the shade, waiting patiently for him, with his drink by her side. "How was Imelda? Did you have your little chat?"

"Yes, we did," Sammy told Katie that he would fill her in later.

Katie stood and got the attention of the guests, "This service today was perfect, and this location makes us all feel wonderful. Thank you everyone for coming today. Please enjoy the fantastic buffet. If anyone wants to take photos, go ahead, the ocean is calm and it makes a beautiful picture. Nick was ready to play some music, which added to the welcoming ambiance.

Once Katie was alone with Sammy, "These two men are very lucky to have met you, Sammy." Katie watched him closely and kissed him quickly. "I walked in on you and Imelda, and I heard my name. I heard your reasons for not marrying me," she whispered as her eyes filled with tears.

Sammy wanted to wipe her tears away, but he wanted to explain. "I do want to marry you. I love you with all my heart and I want to be part of your world—to live with you in Victoria—and I want to be close to Adam, Anthony, and James. The four of you are my life, my whole world. I considered selling this house, but I have one very good reason to hold on to it."

"Are you serious? You want to come live with us?" Katie didn't want him to sell his house. "I can't let you sell this house! It has become the place where all things are made better, and I want you to keep it. I love it here, and I'm looking forward to spending the summers on this beach and being here with you, my love."

"Wow, I didn't expect that. I love you too, my Katie," his arm went around her in a second, and they kissed again. "I want you in my life."

Sammy was blown over with Katie's solution, "There's nothing I would change," she added. "I can't think of one reason for selling it."

"Neither can we, especially when we have all the room you two need." Anthony had his arm around James' shoulder, and passing Sammy and Katie, overheard their conversation. "You two can be together, in our house, as it is split in two . . . well, almost. Katie has a spare bedroom that we can make into a living room. Adam can take the suite next to us. Problem solved."

Anthony was holding James' hand, "We would love it. Please say yes," James had worked out the finer details already, and Anthony was following his lead. "We are both of the same minds. We want you to come."

"My mom, Maria, gave us this idea. She told us Katie was too precious to lose," James stated, and Anthony confirmed the plan would work.

Sammy took a piece of cake from Adam. "Now that's the best wedding cake I've ever tasted." Katie had made it as a surprise for the boys.

Cheers went up to celebrate Katie's tiramisu.

"Adam, what do you think? Should Sammy live with us? You can move into the bedroom next to ours."

"Can we keep Sammy?" the guests started laughing. "Where will I keep my kite? It's safe in Sammy's house."

Sammy was so happy that he was able to keep his beach house and the love of his life. He shared with the guests, "I hope that one day we could pass this house to my grandson, Adam. "So Adam can keep his kite safe."

"I knew you are my grandpa. I knew it!" Everyone cheered again.

"Katie, when you and grandpa get nitched, will you be my grandma?"

Katie asked, "Would you like that, Adam?" He nodded. "You can call me grandma." Adam flew at Katie with open arms.

As everyone celebrated the good news, Jade cleared her throat to gather everyone's attention. "We've got some news, too. Greg will be making his home in Port Hardy. We have found another apartment, and he solved all my work miseries, but best of all, I fell in love with this handsome man. Anthony and James, I blame you! Your happiness is infectious, and we love being here in this magnificent location."

"Congratulations, Greg and Jade!" Sammy toasted, and everyone raised their glasses and cheered.

Alexis and Kurt wanted to share their news as well. "After eleven years of trying, Kurt and I gave up the idea of having a family. A few weeks ago, I announced that we were having a baby." All of the guests began wishing them a wonderful future. "Yesterday, we received more news that our baby has multiplied, and we are having twins! We are twice as excited!"

Maria thanked Alexis for the help she gave to James and Anthony. "I have two things I would like to share with you. It takes a special person to see others needs and help them through the stressful times, and secondly, these babies are a blessing you deserve. Thank you, Alexis, for all that you've done!"

Maria took a sip of water, "Because of James and the love he has for his family, my husband Ray is almost a year sober. Alcoholics have an illness that is difficult to cope with, but Ray kicked the booze out of his life and got his whole family back."

Maria also wanted everyone to know, "When obstacles come along, don't let them trip you up. Jump over them!" Everyone cheered.

"Grandma Maria, can I show you my kite?" Adam asked as he was helping her up from the sand. "It's bigger than me." Ray latched on to them as Adam said, "Grandpa Ray, you can look too. We need wind to fly it."

Sagan stood up, "I have never been so proud of my family. Most of you know that I'm James' sister. This summer, I was prepared to find a job and take some part-time courses at UVic. My parents and I were discussing the cost of a medical degree. It was . . . way out of my reach. A few weeks ago, Anthony and James shocked me when they gave me the cost of my university. They have made my dream possible. My two siblings, Kaitlen and Nick, will benefit from the same trust fund. Thank you for the dream of a lifetime. I love you both. And I will make you proud."

"Hi, I'm Kaitlen. I am still four years from my Grade Twelve prom. I would love to spend my summers in Victoria, so Alexis, remember me if you need a babysitter for full-time hours during summer break. I have taken First Aid courses. Oh . . . and I love kids."

Imelda looked at Anthony. "You deserve a medal, my son. Since my cancer, I have been in a very bad place until you introduced my son-in-law, James, who gave me the name of a doctor, who can and will, help me. I took James' advice, and we called on the doctor together. Now, I am much calmer, less stressed, and on the road to recuperation. Thanks for the support, James. I'm grateful to you both." She smiled.

Eric Gould wanted to raise a glass for the two bravest men he knew, "It's difficult to change your life on a dime and hope you are doing the right thing." He had everyone's attention. "To take and care for another human being who had no one, and to build a family around a child, and to love that child the way they do is a miracle. I want to propose a toast to Anthony and James, and their family and friends."

James stood close by Anthony, who replied to the toasts. "Every person here today has come together for James, Adam, and me. We thank you for being here and helping with the preparations and cooking and the million and one other things that cropped up. Because of your support, we were able to help Adam. As you all know, Adam's mommy went to heaven, and she left behind her most sacred possession, her son. James was Adam's casual care-giver, and when Karen passed, James immediately assumed responsibility for Adam. I also wanted to help and soon became involved. With Eric steering us on, we were committed and able to keep our son Adam safe. We had no idea what parenting would entail, but we were determined to devote everything to bringing up this brave young man. The most important choices we made were gifted from our hearts. We love you, Adam. Everyone here encouraged us and supported us, and because of you, we are, beyond a shadow of a doubt, a family."

James moved close to Anthony, and whispered, "I can tell you a secret. It's in the bank."

Sophie added to the cheers, "We are all here to celebrate Anthony's and James' marriage, and the underlying principle for being here, together, is because they opened their arms and hearts to all of us. They created a huge family. A family I am proud to belong to." Glasses were raised, "I propose a toast to our family!"

"Our family!" was the chorus, loud and clear, which ended the wonderful celebration.